Advance Praise for
The World Is Full of Champions

"*The World Is Full of Champions* is a uniquely fascinating novel of manners that examines overarching questions of family secrets, social pressure, and generational trauma in the little-known world of Philadelphia's black bourgeoisie."

—**Andrea Lee**, Author, National Book Award Finalist

"You need to read this book if you want to understand the clash between want and privilege—and ultimately hope—in Black society."

—**Andrew J. Young**, Civil Rights Leader and former U.S. Ambassador to the UN

"Debut novelist, Julie Sullivan, has written an important book that touches upon a less talked about topic related to social justice in America: the deep chasm between the haves and the have nots in African American society. A must read."

—**Busy Philipps**, Actress and *New York Times* Bestselling Author

"While the book is set in 1980s Philadelphia, this book is highly relevant for our times. Julie Sullivan delves into the behind the scenes matter of U.S. society's little known Black caste system, one that is fueled and fed by historical racism."

—**Reverend Al Sharpton**, MSNBC Commentator and Founder of the National Action Network

"This is a timely and important book that exposes U.S. society at its fringes and how material privilege not only affects the struggles of Black folks from the outside, from endemic racism, but from inside that world as well."

—**Reverend Jesse Jackson Sr.**, Civil Rights Leader

THE WORLD
IS FULL OF
CHAMPIONS

THE WORLD IS FULL OF CHAMPIONS

Julie Sullivan

Post Hill
PRESS

A POST HILL PRESS BOOK

The World Is Full of Champions
© 2023 by Julie Sullivan
All Rights Reserved

ISBN: 978-1-63758-858-1
ISBN (eBook): 978-1-63758-859-8

Cover design by Tiffani Shea
Interior design and composition by Greg Johnson, Textbook Perfect

Scripture quotations taken from the New American Standard Bible, (NASB). Copyright © 1960, 1971, 1977, 1995, 2020 by The Lockman Foundation. Used by permission. All rights reserved. www.lockman.org

Post Hill Press
New York • Nashville
posthillpress.com

Published in the United States of America
1 2 3 4 5 6 7 8 9 10

To Heather, Harvey, Barbara, Deborah, Brittany, Debby,
and Rachel for your thoughtful guidance.

And to my husband Alan, and our children,
Elisabeth, Emily, Grace, Leon, Olivia, and Tamra,
for your love and support.

"A polite and sympathetic attitude toward these striving
thousands; a delicate avoidance of that which wounds
and embitters them; a generous granting of opportunity to
them…all this, added to proper striving on their part,
will go far even in our day toward making all men,
white and black, realize what the great founder of the city
meant when he named it the City of Brotherly Love."

—W.E.B. DU BOIS, *The Philadelphia Negro*

"Opportunities never come a second time,
nor do they wait for our leisure."

—BOOKER T. WASHINGTON, *Daily Resolves*

PROLOGUE

The music recital was over. Day had dipped stealthily into night in Blue Bell, northwest of Philadelphia. A brilliant bolt of feathery orange could be seen from the red barn, brightening the dark sky. Autumn had come early that year to Pennsylvania, and some could be heard complaining that they had forgotten their winter overcoats at home.

Inside the barn, the audience had begun to disperse, but the two women stopped dead in their tracks. Both were stylishly attired. They stared at each other in silence, two wary she-wolves.

Their silence was interrupted by the questioning voice of a small child.

"What's wrong, Momma?"

One of them finally stepped forward.

"Claire, dear. Could that be you?" Georgia asked.

PART ONE

1

Until recently, grief had always been no more than a bit player in her life.

A backwoods country girl until her family migrated north, Bettie Smythe had always taken life in her stride, both the good and the bad, but she'd found a way to embrace the good more often, like savoring maple syrup on a stack of flapjacks. And that made life sweet and true. And for many years, laughter, summer barbecues, and family gatherings consumed her days. Things were happy and grand.

It wasn't really until grief seeped into her world, crawling under the floorboards and entering her soul, that she realized her life had begun to wither on the vine. Still, she was determined to embrace the good wherever she could.

The withering began in earnest on a chilly day in March of '66 when her daughter, Georgia, was six. Mrs. Whitman had allowed Bettie to leave work early to get to the Sojourner Truth Elementary School's kindergarten to see Georgia in her school play. Later, when they got home, she would take great pride in telling her neighbors that Georgia had played the role of Gretel beautifully.

"She spoke loud and clear, and she didn't forget any of her lines," she told them proudly, before going on to describe Georgia's costume, a red felt dress with a white bib that Bettie had made herself. "And her long, black cornrowed braids with golden beads at the end just *dazzled* the audience. There's no other word for it."

"Well," her neighbors said in one way or another, "you can do some hair. We do know that."

Everyone, within a five-mile radius of where they lived in West Philly, knew that Bettie was the expert behind her daughter's long, carefully braided tresses.

When the play ended and the applause had died down, Georgia bounded from the stage and ran straight into her mother's arms.

"Where's Daddy?" she asked, looking past her mother at clusters of moms and dads.

"Your daddy wanted to make it, but he couldn't," Bettie said. "You're a big girl, Georgia. You know your daddy has to work."

Jimmy Smythe always left for work in the mine before sunrise, and Bettie made it her business to wake up even before he did. She had Maxwell coffee and homemade hot and steaming biscuits on the table for him every morning, rain or shine. And after breakfast, they'd always perform the same daily ritual.

"I love you," he would say, leaning in to kiss her. He smelled of the only soap he ever bought, Lifebuoy.

"And I love you, too," she'd reply, and then always added, "Be safe out there, babe."

"Tell Georgia to be good," he'd say before stepping out of the door, dressed in the one, gray woolen coat that he owned.

Then she'd watch as her husband walked out into the murky gloom for his hour and a half commute to Schuylkill Haven in Northeastern Pennsylvania.

* * *

It was past midnight when Georgia tiptoed out of her bedroom wearing her white terry cloth robe, which she had belted tightly around her waist, and her red fluffy Peter Pan slippers. She walked by the cracked brown banister toward her mother and father's room. She knew her father would still be at work and her mother would be alone in their room. She wanted her parents to buy her acting lessons and, based on her success in the school play, she thought that now was the time to ask. In her hands was a big silver piggy bank, and she planned to propose that its contents be used to pay for the first few lessons.

She knocked on the bedroom door. There was no answer, so she knocked again—harder this time—and then pressed her ear against the door. At first, what she heard was barely perceptible, a bare wisp of a noise. But then the sound grew to a soft moan, like the sound of a draft through the window that her father was always promising her mother he'd repair when he could get around to it.

It was only when her mother's moans swelled into perceptible howls that she acted. Georgia opened the bedroom door and saw her mother kneeling beside her bed, on her bare knees and in her white nightdress. Clutched between the fingers of one hand was the corner of the thin brown blanket that covered the bed.

"Momma," Georgia asked, "what's wrong?"

Bettie lifted her face from where it lay on the sheet and looked at Georgia for a moment, as if trying to remember who she was. She opened her arms widely, just as she had at the play earlier that day. Without a word Georgia ran straight over to them and was enveloped in a warm embrace.

"An accident happened tonight," Bettie said, trying to contain herself for her child's sake. "Part of the mine's roof collapsed and fell on your father...."

Unable to keep it together any longer, she let out a searing cry.

"He's gone, Georgia!" she wept, pressing a trembling Georgia close to her chest. "Oh my, he's gone! What's to become of us?"

Georgia felt her soul go rigid. She pressed her face upward, struggling to breathe as Bettie held her even more tightly. She felt lifeless, like the Raggedy Ann doll that never moved from the shelf in her room, an outsized red heart emblazoned on its white apron. She squeezed her eyes shut. It was a mistake, she thought. It just had to be one big fat mistake. Shocked, she lay in her mother's arms as the enormity of her father's death slowly and perniciously began to dawn on her.

"It will be alright, Momma," is all that Georgia could think to say as her mother rocked her back and forth in her arms.

They lay there together until Georgia fell asleep, after which Bettie picked up the slumbering child, took her to her room, and tucked her into bed.

Five hours later, Georgia woke up drenched in sweat, clutching her knees to her chest. She heard her mother rapping at her door, calling her name. But she refused to answer. She shook her head and squeezed her Raggedy Ann doll close to her chest.

2

Spring 1966

During the agonizing months following Jimmy's passing, Bettie ploughed through her grief the best she could, all for the sake of her child. Judge Whitman and his wife, Mamie, her employers, tried to ease her grief by pressing gifts of nice perfume, Tasty Cakes, and Mamie's homemade pies upon her. Judge Whitman often unobtrusively asked if she could use a little extra money, and once pushed an envelope stuffed with cash into her hand. She politely declined.

Each time such offers were made, Bettie replied with a faint smile and the same refrain, "Thanks for thinking of us, but we'll cobble through. It'll be alright. It always is."

Six-year-old Georgia had become the center of her orbit since Jimmy died. Her glistening smile over early morning cornflakes enlivened each day. Her front top teeth stuck out when she laughed, but that was a part of her charm. Over breakfast, she'd parrot out a few jokes she knew, some of which she'd acquired from the Whitmans' youngest son, Lawrence, who she saw on the occasions when Bettie brought her along with her to the Whitmans' house.

After Jimmy passed away, she'd asked her daughter if there was one thing she could have, what would that be.

"Anything in the world?"

"Within reason."

"Long hair."

"You got it," Bettie replied, smiling. That, at least, was something she could do for the child. Folks knew that Bettie was an expert with hair; she practiced her skills on her neighbors, and her shop was the front stoop. She took Georgia's own hair and integrated it with store-bought hair and plaited long braids with beads on the tips of her tresses, which shook back and forth when she played Double Dutch outside with the big girls around her block.

On this bright, sunny spring day, Bettie couldn't help but smile at her humming daughter in the car as they drove from their home in West Philly to the Whitmans' house in Chestnut Hill for their annual Easter Egg hunt. She'd phoned Mrs. Whitman beforehand to say that they would be late because they'd had to wait for a plumber to come to fix a leaky faucet before they set off, and asked whether they should still come. An anxious Georgia waited for the reply, which was, "Of course you should come. We wouldn't want Georgia to miss the fun."

As she and her mother drove up to the home, Georgia noticed many big and shiny cars parked up and down the street.

"Do you think there'll be a lot of people at the egg hunt?" she asked.

"I guess so, honey," Bettie replied as she struggled to find a place to park. "Judge and Mrs. Whitman are important people, so I guess they know lots of folks to invite."

Bettie eventually found a spot to park, and they walked hand in hand to the Whitmans' house. Georgia ran up the steps to the front door and got there before Bettie. She stood on her tippy toes to reach the knocker, but before she could use it, Mamie Whitman opened the door.

"Well, hello, Smythe family!" she said vivaciously as her husband, Theodore, walked up behind her and gently rested his hands on her shoulders. "How lovely to see you both. Do please come in."

"Now Bettie," Mamie said as they walked through, "I want you to put your feet up while Georgia's enjoying herself with the other children. This isn't a workday."

Bettie smiled in reply as Georgia looked up at Mrs. Whitman. She breathed in deeply and smiled, too. Mrs. Whitman smelled sweet, like an unopened Easter basket.

"When do we go out to hunt for eggs?" Georgia asked.

"I'm afraid that the hunt is already over," Mamie replied. "But don't worry. I knew you would be late, so I've saved some eggs for you. But you can join the children for cake and ice cream. Would you like that?"

"Yes, please," Georgia whispered.

"Cat got your tongue?" Bettie prodded. "Speak so that Mrs. Whitman can hear you."

"Yes, please," Georgia said, louder this time. "Cake and ice cream, please."

Bettie scrunched her eyebrows. She wished she had said no to Mamie's invitation. She knew that most of the children would be members of Jack and Jill, the elite social club, and she wondered how they would react to Georgia. But it was too late now for such concerns, so she followed Mamie and an excited Georgia to the dining room, where Lawrence, Robert, and their friends were already seated at the table. Georgia gamely ambled in as well, chin held high as she remembered what her father had taught her.

The children stopped their sunny chatter as they entered the room and looked up at the unfamiliar face. Georgia was directed by Mamie to sit at the empty seat, which was next to Robert and two down from Lawrence, who sat at the head of the table.

Aside from Lawrence and Robert, Georgia recognized only one little girl, Sally, who was in her Sunday School.

"I know you. You're Georgia Smythe," Sally said, taking the end of a long strand of hair and twirling it between her fingers. "You go to my church."

"Yes, I know," Georgia shot back. "Lawrence and Robert do, too," she quickly added.

"I know that already," Sally retorted.

Georgia looked over at Lawrence, who smiled back at her. Both the Whitman and Smythe families attended Oak Street Baptist Church, which attracted Blacks from a wide range of incomes and social classes. But Georgia had noticed that she and her mother always sat upstairs in the balcony, while the Whitman family and Sally's family, along with many other prominent Blacks, always sat conspicuously downstairs in the congregation, close to the pulpit.

Georgia surveyed the faces of all the cherubic-faced girls and dour-faced boys. Around the circumference of the white plates and matching cups, were party favors, including a bubble kit, a box of candy cigarettes, and Georgia's favorite—rolled strips of rainbow-colored candy dots. Each child had also been given a little paper basket to put their found colored eggs into. There was an empty basket at Georgia's place, so she picked up the role of candy dots and dropped it into the basket.

"That's for eggs, stupid. And you don't have any!" Sally said, looking at Georgia.

"Yes, I do!" she replied. "Mrs. Whitman saved me some."

While they waited for the cake and ice cream to be brought out, Lawrence's brother Robert, the spitting image of his father, took a baseball from his pocket and began tossing it up in the air and catching it. On one of the throws, a nervous looking girl, seated next to him, grabbed it and put it in her lap.

"Give it back!" Robert snarled.

"Sing something, and I will!"

After a moment's hesitation he began to sing. It was Fontella Bass's "Rescue Me." The select children of Philadelphia's professional Black class sat riveted in their seats. Robert was a revelation. His voice, like liquid crystal, carried as he sang and could be heard by the grownups in the adjoining room. Bettie, who had joined Mamie in the kitchen to scoop out Neapolitan ice cream, asked, "Who's that?"

Theodore opened the door and the three adults stood huddled by the door to listen.

"You have an outstanding voice, son," his father announced.

Robert beamed.

"Your turn now, Lawrence," Georgia said.

But then, the thin faced girl suddenly tossed the ball she was holding back to Robert. She waited for the adults to leave the room before she said, "That stupid girl's sweet on Lawrence!"

That set a train of taunts in motion that were repeated around the table by the well-heeled children. Distraught, Georgia buried her face in her hands. Her braids fell onto the plate and collided with the chocolate butter cream frosting.

Before she left the house with her mother, Mamie handed Lawrence three Easter eggs to give to Georgia to take home. All three were pink with a bright blue band around the middle. Still reeling from the taunts, her hands trembled as she cupped them. He dropped the eggs into her hand.

"What's the name of the girl who started it?" she asked him.

Lawrence looked at her questioningly.

"The little girl who stole Robert's ball."

"Who?" he asked.

"The girl wearing the pretty silver locket."

"Oh…I think her name is Claire. Claire Sherman."

As she left Lawrence's house, hand entwined with her mother's, she turned back and feasted her eyes on the elegant home's façade. She counted ten shutters in total, all deep green, the color of the leaves that draped gracefully over the boys' bedroom windows.

I'm going to live in a house like this one day, she vowed to herself, as her mother led her back to the car.

3

April 1967

Bettie had given considerable thought lately to the Whitman boys. She had observed how they always seemed at each other's throats, any old season of the year. But it wasn't until Lawrence's baptism day that she began to truly believe there was more than sibling rivalry going on here.

There was more than skin in the game, in fact. There was blood in the game.

"What was that again?" Bettie asked. She transferred the white phone cradled between her ear and shoulder to the other ear, so that she could speak while wiping up spilled milk from the kitchen counter. It was Saturday night and Bettie was preparing hot chocolate, her daily evening ritual.

"I said, you don't have to, but Theodore and I would be delighted if you and Georgia would join us in the downstairs pew for Lawrence's baptism tomorrow morning."

"It's a little short notice...but we'd be happy to join you," Bettie said diffidently, looking out from her window at the rain-splashed neon sign of Billy's barbershop.

"Thank you," Mamie said, and Bettie sensed an irritated edge in her employer's voice at her hesitations, so she was grateful she hadn't declined. It was Jimmy who had encouraged her to join the Whitmans' church, one of the largest Baptist churches in town. Oak Street Church was the church people of every income bracket flocked to every morning to hear Pastor Blue's sermons, a fervent blend of fire and brimstone sprinkled with a good dose of advocacy for social justice.

She'd initially not wanted to attend, knowing that she, like all the others, would be on parade. But Jimmy had said, "Don't be like them. God don't care nothing about what you wear. He's got better things to do…. Least I hope so!"

At the mention of Lawrence's baptism, her thoughts turned toward Georgia. Why hadn't she tried harder to persuade Georgia to be baptized? How could something so fundamental to her faith be overlooked?

"There will be a reception at the house after the baptism and I would like for you and Georgia to be there."

"Mrs. Whitman, I don't feel comfortable—"

"Please, Bettie," Mrs. Whitman interrupted. Bettie could almost see her tightly pursed lips. "I'm not going to take no for an answer."

* * *

For Lawrence's special day, Bettie ended up fishing a knit dress out of the bottom drawer of her bureau. For some reason, the color of it reminded her of green sewage, so she hadn't worn it since hosting a small celebratory dinner in honor of Jimmy's eventual completion of his GED.

Determined to get to the Whitmans' church on time, she'd deftly flipped what would have ordinarily been a casual Sunday over like a pancake. She urged a cold cherry pop-tart on her daughter, pushed a week's worth of ironing aside, and left a stack of dishes in the sink. It wasn't until after they met up with the Whitmans outside the sanctuary that she found time to exhale.

"Well, Georgia, don't you look lovely," Mamie said, bending down to compliment Georgia, who wore a hand-sewn blue and white paisley smock dress and black Mary Jane shoes.

An usher greeted them. "Good morning, Judge and Mrs. Whitman!"

He indicated for the group to follow him down the aisle. They walked in single file behind the middle-aged usher, short in height but oozing stature.

Bettie stuck her hand out. She realized that she recognized him.

"I'm Mrs. Smythe."

"Oh," he said, revealing a brilliant white, mile-long smile. "Jimmy's wife!"

As he led the way to their seats Bettie noticed that the man's right forearm was pressed flat against his back at a horizontal angle, as if firmly glued in place. It didn't waver, not even by a millimeter. She smiled to herself. It was obvious to her that he'd been instructed to do just that, and she knew from his neatly pressed suit and the way he held his head aloft that he took great pride in his role.

As she followed Miss Mamie and Judge Theodore to their customary seats in the second row from the front, Bettie's gaze fell upon the people sitting in the balcony, some of whom were her friends. One of them recognized her and began waving vigorously with a fan that she held in her hand. Bettie waved back. And for a second, she thought about joining her friend in the balcony so as to be far removed from the scrutiny she felt, whether real or not, by the prettily dressed congregants in the main sanctuary.

"Is that a friend?" Mamie asked.

"Yes ma'am," Bettie said, turning her eyes from the balcony in case more of her friends recognized her. As she did, she became aware of the jumble of heavy perfumes that seemed to assault her from all angles. As they sat down, Bettie self-consciously lowered her hand to her lap to cover the small spot on the front of her dress—an old cranberry juice stain.

Georgia was sandwiched between herself and Judge Whitman and fidgeting to no end. Bettie rustled Georgia's hair to get her attention, then pressed her index finger to her lips. "Stop it," she whispered fiercely. Georgia was scratching her legs, encased in little girl's white patterned tights. "Now didn't I tell you to put lotion on those ashy legs this morning?"

Georgia grimaced at her mother, then started biting her bottom lip. But at least she stopped fidgeting. Distracted, Bettie turned her head to the right. Robert and Lawrence, she noticed, were behaving. She had known the brothers since she had started working for Mamie and Theodore in 1964, when Robert was three and Lawrence was one. She wouldn't admit it to anyone, but she was privately pleased with the role she'd played in helping to raise these boys.

She turned her head to look at them now. Robert's attention was fixed on the alto soloist while Lawrence sat frozen in his seat, little droplets of perspiration visible on his forehead. Bettie recalled a conversation she had overheard at the Whitmans' house on Friday between Judge Whitman and Lawrence. The memory of it made her wince.

"Now, remember son, you will be baptized tomorrow."

"Like Robert."

"Yes, that's right. Now Lawrence, remember what the pastor asked of you. Do you accept the Lord as your personal savior?"

"Sure. Does he accept me?"

"Don't you sass me, boy."

The judge's voice, to Bettie's ear, had a rough edge to it.

"He won't, unless you stop your misbehaving ways," Lawrence's father had added sternly.

She tried to put that conversation out of her mind as she directed her eyes toward the front of the sanctuary. The youth choir was clad in long, flowing gowns of gold and white. They belted out "Goin' Up

17

Yonder," Bettie noticed, as though they were teed up to go just there. She tapped her feet to the music and politely clapped along with the others, her head moving from left to right. The choir's zealous rendition was sung as though their lives depended on the performance and, at its conclusion, many of the ardent parishioners shot up from their seats and amens were shouted high to the rafters.

Bettie was left breathless by the end of the sermon. It was delivered by Pastor Simon Blue, who hailed from Rhode Island but could deliver a sermon as though Kentucky was in his bones. As the sermon drew to a close with a call and response, the pastor took out a handkerchief to wipe his face, which was bathed in sweat. He began to sing his sermon, each cluster of words punctuated by the organist thumping out a reedy chord.

Bettie looked at her Timex. She knew what would be next and stole a glance at Lawrence, whose expression was firm. She could tell that he was anxious.

"Here," she said, reaching over Mamie to hand the boy a peppermint, which he accepted with a smile. "And here's one for Robert, too," she said, and then gave one to Georgia.

Bettie patted Mamie's lap reassuringly as Lawrence was led by one of the ushers, along with others who were to be baptized, to the side of the church. They reappeared shortly afterward in the Baptismal pool.

"Lawrence!" Georgia whispered excitedly to her mother. "There he is," she said, pointing.

It did not escape Bettie how Georgia said the boy's name softly, like velvet.

Bettie sighed, noticing that Lawrence was a somber figure, unsmiling and dressed from head to toe in white. She watched as the pastor opened his Bible to read in a voice that was inaudible to the congregants. Only his lips could be seen. Suddenly there was a sharp movement and Lawrence's head fell backward. There was a splashing sound, and as he rose, the sound of coughing and sputtering.

"I didn't do that," Robert told his mother.

"Do what?" Bettie heard Mamie ask.

"Cough and get water all up my nose like Lawrence did."

* * *

After the service was over and Lawrence had rejoined them, the two families clustered together in the church foyer for a few moments before setting off for the Whitmans' house. Bettie and Georgia arrived after the Whitmans and made their way to the front door, which was at the top of two flights of steps. The house was a three-story turn of the century Tudor, made of thick, quarried, big gray stones that reflected the strong sunlight.

As they entered, a pair of child's galoshes were parked by the door. Georgia picked them up to look at them.

"Are these Lawrence's?" Georgia asked innocently, turning her head to look at her mother.

"Are they yours, Georgia?"

"No," she said.

"Well then, put them down," Bettie said firmly.

Georgia looked mournfully down at her shiny black shoes that were too small for her. They had been a hand-me-down from a second cousin whose name she couldn't remember.

"Hello, Bettie, Georgia. Come on in ladies," Mamie said as she opened the door. She bent down to speak to Georgia. "Lawrence and Robert are in the playroom, Georgia. You know where that is, don't you? Just go upstairs, then turn at the landing,"

Bettie had been told by Mamie more than once that the stairs had been constructed from original walnut boards, a prized selling point of the classic German-style home. This meant nothing to her, but *everything* to Mamie. But still, each time she mounted the stairs to clean, she couldn't figure out what was so special about the house's old wooden stairs.

"Is she OK?" Mamie whispered to Bettie. She'd noticed Georgia hobbling up the stairs.

"Shoes too small," Bettie said, in a matter-of-fact manner. "Don't worry, Mrs. Whitman. She'll be fine. Leather stretches."

When Georgia turned around and smiled at her mother and Mamie at the top of the landing, Mrs. Whitman smiled generously back. Internally, though, she was giving a sigh of relief that she'd decided against inviting Claire, the daughter of the Scotts. She was the same age as Georgia and a delicate little hothouse flower in the mold of her exquisite mother. She couldn't imagine that child ever wearing a shoe that had not been fitted with precision.

Afternoon light poured through the colorful Victorian stained-glass windows on either side of the front door, the thick beveled glass casting a comforting reddish glow onto the two women standing there. Mamie draped her hand lightly around Bettie's waist. She had already changed from her dress with the white Peter Pan collar into a blue cotton camp shirt and black linen pants. As Mamie stood next to her, Bettie self-consciously moved her hand over the stain on her dress.

"I'm so glad that you came," Mamie said warmly. "You're like family."

"We wouldn't have missed it," Bettie replied as she followed Mamie into the kitchen.

"I've already taken care of lunch, so all we need to do is sit down and eat."

"Yes, ma'am," Bettie said. "But won't you let me help you, Mrs. Whitman?"

"Certainly not!" Mamie said as she put on bright red oven mittens and pulled a pan of buttery pound cake out of the oven. "I won't hear of it. You and Georgia are here as guests and, as I said, everything has already been taken care of."

They walked through the house to the living room, where Judge Whitman and their friends the Scotts were deep in conversation.

"Robert's really a chip off the old block," Bettie heard Dr. Scott say, and as she walked into the room, she saw the judge nodding vociferously in agreement.

"Hi, Bettie!" Dr. Scott said as he saw her. "How are things with you these days?"

"Better than I have a right for them to be, Dr. Scott," she replied.

She walked across the room, and as she did Dr. Scott rose from his seat.

"Call me Sherman, please. It's good to see you, Bettie. I hope that you're both keeping well."

"Georgia and I are both as well as can be expected, I suppose."

Bettie had seen the Scotts once or twice before at the Whitmans' residence. Whenever she saw Sherman Scott—she didn't know if it was the way his horn-rimmed glasses always rested on the edge of his nose, or the intensity of his inquisitive eyes—she always thought of someone who belonged in a library in front of a stack of books. Mrs. Scott, on the other hand, was a creature of fashion. She recognized her type. She was one of the millions of middle-aged adherents to magazines that featured women much younger than themselves. She noted Mrs. Scott's long limbed, graceful physique. Always shy in polite company, Bettie's eyes were drawn downward, to her thin ankles, encased in tan lace-up sandals.

Bettie breathed in deeply. Well, since she was an invited guest, damn it if she wouldn't play the role to the hilt. She sat down next to Mrs. Scott on a walnut brown straight-backed chair and placed her purse beside her, thinking how strange it looked there instead of its normal perch, which was the ledge at the side of Mamie's kitchen sink.

Then she noticed Judge Whitman looking quizzically at her. Theodore was tall with a high forehead and finely proportioned features. His eyes happened to be light brown, but it wasn't the color of his eyes that were appealing. It was the contrast between the color of his eyes and the heavy black lashes and eyebrows above them that lent him a roguish charm. Bettie noted that Judge Whitman's eldest son, Robert, had inherited an exact replica of his father's eyes.

Bettie looked at him, expecting him to say something. But he didn't, so she turned back to Sherman.

"Well, to tell you the truth," Bettie told him, "Georgia and I have struggled some since Jimmy died."

Judge Whitman cleared his throat and averted his eyes to look at the ivy that fringed the big picture window.

"Is there anything more that we can do, Bettie?" he asked with sincerity.

"Well, there is one thing you could do for me that would set my mind at rest," she admitted. "I know that you are on the board of Colsol, the mining company that Jimmy worked for. Could you find out for me why he died?"

Surprised and seemingly uncomfortable by Bettie's sudden question, Theodore said, "As you know Bettie, mining is a treacherous job. One that he chose, knowing the risks."

He stole a look at Mamie, whose head was bowed.

"I'm very sorry for your loss, but regrettably accidents do sometimes happen."

"They said that the roof of the mine collapsed on him. How did that happen? It would have to be a safety lapse, right?"

The room fell silent.

"Ain't that a safety lapse, Judge Whitman?" she demanded.

Mamie stood up and rushed over to Bettie, draping her arm around Bettie's shoulder.

"Now, now, Bettie," she said soothingly, pushing a stray hair back from the side of Bettie's face. "This has been a really rough week for you, hasn't it? You've been under a lot of stress."

"I could raise your salary if you're having trouble making ends meet," Theodore said, acutely aware that their good friends, the Scotts, were listening intently.

"Thank you, Judge, but I don't need charity," she said firmly. "You pay a fair wage for what I do, and it wouldn't be right to ask for more."

"Yes, that's right Bettie," Shirley said. "We women are beyond that. What we want is respect."

"All I want, Judge Whitman," Bettie said, "is for you to help me and Georgia get some answers."

Theodore moved forward in his seat.

"Bettie, I'm afraid that there's nothing I can say right now. The accident is still being investigated—"

"Answers, Judge Whitman," she said, cutting him off. "Please. I need answers."

The tension was thick, and grew even more so as a disquieting calm descended on the room. "I'll find them for you, Bettie," he finally said, in a voice that was equal parts firmness and exasperation.

"Jimmy would sure be so proud of how Georgia is turning out," Dr. Scott interjected, seeking to lighten the heavy mood that the conversation had wrought.

He looked from Judge Whitman back to Bettie.

Smiling brightly, he said, "Georgia's blossoming into a beautiful young girl."

"Thank you, Dr. Sherman," Bettie said.

Theodore coughed loudly and turned his attention back toward the group. He still had bad dreams about Jimmy Smythe. Jimmy, with his lean, elegant bearing and kind smile, was an unusual sort to be found working in the mines. He could have been a matinee idol, but instead he was just Jimmy, the gentle soul who, at the end of the day, washed off the grime from the mine and put the apprehension from working there to the back of his mind. Theodore would never forget Bettie ringing him the night of the accident. It was just after midnight, and it took him several moments before he realized that it was Bettie yelling hysterically that her beloved Jimmy was dead. The investigation into the cause of the roof collapse was still ongoing and he felt irritated and embarrassed that he could not yet provide Bettie with the answers she sought.

Dr. Scott, knees sewn tightly together as he sat stiffly on a wing chair that had been inherited by Mamie, glanced at Theodore. A sociology professor, Dr. Scott had deep, permanent worry lines creased on his forehead. He put down the magazine he had picked up from the coffee table, which he had previously been engrossed in.

"Teddy, you're not going to stay on the board of Colsol mining after what's happened, are you?" Sherman asked inquisitively, taking off his glasses to get a better look at Theodore.

Theodore flushed red and turned toward his wife, his eyes mutely begging for help. Mamie deftly changed the subject.

"Any one for some hot quiche Lorraine and potato salad?" she called out.

Each table place was adorned with silver forks and knives over buttercup yellow folded linen napkins. A spray of freshly cut flowers in a glass vase adorned the table.

"Mrs. Whitman, would you mind?" Bettie asked, pointing toward the kitchen. As Mamie followed, Bettie was wringing her hands as she hurried into the kitchen. She had picked up her purse from the floor and now clutched it to her chest.

"Yes, Bettie?" Mamie said.

At that same moment, Lawrence came downstairs.

"I'll have some of that quiche, Momma!" he said.

"You could hear me from upstairs?" she asked.

"I can always hear you, Ma," he said, grinning ear to ear. Favored child that he was, he seemed aware of the special niche he filled in his mother's heart.

Bettie quietly marveled how Lawrence, the stoic little figure in the Baptismal pool, had reverted so quickly back to his usual charming self. She, too, couldn't help having a soft spot for this bookish, artistic child, who seemed to always be met with wrath from Judge Whitman for no apparent cause.

"I've set the children's table on the porch, Lawrence. Go along upstairs and corral everybody down," Mamie instructed.

She then closed the kitchen door behind herself and Bettie.

"I know what you're going to say, Bettie," Mamie said. "Don't think I don't."

Bettie didn't reply. Instead, she fell into work mode and began washing the large bowl that Mamie had used for the cake dough, placing it in the kitchen sink and filling it with hot sudsy water. She washed and dried it before putting it away. The kitchen was now nearly as spotless as when she'd left it after work on Friday.

"Now, please just stop it," Mamie said, reaching out to gently grasp Bettie's arm.

Bettie turned around to face her.

"I want you to relax," Mamie said. "I know that the Scotts can be a bit…"

"That ain't it," Bettie replied. "I need to get home. I've got things to do before work tomorrow."

"OK, Bettie. I understand. You go ahead upstairs and collect Georgia. I'll make a plate for you to take home."

Bettie and Mamie locked eyes, mutely understanding each other. Then Bettie smiled and headed toward the stairs. She found Georgia on the landing, seated cross-legged on the floor, shoes strewn to the side and staring out of the window.

"Come on, Georgia. It's time to go home."

Ignoring her mother, Georgia continued to look out of the window, so Bettie went over to see what was capturing her attention.

"Oh, my God," she said. "Lawrence and Robert are fighting!"

Bettie could see that the Whitman brothers were writhing outside on the ground in the backyard. Georgia scurried to her feet, picked up her shoes, and ran downstairs.

"Wait. Georgia, stop!"

She followed her daughter down the staircase and toward the backdoor that led outside to the yard.

"Did so!" Lawrence yelled.

"Did not!"

"I saw you. Don't lie! You let Tom and Elijah beat you up. Right on this very spot!"

"They called me a bad name! They could have killed me!" Robert yelled.

"What did they call you?"

"They—they called me a queer!" Robert shot back.

"Well, maybe that's because it's the truth!"

They tumbled roughly in the green grass. Lawrence was on top at first and then Robert managed to get the better of his brother. Robert triumphantly sat on Lawrence's back. He yanked his brother's arm from the ground over his back.

"Say uncle!" Robert demanded.

Lawrence groaned as Robert pressed his body harder onto him.

"Say it! Say uncle!" Robert repeated, glancing frantically around.

"My arm hurts!" Lawrence yelled. He looked up toward Georgia, who was standing next to the fighting boys.

"Momma!" she called, just as Bettie arrived at the patchy spot of grass by the boys' long-neglected tree house in the corner of the yard.

"Help! Robert is hurting Lawrence!"

Theodore suddenly appeared, slice of cake, wrapped in a white paper napkin, still in his hand.

"Now what's going on here!" he bellowed. "Break it up!"

Robert was still seated on top of Lawrence as he loomed above them. At the sound of his father's menacing voice, Robert got off his brother. Lawrence rolled over onto the grass, clutching his hurt arm.

"Lawrence! This has your signature written all over it," Theodore said. "I don't even have to ask to know who's behind this."

"That's not true, Dad! He hurt me!"

Lawrence struggled to his feet and was facing his father as Robert, embarrassed, looked on. Bettie could see that Lawrence had started to cry. She and Georgia looked on with horror as Theodore slapped Lawrence hard on his right cheek.

"Don't you *ever, ever* fight with your brother again," his father said.

"No, no, Judge Whitman," Bettie said, taking a step forward. "This ain't right now." She looked at Lawrence, who had lowered his head and was crying. "I'm going to go get Mrs. Whitman."

Georgia stayed behind as her mother ran back to the house without looking back. A chastened Lawrence stared at his brother.

"But Robert's the one who hurt me!" he told his father. "Robert, say something!"

Robert stared back at Lawrence. He tightened his lips and said nothing. So, Georgia moved forward to stand between Lawrence and his father. Judge Whitman looked down at her. She confidently stuck one stockinged foot forward as if she were performing a ballet move. Her white stockinged feet were fluorescent green with grass stains.

She looked up at the judge.

"You got that wrong, sir," she said.

"What did you say, young lady?"

"You got it wrong Mr. Judge," she said, her nose turning up in the air. "Robert hurt Lawrence, not the other way around. I think you even saw that."

She knew all eyes were on her. She swirled around, allowing the hem of her dress—the new one she was so excited to wear today for Lawrence's baptism—to sashay around her. Then she ran as quickly as her feet could take her back to the house, nearly colliding at the back door with an anxious Mamie, who had left her guests to find out the cause of the trouble between the two boys.

* * *

On the drive home, Georgia took both hands to lean over and pry off her shoes and stockings. She raised her bare feet in the air and propped them on top of the dashboard.

"You better take those feet off from my dashboard. Do you hear me?" Bettie said, taking her eyes off the road for a second to glare at her daughter until she complied.

"By the way, what happened back there, Georgia?" she asked.

"What?"

"What did you say to Judge Whitman? I hope you didn't sass him."

"All I did was tell the truth, Momma."

"And what is the truth? I want to know because Judge Whitman came back to the house, huffin' and puffin', muttering about how you reminded him of one of his rude law interns. He even asked me if I allowed you to disrespect me at home?"

"I didn't sass him, Momma. I just told him that it was Robert that hurt Lawrence, not the other way around. You always say that I should tell the truth, so that's what I did."

Bettie sighed, then fell silent as their compact car drove from the green haven of the suburbs to the tightly packed row homes that populated West Philly.

* * *

That evening, before turning in, Whitman stepped outside to be nourished by an indigo sky, cut through with rhubarb-colored ribbons from a setting sun. For a moment, the altercations of the day were forgotten. He sighed, reflecting on his life. He hadn't done bad for the grandson of a Tennessee farmer. But the dark parts of his past were still hard for him to deal with, even after prayer, even with his stellar career. His father's penalty for him, even for the most minor of infractions, was a slow walk to a pine tree in the back where he would be asked to tear down a thick branch of his choosing. Large or small, his father would manage to wield that stick and use it to whip him good. But despite the beatings, life was good and sometimes he longed for schoolboy days, catching 'coons in the backyard of his grandfather's farm.

He'd been lucky to get an education and elevate himself in the world—all the things his parents had hoped for him. He'd since cultivated a clique of white friends whom he played racquetball with. They never asked him about his childhood, and he never told them. That suited him just fine.

He knew that most of them considered him an equal, just as Martin Luther King, Jr. had told them. It wasn't the color but the character that makes a difference. But oftentimes color trumps character for folks that looked like him.

Being equal, everyone was expected to pull their own weight, to raise themselves up by their own bootstraps. That's what he had done, and it had been tough. But, he smiled to himself, toughness is a leavening thing.

There were two worlds, he thought as he contemplated the sun sinking below a gorgeous purple sky. Both of them he knew well. He rubbed his chin, pondering. If he was honest with himself, for folks like Bettie and Jimmy, their bootstraps were simply too short to get a good grip. That thought brought shame for him, and a recognition of his own borrowed identity.

He patted his front pocket, fishing for a Camel unfiltered. Although he had quit smoking, at certain times when under stress he instinctively reached for a pack of cigarettes that was no longer there. *Why does Lawrence irritate me so and bring out my dark side*, he asked himself as he turned to go back into the house. *Is it my fault or his?*

4

"Boy, will you stop walking on my just mopped floor?" Bettie said to Lawrence as he came into the kitchen.

She playfully shook the mop at him as he held his hands up in front of him.

"Don't shoot me now, Bettie!"

"Well, you better get off my floor, boy, before I do!"

Lawrence flashed a wide grin as he side stepped to the corner of the kitchen. She beamed a smile back at him as though he were her son. She was only half listening to her cousin Rebecca on the other end of the phone.

"Get on out of that funky city of yours and soak up some of this good old country air!"

Bettie put the mop aside and used one hand to sponge off the kitchen counter while her other hand held the phone to her ear.

"Hush. Didn't I tell you not to call me at work?"

"Well, Jed and I now live in a farmhouse at the end of that same dirt lane where Granddad built his farm. We bought it a while back after I sold the hairdressing business I inherited from Mamma."

"I loved visiting your grandad's farm," Bettie said, making herself busy now by sponging off crumbs from a coffee cake one of the boys had left on the table. "Do you remember how Sam, Claudia, you, and I used to pile onto that bed in the guest room and we'd all laugh about nothing 'til two a.m.? Remember how clean your grandmother's sheets were?"

"Girl, I remember. My grandmother didn't mind us making such a hoot and holler. She'd come in before bedtime to push back the curtains and open the screen windows wide. 'Ain't nothing better than a little country air for my country girls,' she'd say."

"I remember, Rebecca."

"So why don't you and Georgia come visit us?"

Bettie hesitated.

"No need to worry," Rebecca interjected. "Things have *changed* in this neck of the woods, don't you know. There are a lot fewer rednecks. Now, I'm not going to go so far as to say they disappeared. As God is my witness, they haven't. But they are no longer in the numbers they once were. Nowhere near, in fact."

"Let me think about it," Bettie said, but she was already working out the logistics in her head. "I'll give you a call this evening."

* * *

On the Monday before the trip, Bettie asked Mrs. Whitman for an extra day.

"I'd like to take off this Friday, if that that's OK. My cousin Rebecca has invited Georgia and me to her home in Virginia. I'll make sure that all the laundry's done by Thursday."

"That's fine with me, Bettie. A few days in the country will do you both good. You two have a good time."

As the Greyhound lumbered over empty brown country roads on a bright blue morning, Bettie tried to doze, but to no avail. Eight-year-old Georgia was talking nonstop.

31

She opened her eyes to see Georgia's nose pressed against the window of the bus. Transfixed by the acres of green and brown, she shot out questions.

"What's that?" Georgia asked excitedly, her finger pressed against the window.

"Cotton, child," Bettie replied.

In the wake of Jimmy's death, Georgia's natural humor had seemed to peel away like stewed chicken meat falling off the bone. It seemed back now, and she could see that Georgia was regaining her spirit. The questions kept coming, but then Georgia settled down and scanned the white expanses of cotton. Blankets of white fluff were hoisted on top of the black, spindly shoulders of branches that held them up to the sun. The cotton clung to its spiky branches as far as the eye could see.

Mother and daughter were flat-out tired when, after eleven hours, they arrived at the Greyhound bus station in Roanoke. They were met by Jed, Rebecca's husband. Bettie sat next to Georgia on the torn leather seats of his red pick-up truck for the drive to the farm.

"The grass is so *green*, Momma!"

"Yes, baby!"

Jed took his eyes off the road for a moment to peer in his rearview mirror at the excited child, whose pigtails were pressed upward on the seat.

"It's her first time in the country," Bettie explained.

"That's alright, Bettie. It's good that she's taking an interest. The South isn't just our history, it's her history, too. Can't escape it."

Georgia fell silent. So did Bettie.

Close to her cousin's house, Georgia struck up a game of twenty questions with her mother. She was forced to speak over the music that Jed had cranked up, which had been Jimmy's favorite: Ray Charles's "What'd I Say."

Rebecca was waiting for them upon their arrival. From the moment the truck drove onto the gravel driveway, they could see her vigorously waving her hands as she stood by the front porch. Bettie admired her cousin's espadrilles as she bounded toward them.

"Safely delivered!" Jed called as he hefted Georgia out of the truck and set her on the driveway. He then lifted Bettie's battered suitcase that she'd had for decades, not seeing any good reason to buy a new one, and Georgia's little red one from the bed of the truck.

"How are you doing, Sissy?" Rebecca affectionately asked.

Bettie hadn't heard the word *Sissy* in a long time. It was short for *sister*, and she drew comfort from it. Having had no biological sister, her cousin had always been there for her as a surrogate sister. As they hugged, the beige, wide brimmed straw hat that Rebecca held in her hand accidently scratched Bettie's bare, brown arms. She smelled of what she had always smelled of for as long as Bettie could remember. It was a scent called *Youth Dew*.

Bettie stepped back to examine her cousin. Rebecca's face was scarcely different than when they were schoolgirls. The same toothy, ebullient tomboy grin as in the days when skipping was not just for beautiful days, but any old day. The same happy-go-lucky child who preferred male company on her backyard firefly hunting escapades, and the girls didn't begrudge her one bit, because they all wanted to be like her...like Rebecca.

Rebecca turned toward Georgia and said, "Come here, girl. My, aren't you pretty."

Georgia had a second's reprieve before being swallowed up in Rebecca's ample arms.

"I'll take that," Rebecca said, reaching for the handle of Georgia's suitcase and lifting it effortlessly into the air. Then they proceeded to walk through the long thick grass and toward the country farmhouse. Rebecca's arm was interlinked with Bettie's in front. Georgia trailed from behind.

Rebecca stopped as they were walking, as though she'd forgotten something in the truck. She turned her head around, smiling expansively at Georgia.

"Do you like pecan pie, child?"

"Yes, ma'am! I love pie," Georgia replied with a smile.

"Not 'ma'am'—you're aging me now. Just call me Aunt Rebecca." They all laughed.

Awaiting them on the porch, on a long table covered in a pink and purple flowered plastic tablecloth, was a platter of roasted chicken and salad, a pitcher of sweet tea and crusty, buttery, and lumpy pecan pie that made Bettie's mouth water just upon sight. The rickety stools didn't bother them. They ate until they were full, and then they ate some more until there was nothing left on the platters.

Later that evening, after the dishes had been cleared, Bettie followed Rebecca and Jed outside to the wide front porch that was graced on either side by two Magnolia trees, their fragrant blossoms scenting the night air.

Before stepping outside, Bettie instructed Georgia to stay inside and draw. Rebecca had placed some paper and a tin cigar box full of crayons on a small card table in front of the large picture window in the living room.

"I've kept those crayons all these years," she said. "I bought them for my nephew. He's all grown up now, but I was hoping that someone like you might come and visit me one day and enjoy using them."

"Thank you, Aunt Rebecca," Georgia said. "I'll be very careful with them."

She reached for the orange crayon, then the brown, and began to draw, happy to be alone with her thoughts.

Outside on the porch, Rebecca placed two glasses on the table and poured a splash of brandy into them for Bettie and herself. Jed, a teetotaler, poured himself a tall glass of homemade lemonade and a smaller glass, which he took to Georgia.

"A long time ago, I got in a fight that ended badly and which I'd rather forget," was all Jed had to say by way of explanation when Bettie asked on his return why he didn't drink.

Truth be told, she didn't know too many Black people who'd stopped drinking entirely. They might have sidled from the hard stuff onto wine, but she couldn't think of any she knew who'd stopped for good. As for her, she enjoyed a spot of Remy once in a while.

"You want?" Rebecca asked her, pointing to her empty glass.

"You can put a splash in there, sister," Bettie said with a smile on her face.

It was quiet outside, there in the country, she thought. No sirens, no sound of busses or trains going by. A kind of peace that she had forgotten could exist. She watched as both Jed and Rebecca closed their eyes, enjoying the respite of the soft, summer breeze. Then, she opened her mouth and the words just flowed out of her.

"It wasn't supposed to happen like that. Jimmy dying out of the blue, so young."

Bettie felt fine and able to contain the emotions that suddenly threatened to surge through her. That is, until she felt a touch on her sleeve of her knit sweater. Startled, she turned and saw that it was Jed looking down at her with his large, brown, luminous eyes.

"We are so sorry, Bettie. You know, you and your sweet Georgia are always welcome here. It's good to see you back home."

The lingering way he said *home* made her feel that she was an object of pity. That was the moment that the floodgates opened, and she began to cry. Uncertain how to respond, Jed stood next to her and winced.

"Awwww," he said, sounding like the wind whistling through the woods.

"Come and sit down now, Jed, and leave her be," Rebecca abruptly ordered. "She and Georgia have been through a lot, and it's only natural for her to cry when she's with family."

Then, turning to Bettie, she said, "It shouldn't have happened, Sissy. Shouldn't have happened. I'm talking about your Jimmy. There was something wrong with that mine that the roof collapsed on him like that."

Jed walked over to the front door and opened it wide enough for the light inside to merge with the moonlight so that everyone could see one another.

"I saw Judge Whitman's face on TV a few months ago," he said, sitting himself down now on the porch rocker with floral decorated seat cushions. "He was on a special to talk about Justice Thurgood Marshall. He did a fine job, in my opinion, but I seem to remember that they said in the introduction that he was on the board of Colsol mining. Ain't that the company that Jimmy worked for? I seem to remember it from the news clippings you sent us about Jimmy's death."

Bettie stopped sobbing and looked hard at Jed. She took another small sip of her brandy.

"Yes, you're right," she said. "Jimmy did work for Colsol, and the judge is still on the board."

"That ain't right," Rebecca said. She hugged herself and rocked back and forth in her chair. "It just ain't right. What's he doing staying involved with that company after it killed your Jimmy?"

"He says that he wants to stay on the board until after the investigation report is issued," Bettie replied. "Then he wants to make sure that any safety violations are taken care of so that no more men die like my poor Jimmy."

There was a lull in the conversation as Jed put his half-drunk glass of lemonade on the table, smiled a little awkwardly, and cleared his voice.

"Now Bettie," he said. "It's none of my business, I know, but you need to hold that judge to his word. The company owes you an explanation about what happened to Jimmy and it needs to fix whatever went wrong. Ain't that right, Rebecca?"

Rebecca reached out and touched Bettie's hand, which felt cool on Bettie's warm skin.

"Jed's right, I guess," she said. "But I still think he should resign from Colsol after what's happened. It just don't seem right for him to stay on there."

Bettie was about to speak when a red Mustang, flashing in the moonlight, careened by and startled her. A chorus of laughing male voices rose into the night as the car passed by. She felt the skin on her arms prickle and sat bolt upright.

"White or Black?" she asked, a little shaken.

"Don't you worry about them," Jed said. "They're rednecks alright, playing their Johnny Cash tapes. But these ones? They're harmless. They come over to our place for fresh corn by the bushel."

He looked at his wife and smiled.

"Rebecca gives them to the boys' parents. Damned smart lady she is. I know that the Klan is still around these parts, but not every white person is in the Klan. Still, it doesn't hurt to be on the right side of your white neighbors."

Bettie turned and looked out into the woods that surrounded the house. The scent of magnolia marinated the cool night air and settled pleasingly over her. But the mosquitos were on parade, so they decided to go inside.

They found Georgia still seated at the card table, engrossed in her drawing. The cookies that Rebecca had left for her had been devoured and the juice fully drank. Jed decided to call it a night and went upstairs after pecking his wife on the cheek. Bettie and Rebecca walked over to Georgia.

"Now let me see," Rebecca said, kneeling on the floor beside Georgia. "What have you drawn?"

"This one's at my school. There's my teacher," Georgia said, pointing to a stick figure of a lady with rectangular blocks of hair on either side of a brown colored face. She told me…"

She paused to finish coloring in the one of the desks.

"She told me when my daddy died that sometimes God wants to be with his special people. She called them his champions. And sometimes, just sometimes…"

"Sometimes what, baby?" Rebecca said, as Bettie drew in closer to get a better look at the drawing.

"The teacher said that people are like flowers and sometimes God plucks up his best flowers early from earth for a very special purpose," Georgia said, her eyes still glued to the paper where she was putting the finishing touches.

A pause followed that was filled by the sound of thick Crayola crayons scrawling on paper.

"Hey, where'd that come from!" Georgia cried. Bettie's tears had fallen onto Georgia's drawing to form a watery splotch.

"Oh, no!" she said, quickly wiping her eyes.

Georgia looked up to the ceiling and then back down again at Rebecca.

"It must be a leak in the attic," Rebecca said.

"But there ain't no rain," Georgia replied.

Rebecca leaned over and inspected the picture more closely, allowing Bettie to gather herself.

"And who is that?" Rebecca asked, pointing to a stick figure sitting at a desk.

"Well, that's me, silly," Georgia said.

Bettie drew closer and both women looked intently at the drawing. They smiled as they saw the teacher was leaning over the desk, and in her hand was a cone with a big blob of pink colored ice cream on top for Georgia. Then Bettie noticed something.

"Georgia, since when is your hair yellow?" she asked.

Georgia put down her crayon wearily and sighed. She stared up at her mother quizzically.

"Don't you see, Mom? Don't you get it? That's me! And that's the color of hair I'd like to have."

Embarrassed, Bettie turned her bewildered face toward her cousin.

"I don't know where she gets such foolishness from," Bettie said, in an apologetic voice. Turning back toward Georgia she asked, "Is being Black not good enough for you? You should be proud of who you are—a beautiful Black girl with lovely black hair."

She knew as soon as she spoke that she'd chosen the wrong words. The hurt that glazed her daughter's eyes registered deeply with her and compounded her sense of helplessness. Silence settled in and, after a few minutes, Rebecca spoke up.

"Let's go to bed. Everything looks better in the morning," she said wearily. "Now there ain't nothing on the schedule over the next few days, unless you want to help me collect some eggs from the chicken coop. Later tomorrow, you and your momma can join me to go into town. We can stop off at the curio shop and we'll buy you some home-made, freshly churned ice cream. But right now, let's tuck the day behind us."

A short while later, Bettie and Georgia crawled into the guest room's queen-sized bed that was covered with a fresh white cotton quilt. For the life of her, Bettie thought that the quilt smelled like the clear, gurgling creek water that she and Rebecca used to slosh their bare feet around in as children on lazy Saturdays. She inhaled slowly, wiggling her toes under the cool, clean sheets. It smelled of safety, she decided. She smiled and breathed in again, consciously lowering shoulders that were tense from day after day of toil. She allowed herself to drift off to sleep, lulled by fresh country air.

* * *

They had to leave on Sunday so that Bettie could get back to work. The day came too fast as far as she and Georgia were concerned. It had been a good visit for them both, she decided. The healthy country air seemed to have injected new energy into Georgia, and Bettie had enjoyed reconnecting with where she came from. Things would be good; she'd decided that as she found herself looking down from the top of Rebecca's narrow stairwell. Georgia was walking slowly down the stairs ahead of Bettie, as if in a processional, in her just pressed white cotton pink and white smock dress that she'd picked to go home in.

Things would be far better than before. She and Georgia would find a way to press on, just the two of them. As Bettie lugged her daughter's suitcase behind her, thumping against the balusters, she watched as Georgia walked gingerly in front of her as though not to crease her new shoes.

Goodbyes were said after a breakfast of hot buttery cloverleaf biscuits, sausage, and scrambled eggs. Bettie wiped the grease from her lips and then took the same beige linen napkin to wipe the corners of Georgia's mouth. They walked out to Jed's pickup truck in line formation, Georgia clutching her mother's elbow. As they got to the truck, Bettie watched as Rebecca bent down and slipped a gift under Georgia's arm.

"Oh, thank you!" Georgia said.

Bettie also got a gift, which was passed through the truck's open window. It was immediately recognizable. The gift was wrapped in aluminum foil and was oblong shaped.

Bettie lifted the package to her nose. "Mmmmm. I could smell the cinnamon from all the way upstairs. I know exactly what this is—my favorite. It's Brown Bettie?" Bettie said teasingly.

Rebecca smiled from ear to ear, her smile dissolving into laughter. "We don't call it that no more. It's called apple crisp now."

"Well, I'll have you know that Georgia and I will have eaten this here Brown Bettie before we even get back to Philly!"

As Rebecca leaned against her aluminum postbox and waved to them amidst the emerging light of morning, Bettie cranked her window down and waved back.

"I love you, Sissy!" she yelled out into the blue as Jed put the truck into gear and the three of them drove off, waving vigorously until Rebecca receded into the distance.

Rebecca watched until her husband's red truck disappeared into a big cloud of brown dust. It was only then, she told Bettie when they next spoke on the phone, at the moment her husband's creaky old truck turned the bend, that she started to cry.

"I suppose some of Grandmom's voodoo must have rubbed off on me a little," she said. "Because there was just a smatter of tears at first. That's always the case whenever guests come and go. Just my way. But then it was suddenly a wind gust of tears. You hear me?

"Crying I just couldn't contain, girl. You understand? If any soul had asked me why the tears, I wouldn't have been able to tell them a damned thing. I had an inkling, though. I had a feeling of trouble coming on, somehow. I just couldn't tell what direction that damned storm was coming from. But I knew it was coming."

5

Georgia pressed her present tightly to her chest all the way from Rebecca's home to the small bus terminal on Jefferson Street in Roanoke. She was lost in the pleasant memory of the weekend, swimming in the clear water creek down the hill from Rebecca's home, unaware that by the end of the day a choice she would make would loom large over her days for some time to come.

Jed quickly unloaded their suitcases and said his goodbyes right there and then.

He'd planned it just so because, while he enjoyed being with Bettie and Georgia, he was anxious to get to work. He stood on the curb alongside the two and looked down at the pavement. Long red streamers had fallen off one of the streetlights, which were still beribboned. A large banner was stretched pole to pole, and read: *The Historical Society of Roanoke Women's Parade.*

"That's one we've missed," he mumbled. He looked up at the banner and then down at Georgia. "Guess we didn't get the invite," he said and winked.

"Well, Sis, you have a good trip back."

"Are you're my mother's brother?" Georgia asked, holding her present in one hand and the handle of her little suitcase in the other.

"No, I'm not," he said and smiled broadly. He raised his hand and covered his eyes to keep the bright Virginia sun out of his eyes. "But your mom is like a sister to Rebecca and me, which means that you are a treasured niece to us." He reached down and gently tousled Georgia's two braids, which were held together at the back by a long strip of soft black velveteen ribbon.

"Praise God," Bettie whispered.

Georgia thought she was praying for a second. But then she realized she wasn't. She was just being Momma and giving thanks.

They said their goodbyes to Jed then the two of them walked hand in hand into the bus station. It was a plain brick building, with simple glass windows on either side of a big red door in front.

"We're early!" Bettie pronounced. "But if you got to be somewhere, it's best to be there early," she added, looking down at her child.

"Uh-huh," Georgia said, preoccupied by the present clutched to her chest.

"Can we sit over there, Momma?" Georgia asked. She pointed to the corner of the room. Sunlight dappled the red upholstered bench.

"Sure honey."

Two white families were seated on the other side of the room, each surrounded by their luggage. Their bench was much longer than the one where she and her mother were seated, but it was covered with the same waxy red upholstery.

While her mother glanced through her *Redbook* magazine, Georgia applied a child's detective eye to her subjects. She gingerly took a red lollipop out of the little white leather Easter purse that she'd been given by her mother for Easter service at Oak Street Church and now took everywhere with her. She peeled the wrapping off the lollipop, then used a fingernail to tear off a tiny bit of plastic that had stuck to the candy. Sucking on it, she stared at two young families seated across the room.

She narrowed her eyes. She could separate the two families only by the fact that one mother was blond and the other brunette. The blond-haired mother looked over at her for a second, her curious eyes burning into hers. Georgia smiled but she could see that her smile somehow was unsettling to the lady, like an irritant. The lady smiled briefly then turned back to the conversation she was having with the brunette mother.

As Georgia watched the families, she decided that their sameness came on account of one obvious fact. They were white and she was not. That's the main thing that made them seem the same.

She continued to watch them as she sat next to her mother, the square-shaped gift wrapped in pink tissue paper that Aunt Rebecca had given her pressed into her lap. Each family had a mom, a dad, and a little boy. The mothers were chatting with each other, blue eyes flashing, hands moving animatedly in the air. Georgia noticed that while the mothers spoke to one another, the fathers sat glumly on the bench behind newspapers that partially obscured their faces. As she watched the boys play, bright sunshine poured into the room, warming her cold body and illuminating the spare waiting area of the bus station.

The boys raced back and forth across the room, laughing and eyes wild. Both of them wore their hair long, like girls Georgia thought, and their hair flew up as they ran. She watched as a tall mustached man dressed in a stiff white shirt and navy pants, gold badge flashing, stood in the middle of the floor. He took no notice of the playing boys, she saw, just as the boys took no notice of her. But his eyes did lock briefly with Georgia's.

"Why don't you open your present now, Georgia?" Bettie asked nervously, noticing the silent exchange between Georgia and the grim-faced guard.

Georgia had always had the manner of delicately opening presents since the time she was little. But this time, she did not do that. She tore off the tissue paper, allowing the pink paper to fall to the floor by her feet. She let out a whoop. It was *Corduroy*, the book she'd told Aunt Rebecca she'd wanted for Christmas but didn't get. The guard looked over disapprovingly at her. As he did, Georgia turned to look at the boys, who now had taken off their sneakers and were playing hide and seek in their stocking feet.

"*Corduroy*, Mom!" Georgia exclaimed, turning her face from the children to her mother.

Bettie cast a stern glance in the direction of the guard who was only standing a few yards from where they sat. She turned toward her daughter and smiled, eyes crinkling at the corners. She took a quick look at her watch, then turned her head to look at the far side of the facility where the ticket office was located. There was no queue, so she stood up and said, "Georgia, I want you to sit right here and watch our luggage while I go check on the tickets."

Georgia pouted.

"It's OK. Ain't no one going to bother you," Bettie said. "I'll just be over there, so just stay and behave yourself." She took a quick look at the guard, who had moved from one side of the room to the other. "You just read your *Corduroy*. You hear me? I'll be back in just a few minutes."

Then she bent her head toward her daughter's so that the sides of their heads touched gently against each other. "Don't you pay those little boys no mind," she whispered. "You just sit here and be quiet and don't move until I get back. Keep an eye on our bags. You hear me?"

"Yes, Mom."

But only a few minutes after Bettie left, Georgia had an urge to use the bathroom. She squirmed in her seat and fidgeted with the black ribbon that Bettie had used to tie her two braids together. It came away in her hands as she fixed her eyes on the boys who were now seated back with their parents. The thin blond mother had taken some food out of a bag that was wrapped in waxed paper. She was wearing a red and green plaid twill kilt. Both boys stood by the lady's knees as she unfolded the paper to reveal a huge, buttery cinnamon roll. The boys were told to stand back as she broke the pastry in two,

45

handing each one a white cotton napkin that they greedily snatched from her hands. As the brown-haired boy reached for his half, he glanced at Georgia, seated alone on the bench. She saw him looking at her two braids.

Earlier that morning, Georgia asked her mother, "Why do you have to tie my braids back?"

"Those braids might be fine at Sojourner. That's a *progressive* Philly school. But your braids hanging out around your shoulders may not be OK here. This is still the South, remember."

Her locks were flowing down the front of the smock dress she wore. She used one hand to push back one side of her braids. And then the brown-eyed boy, who she now noticed wore glasses, suddenly smiled at her. And that bright soft smile, even with the bit of cinnamon bun that she could see was caught between his teeth, was something beautiful to her.

She smiled warmly back. But it only took the boy's mother to glance her way for Georgia to quickly look away. Her eyes landed on a door to the left. A sign announced that it was the Ladies' Room. Without looking back, she picked up the red hardback book, shiny and smooth from being just opened, left the suitcases, and entered the bathroom.

She decided to get started on reading the book as she sat on the toilet. It felt peaceful and quiet in there until she heard voices.

"But y'all, what did I do?" The faint sound was that of a little girl, a little Black girl she thought, maybe the same age as her.

"You mean to tell me that you got to *ask* what you did? Didn't you push in front of my friend here to get to the only stall open before she did? Don't you know that just because there ain't a Colored Only sign over the door don't mean you get to act like an uppity nigger and get away with it?"

Georgia stood quietly behind the door of the stall, feeling compelled to listen.

"Please, please don't!" Georgia heard, just in time to step out from behind the door and see a little girl kneeling on the floor in front of the toilet and held down by two older girls. The bigger girl was pushing her head, while the other girl was holding down her struggling legs with all her weight.

Suddenly, Georgia heard the toiled being flushed. She clutched her stomach, and as she did, the book dropped to the floor. The girl that had pushed the smaller girl's head into the toilet turned and saw her. She had let go of the Black child's head, who now turned toward Georgia, her face and hair dripping with water, and yelled, "Please get help!"

"You tell a soul, little nigger," the menacing voice of the bigger girl said, "and trust me, it will be your turn next. I'll flush that nappy head of yours, beads and all, down the toilet."

Georgia couldn't see the face of the other girl that was pressing on the Black child's legs, but she could hear her laughter. She stood paralyzed for a second; her eyes were glued to the heart-shaped brown face of the terrified little girl. Then she picked up her book from the floor and ran out of the bathroom so fast that she almost ran into the guard who was standing by the vending machine.

"Whoa, whoa, young lady!" he said, lightly taking hold of her shoulder. "Now what're you running from?"

"I—I—there's a girl…"

Georgia stared, eyebrows furrowed, at the guard. She couldn't decide for a second whether that was friendly concern emanating from his light gray eyes, or something entirely different, something hostile to her kind. Confused, she looked around the station. The two families were no longer there, and her mother was standing by the suitcases, her face somber.

"Oh, oh…my mom's there."

She pointed in the direction of where Bettie stood.

"Well then, I guess you'd better go to her," he said quietly.

Georgia ran to her mother and buried her face deeply into the front of the light blue cotton blazer that she had seen her mother carefully iron only the night before. It smelled, for the life of her, like the creek she'd swam in by Rebecca's house.

"Now didn't I tell you to wait with the suitcases? Didn't I tell you?"

Georgia lifted her face. She'd started to sob. Big, fat, doleful sobs, soaking Bettie's blouse.

"Now it ain't all that bad, now," Bettie said, patting Georgia's hair. "I see you just needed to go to the bathroom. I'm not mad at you. I was just worried about where you were. It's time to go."

Georgia politely did as her mother asked, grabbing the handle of her little suitcase and following her mother as they walked to the bus. They left their bags at the rear of the bus to be loaded. When they boarded the bus, she looked for the two families but couldn't see them anywhere. So, she settled down and opened her book. For a while, it kept the memory at bay of how she'd let the little girl down…but when she had finished the book the tears came. She kept her head turned from her mother so that she couldn't see her crying as she racked her brain, trying to understand why she just didn't do what the little girl had asked her to do—to go get help.

It was nighttime when they arrived in Philadelphia. As they walked to their small row home in the pitch-black darkness, fear gripped her, tightening inside with every second while she waited by the bags as her mother opened the door.

* * *

Over breakfast the next morning, Georgia sat cowed in her seat.

"Lift your head up and eat your cereal," Bettie said.

It hadn't escaped her that Georgia had hardly said a word on the bus ride home.

"Something happened back at the bus station, didn't it?" she abruptly asked.

Georgia didn't reply, head hung low over her bowl of uneaten Cheerios.

"Talk to me, child," Bettie said sharply. "Did something happen at the bus station?"

Georgia wearily lifted her head and nodded.

"Did something happen when you went into the bathroom?"

Again, Georgia reluctantly nodded her head.

"Then tell me…what happened in there?"

"Two big white girls with a little girl."

"What color was the little girl?"

"Brown," she said, pausing to indicate to her mother the back of her hand.

"And where were they?"

"In the stall next to mine," Georgia said, evading her mother's penetrating eyes.

She dipped the end of her spoon into the cereal, which had gone mushy. Bettie waited patiently as she used the tip of her spoon to stir the soggy cereal around and around in her bowl. Then she watched as Georgia removed the spoon from her bowl, placed it neatly on the placemat, and stood up.

"Where you going, child? You haven't asked to be excused from the table!"

Georgia paid no mind to her mother, sullenly walking past her and out of the kitchen.

"I'm tired, Mom. Don't you get tired some time?" she said.

"Little girls aren't supposed to get tired," Bettie called tensely to her daughter as she walked up the stairs.

"Well, I'm not every little girl," she hollered back, her mind consumed by the memory of the little Black girl. That girl with the dirtied soles of those pretty pink sneakers poking out from under her. The pretty little girl whose head was held down in the toilet.

6

There were Black folk and then there were *Black* folk. And no Black bourgeois female with a grain of sense crossed the svelte and effortlessly charmed Jemma Lavington. She was the lynchpin of the Black Philadelphia social set and, as such, Jemma's approval was fervently sought by the *climbers*, anxious to gain entry into the tightknit professional Black community.

Would-be members of that social set were scrutinized by Jemma and her friends for excellence and distinction in education, in the arts and in civic affairs. The tailors they used, the stores they frequented, the intelligence of their children, were all carefully examined before Jemma bestowed her seal of approval. Members and their progeny ranged from first-generation graduates of prestigious universities to successful artists, medical doctors, and lawyers. All were prominent self-made men and women and Mamie Whitman had been, for some time, a beloved member of the set.

Jemma had been president of the Philadelphia Circle, an exclusive club for professional Black women and the wives of prominent Black men for three years. Her taste and pedigree had never been called into question since it was widely known that she had traveled extensively

50

throughout Europe and was a grandniece of Ossawa Tanner, the famed 19th century Black oil painter. She'd abandoned her role with the club in February in order to accept an invitation to be a member of the Pennsylvania Horticulture Society, an offer that had no precedence in the Black community and which was heralded in the *Philadelphia Tribune*. The society had become keen to demonstrate inclusiveness, so Jemma was given carte blanche to cultivate sponsors for the Philadelphia Flower Show and determine the range and types of exhibits. Her favorite, the Dragon's Mouth orchid, would be on prominent display this year.

Jemma tended to hold herself aloof and had few friends. But Mamie Whitman was one of them. Their bond had been forged some years ago during a soggy summer weekend in Atlantic City. She and Jemma had spent a Saturday biking up and down the wide gray boardwalk, while the men sat bundled in tall-backed maroon leather chairs in the hotel's lounge drinking scotch. The day's sharp coolness had made them famished by dinnertime and the four-way banter over a three-course meal and two bottles of Merlot in the hotel restaurant was one of the most pleasant evenings she could remember.

This Wednesday, Jemma was holding a small dinner party at her house for her niece Estelle, and she had invited Mamie to come over before the other guests arrived. The Tudor style house presided at the top of an acorn strewn street in the coveted Main Line district of the city. The arched doorway was set in quarried stone and the walls of the pitched roof house were covered in green ivy. Long, thick black strips of timber crisscrossed the nutmeg-colored walls, intersected by steepled windows. The doorway was reached after two flights of stone stairs.

Mamie had visited the house on many occasions and had always been impressed by the stylish precision with which Jemma decorated her home and cultivated her gardens. Lately, it seemed as though Jemma had tried to use her newfound interest in the horticultural society to improve her front yard. This time, as she drove up, Mamie noticed that a carved stone rabbit the size of a large dog had been moved from the entry way to a more prominent position at the foot of the driveway. As she walked toward the house, a pretty array of red and white petunias—cascading from the sides of rustic brown flower boxes—caught her eye. She rang the doorbell and within seconds, Jemma appeared, hair coiffed in a dark brown bouffant that rose like a fountain over a face whose eyes seemed fixed in a look of perpetual curiosity.

"Hey, girlfriend!" she called as she saw Mamie. She was carrying a sprig of lavender from her garden in one hand. Mamie had to smile. Jemma had always had a green thumb.

Mamie followed Jemma from the wood paneled foyer, past the library and dining room, to the porch area. It was glass enclosed, just like Mamie and Theodore's, but an order of magnitude larger and brighter, brimming with African violets and all manner of colorful garden cuttings. The late afternoon sunshine speckled the flora, giving the room the feel of being in a glossy rain forest.

"And Joshua?" Mamie asked, silently admiring the home and wishing it were hers. "Where is he this evening?"

Everyone in their set, but seemingly not Jemma, knew that her husband had a serious roving eye. He was a second-generation dentist and the hardworking son of hardworking Caribbean immigrants who never took no for an answer if it impacted his financial well-being. His studied and disciplined manner and the pairing of his intellectual nature was evident in his keen, bright eyes. He was precise about the clothes he wore on his back and his hilarious stories made him a lightning rod for the ladies.

"He's at the nineteenth hole after his round of golf," Jemma said without turning her head around as she led Mamie into a chef's kitchen to await the other guests.

"This time of the day?" Mamie said, but then, like a used Kleenex, dropped it.

Jemma made Mamie a pot of Earl Grey tea and then insisted on sharing a juicy bit of gossip that was just too delicious to keep to herself.

This story was absolutely true, she said, no lie. It had circulated among the members of her bridge club. According to Jemma, who was well known for repeating and embellishing such accounts, it concerned a light-skinned Black couple from Upper Darby who had fallen in love at fifteen and married at twenty-one. After years of hard work and long hours, they were cocooned in a modest house that they bought in the same suburban community in which they had grown up.

There, they found fringe acceptance among their white neighbors. No one spoke ill of them, this model Black couple with their pale skin and pleasing demeanor. The couple retained their acknowledged status even after Black families slowly began to trickle into what had once been a white enclave. After a while, even they, like their new Black neighbors, began to face instances of bias—the callously thrown coins on the grocery counter and the overheard whispered slur. But they, nevertheless, remained accepted members of the community, albeit lesser and lesser as the days went by.

"And so, Mamie, do you know what happened after the young man was offered a job at the Navy Yard?"

"Not a clue," Mamie replied.

"Well, I was told in the strictest confidence that this couple, once they arrived in Philly, were thinking about having a child. But then they discovered that in this polite society, any skin color that varied between that of a brown paper bag and a Cadbury chocolate bar was vulnerable to a veritable book of slights that they had never read.

"They were then torn between the joy of having a child, the product of their own loving union, weighed against the possibility of the child showing color at all. So, they chose the safest route—"

"Let me guess what that was," Mamie interjected. "It was to have no child at all."

"Have you heard that story before?" Jemma asked, disappointedly.

"Yes, I have, and I'd advise that you drop it like a hot brick. It makes you appear…"

"Unseemly?"

"Well, that's not quite the word I would have chosen, but you know what I mean."

Jemma moved on to less controversial topics as Mamie silently admired her friend's good taste. The Limoges dining set that had been set out may have been slightly over the top for the dinner party on hand tonight, but the intent was good and spoke for itself. The party was in honor of her stunning niece Estelle, and Jemma was always one to make people feel welcome.

*　*　*

After introductions had been made and drinks had been poured, everyone was directed outside to a table on the porch so they could admire the grounds of the house. It was a small gathering, just the four of them, and little beige cardboard name cards in front of brown placemats indicated where they should sit. Mamie noticed the deep orange color of the linen napkins—russet, she decided. Russet was not a summer color and not one she would choose, but somehow it worked. It appeared both unfussy and elegant.

"What was that again?" Mamie asked.

Sigrid, the wife of the artist, Jeremiah Wollstone, and one of Jemma's guests, was laughing. Mamie had known Sigrid since childhood, having attended the same segregated elementary school. She knew her to be the type of person who used laughter as a form of verbal punctuation. All of her sentences ended in a laugh, while breathy giggles indicated the commas.

"You were in a world all of your own, weren't you, Mamie?" Sigrid said, followed by an inevitable chuckle. "I asked how you are."

"Oh, I'm just fine, Sigrid. Thank you for asking."

Mamie took her seat in front of her name card. She was next to Jemma's niece, Estelle, who was across from Sigrid. The smell of something succulent wafted in from the kitchen. Oh, yes, Mamie remembered. Jemma was serving pot roast au jus with fresh horseradish, which, Mamie thought to herself, was just the perfect dish for the evening.

"How are you, Mrs. Whitman?" the guest of honor asked. She extended her hand.

The second she did, Mamie knew instantly why she may have been corralled into a dinner party for four on a weeknight. The girl was exquisite, from her curly brushed black chignon to her artfully painted lips, which were in that moment taking a sip of iced Evian water. Her thin, dark brown body reminded Mamie of an exotic bird perpetually poised for flight. It had always boggled Mamie's mind how plain white women could manage to get themselves hitched at nineteen, while gorgeous creatures like Estelle were left wallowing. The calculus wasn't there.

"I'm just fine, and congratulations," she said, reaching across the table to hand Estelle a graduation card that had been signed by both her and Judge Whitman. "And Haverford!" she added gaily.

As they dug into their appetizers—a medley of creamy brie and roasted tomatoes—Estelle put her right hand out in front of her.

"Thanks, Aunt Jemma, for the beautiful ring!" she said.

Estelle's white gold ring, the center point of which was an elegantly shaped letter E, shimmered in the evening sunset.

"Lovely," Sigrid and Mamie both said simultaneously. "It's so chic," Mamie added over Sigrid's laughter, "and so thoughtful of your Aunt Jemma."

The conversation stopped for a moment.

A slightly heavy-set young woman walked onto the porch. Annie was Jemma's newly hired maid, who had responded to a want ad in the local Main Line paper. It had never occurred to Annie that the person placing the advertisement would be a Black person. She was Puerto Rican, and she had a certainty that the lady of the house would be white, simply because she'd never seen a brown person in this elite neighborhood. But she was wrong, and moreover pleasantly surprised when she was hired, despite her lack of experience. She'd been thrown out of her mother's house and was living in a girls' home, trying to put her life back on track. Annie cleared their appetizer plates away and then brought out steaming plates of pot roast. She reached down at each chair, carefully placing the plates in front of each guest.

"Is there anything else you'd like me to do, Miss Jemma?" she asked.

"Thank you," Jemma said politely, "but we're fine for now."

They began to eat and, after complimenting Jemma on her wonderful food, the four women began to chat about other topics.

But while the others talked, Sigrid remained silent for a while. As the artist Jeremiah Wollstone's wife, she harbored no false illusions about her position in society. She knew that her club and bridge memberships were more related to her husband's prestige than to her own. And while Mamie could trumpet her ancestral pedigree from Essex County—*Don't you know that my people go back to Jamestown? The African, the English*, and *the Scottish?*—Sigrid had no such golden background to share or chic riffs to trot out. She was, and always would be, known as the wife of Jeremiah Wollstone, the acclaimed—if slightly unstable—Black artist, whose work was regularly exhibited at the Philadelphia Museum of Modern Art. He was a rebel, a genius, and despite being a pan-Africanist, a darling of the Eastern Seaboard art and business world.

Sigrid quickly glanced at Mamie, who was attired beautifully yet simply, as usual. Very Parisienne, she thought to herself. Of course, she knew that Mamie's life had not entirely been a crystal stair. There had been whispers about a possible affair...on Mamie's side. Something like that just wasn't done. But that was years ago; the rumors were firmly quashed by her very best friends. Her attention was brought back to the conversation as Estelle spoke of a recent relationship.

"His name is Jonathan Matthew."

"*Jonathan Matthew*," Mamie repeated.

"He attended Princeton and we met over the summer in a philosophy class at Haverford."

"And?" Sigrid asked.

"We fell in love," she said somberly, a fresh breeze lifting a piece of hair from where it had been undone from her bun.

Estelle lifted eyes in a way that showcased thick, black eyelashes.

She looked straight at Jemma, who returned her gaze without blinking.

"We did," she said determinedly. "But—well..."

She pursed her lips tightly before continuing.

"It all came to a head in December when he invited me along on a skiing holiday with his family in the Poconos. I was so excited!"

Sigrid listened intently, ignoring the juicy morsels of meat and vegetables that remained on her plate.

"I had never skied before, so Jonathan Matthew..."

Mamie interrupted, "Jonathan Matthew, as in, Matthew is his last name?"

"No," Estelle replied. "Matthew is his middle name, but he is known by both names. Never anything else. Always Jonathan Matthew."

"That is such an affectation," Mamie said.

"As I said, I'd never skied before. I was nervous I might make a fool of myself in front of his family. He took me to a ski resort for a long weekend and spent hours teaching me.

"I rented my boots and skis. It was exhausting, but eventually I learned the basics, from turning, stopping, how to get on and off a ski lift, and how to get up when I fell down. But at the end of the weekend, I was able to tackle the easier slopes, confident that I wouldn't altogether disgrace myself. After that, I couldn't wait to go. I would meet his family. Finally. His father had rented a van the size of a bus. We were all to drive up together to the ski resort.

"When we arrived at the house, I could see the van outside stacked with suitcases in the back. We walked hand in hand into the home. I carried a navy ski jacket over my arm."

She paused to look at Jemma.

"The jacket that Jonathan Matthew had bought for me," she said demurely.

"They extended their hands to greet me," she said, smiling gently, as though recalling the scene. "I was impressed by his father. He had such a kind smile. This was a family, I thought, who…who might…"

"Accept a Negro girl in the family?" Sigrid blurted out, tact not being her strong suit.

Mamie, glancing briefly at the girl's high-cheek-boned face, tried to make amends.

"Give you the sense belonging?" she suggested.

"Yes, I suppose so," Estelle said. "But something began to go wrong. I began to feel something was just off. And just as that thought struck me, his mother began to speak."

She paused again, and in the bluish light of early evening, looked out into the eyes of the three older women around the table.

"'You're not planning to accompany us on this trip, Jonathan Matthew, are you?' she said. 'It was your father's and my understanding that you were going to house sit for us.'

"I looked into her eyes, which until then had seemed so cheerful and inviting.

"Jonathan Matthew and I got the message pretty quickly, and in the time it took for my heart to sink, all of my hopes and dreams were swept away."

Sigrid sighed deeply, able to be heard by all.

"His parents then left for their skiing holiday, leaving us behind in the house. He didn't take me in his arms; he didn't apologize. He just stood numbly by.

"I asked him to drive me to the train station, and as he got behind the wheel, he frankly seemed relieved that it had ended this way. I caught an Acela home and cried for weeks."

Estelle, then bravely managing a slight smile, said, "Since then, skiing has never had the same cachet for me." She tried to make light of it, but her resolve segued into hot, salty tears.

"Now, now," Mamie said. "As my husband, Judge Whitman always says, let's just deescalate the drama. None of this was your fault. The blame lies with your, your…"

"Jonathan Matthew," she interjected softly.

"Let's just say Jonathan," Mamie said. "The blame lies with Jonathan for not speaking up, and with his parents for distancing you."

She took a Kleenex out of her purse and handed it to Estelle.

"They were damned lucky that you even looked at their son, girl."

"Truly," Sigrid said, chiming in. "I'm so sorry that you've had to face such blatant bigotry. For some reason, it reminds me of the time many years ago when I was six and Momma took me to a ballet school in Bucks County to meet its grand dame, Madame Olga Krashinsky, who was recruiting new talent. I loved ballet and had taken lessons from the age of four.

"I still remember the ride there. All of the bugs flew in because Momma insisted that we keep the windows down. She always told us that fresh air was free and good for us.

"When we arrived at the ballet school, it stood alone like a little red house straight out of a fairy tale on the top of a hill. There were little wooden steps built into the hill that we walked up. It was a beautiful day, and I was in a good mood.

"We went in and waited, but then when the time came, Momma told me to go into the studio by myself. Momma could always pass for Italian, but as you can see from my nose," Sigrid pointed to her lovely nose that screamed personality, "that game wasn't going to work for me. 'Now just be yourself,' were Momma's exact words as I walked into the studio.

"I arrived with my pink ballet slippers swung over my shoulders and I was shaking like a leaf. I remember that. I also remember that my white stockings were itching my legs like nobody's business.

"The door finally opened and there was Madame Olga. She was white and taller than Momma but around the same age. Her tights were white, and her leotard was black, exactly like mine under my white cardigan and blue jeaned skirt.

"I looked around the room, at the high beamed ceiling above the smooth ballet bars and wide picture windows. This is where I belonged, I decided. This is who I am; this is where I want to be.

"I turned toward the distinguished looking Madam Olga, and as she bent down on her knees to my eye level, I envisioned myself standing at the bar with the other girls. I smiled brightly at her, as Momma had instructed me to do. But then she spoke in a very quiet voice.

"'Oh, my. You're not a colored girl, are you?' she said to me."

Estelle paused. She took a sip of water and could barely place the glass back down without the water cascading over its edge. Jemma hurriedly walked over to her, her pearl necklace clinking against her sorority jewelry. She patted Estelle's shoulders.

No one spoke for a while. And as the sky darkened, moonlight fell upon the faces of the guests as they contemplated the flickering candles that were in two brushed silver candle holders in the center of the table.

"That's quite a story," Mamie finally said, after searching for the right words. "It's amazing that the teacher would humiliate you in that way. How long has it been since Brown v. Board of Education?"

"We keep saying, things are changing. Things are getting better," Jemma said. "But truly…has the train even left the station?"

Estelle shook her head vigorously. "Excellent question," she said. "From my vantage, no."

Jemma threw a sympathetic glance toward her niece, who looked small and forlorn. "Give it time," she said. "Things take time."

"The Negro's lament," Sigrid said, in direct response to Jemma's platitudes.

The awkward moment ended only when everyone's eyes turned toward an unkept boy who, out of the blue, suddenly appeared on Jemma's patio. The boy wore a white t-shirt that only partially obscured a round belly that poked out from under the shirt and over black jeans, which had been shorn at the knees. As the boy walked purposely to the table, everyone turned toward him except Jemma, who, ignoring the child standing plainly in front of her, said irritably to no one in particular, "Where the heck is she? Why doesn't she come and take the plates?"

Estelle took her eyes from her plate. She shook her hair and allowed her tan-colored eyes, unusually arresting in her brown face, to rest on the boy.

"And who are you?" she asked, a gentle smile at play on her lips.

Nonplussed, the boy looked at Jemma and then back to Estelle.

"I'm Carlton Lavington," he mumbled. "Who'd you think I was? The milkman?"

No one laughed since it was clear as the guests scrutinized Jemma's son that he had not uttered the words with that expectation. It was evident that the boy drew no warmth from his mother. She continued to ignore him, turning to angrily swat away a pesky mosquito that had just drawn blood from her arm. There was little physical resemblance between Carlton and his parents. He was short for his age and had certainly not inherited their instinctive ability to act or speak appropriately in social situations.

"Did you forget your manners, Carlton?" Jemma finally asked through her teeth.

"Oh!" he exclaimed, making a little circle with his lips.

"And how do you do?" he asked Estelle, bowing low from his waist.

His theatrics oozed sarcasm, shot through each syllable of his response. Furious, Jemma stared at her son and then walked over to him. Turning her back to her guests, she asked, "Why are you disturbing my party?"

The question was asked softly, and yet to each guest it was as though she were speaking to someone other than her son. She waited for him to respond, and when he didn't, Jemma turned around and spoke directly to her guests.

"He's not like this usually," she murmured apologetically, taking the back of her hand to wipe the sweat from her forehead.

"Now, Jemma. Leave the boy alone," Mamie said soothingly. "He's not a disturbance at all."

Ignoring her, Jemma spoke to Carlton again. "What is it you want?" she asked.

"Dinner, Ma. What else?"

"But Carlton, I distinctly told you…" Jemma began to say, before grabbing hold of his hand and rushing toward the kitchen.

Minutes later, she returned with an anguished Annie. Mamie could see from her full, dimpled face, that she was younger than she had originally thought. She could even be as young as Estelle, Mamie thought, whom she knew to be twenty-two.

"Did you forget what I told you yesterday, Annie?"

Annie nodded her head nervously in response. She cocked her head slightly to the left, taking a moment to steal a shy peak at Estelle, whose eyes were focused on her plate.

"Did you forget what I told you yesterday?" Jemma asked again.

Again, the frightened girl didn't reply. She looked up at the sky as though the answer lay somewhere amidst the glossy black night and stars.

"I told you that I wanted the plates to be removed promptly from the table after the guests were finished," Jemma said sternly, and with evident exasperation. "Was that too much to ask?"

Annie lowered her head and looked around the table, as if seeking support from Mamie, Sigrid, and Estelle. They looked at her with sympathy, flabbergasted at Jemma's public taking down of the shy defenseless girl.

"Well, what do you have to say for yourself?" Jemma asked, raising her voice.

Annie looked down at the floor and quietly answered her employer, "I'm sorry, Miss Jemma. You did tell me that. But I looked in a few times and, although your guests were not eating, they were chatting and there was still food on their plates. I didn't want to interrupt the conversation."

Jemma glared at her, and the girl quickly got the message. She went from guest to guest, quickly stacking plates on her strong, adroit arms and retreating with them to the kitchen.

Jemma had tired of the mosquitos, the shiftless maid, and the dinner party that had gone awry. She checked her watch, wondering when her husband would return. All she wanted was a shot of brandy followed by a warm bath and the feel of her Egyptian eight-hundred-thread-count cotton sheets beneath her toes.

"You'll know better next time," Jemma shouted after her as Annie sped into the kitchen. "Now, who would like coffee?" she asked.

Everyone declined.

"Well, I'm so sorry about that girl. But I'm sure she'll remember next time."

"Remember what, exactly?" Estelle asked, in her cultured, tempered voice. "What exactly did she do wrong?"

Sigrid, reluctant to say anything that might disrupt her friendship with Jemma, turned away and remained silent. Mamie cleared her throat, then gently pushed away her empty glass of wine.

"Remember…" Mamie said, as though musing upon the word reflectively. "The word you used was *remember*, wasn't it, Jemma?"

Jemma turned her head away. Mamie's voice, stripped of convention, was now raw.

Embarrassed that her very good friend was about to take her to task, Jemma looked down at her hands clasped on her lap.

"You do remember chitterlings, don't you Jemma?" Mamie continued. "Smelled God awful but tasted divine. Remember them?"

She turned toward Estelle. "I bet you that your Jonathan Matthew doesn't know anything about chitterlings, but we do, don't we Jemma?"

Jemma returned Mamie's gaze.

"Do you remember your mother waking up at dawn to climb down her stairs in the dark and make you all buttermilk biscuits that melted in your mouth? Made the house smell like heaven. At least that's what you told me.

"You also told me how your momma's fingers were still sticky with dough when she put glasses of orange juice in front of you all every morning. I remember you telling me that."

Mamie folded her hands on the table and looked directly at the silent Jemma, who was slumped in her chair.

"So," she said in a measured voice, "I think you should just take care to remember who you are before you get on your high horse, acting like some fancy white lady.

"Remember that Annie is the same God given color as you. She wears scuffed black work shoes and you wear overpriced espadrilles. Just remember that they are both worn on brown feet. You should remember that!"

Stunned and defeated, Jemma stood up and stormed out, leaving her guests behind her. They stared at each other for a few moments, eyebrows raised. Then, Mamie encouraged everyone to quietly leave, explaining that she would go to Jemma.

Mamie caught up with her in the kitchen. Jemma was hunched over the kitchen table, sobbing heavily. The water from the sink was running and the oven was on. Someone had forgotten to turn them off. Annie and Carlton were nowhere to be seen.

"Just let it go," she said soothingly, gently rubbing Jemma's back. "I'm sorry if I upset you, but I felt it had to be said about Annie. No one deserves to be treated like that. But it's not like you, Jemma. What's wrong?"

"You're right," Jemma said through her sobs. "But you don't know me."

"What you mean?"

"You don't know what it's like for me, putting on lipstick every morning, wearing a smile for the world to see, when the reality is that the man you pledged your heart and soul to ain't faithful to you. He always says that he's at the nineteenth hole, but I know for a fact that often he's nowhere near the golf club."

Mamie instinctively reached out and grasped her longtime friend's hands in hers. Jemma bowed her head, and as she did Mamie felt her friend's tears fall on the back of her hand.

"But it's not just Joshua…it's Carlton as well," Jemma said, her voice beginning to tremble. "That's why I'm so on edge."

"Tell me about Carlton, Jemma. He seems so different than when he was little."

"He's being bullied at school," Jemma replied. "Unmercifully… they call him…"

Mamie was prepped for the most offensive or derogatory word she could think of, so when the word "meatball" finally came out she had to stifle her urge to laugh. She was thankful she did.

"The other boys pummel him in the playground," Jemma said in a near whisper. "And this goes on in a good Quaker private school."

"Is Carlton the only Black boy in the class?" Mamie asked.

"No, there's one other. He wears his hair slicked straight like an Italian. But if you told him that he's just as Black as Carlton, he'd swear you were telling a lie."

"Then why don't you put Carlton into a Black school?"

"Do your boys go to a Black school, Mamie?" Jemma asked, looking Mamie straight in the eye.

"No."

"Then why should mine?" she said smartly.

An uncomfortable pause lingered until Mamie picked up the plate covered in aluminum foil that Jemma had made for Theodore.

"You can get it back to me at any time," Jemma said, pointing to the China plate.

Mamie was about to leave, but then she turned back and hugged her friend.

"Why don't you and Joshua get out of town for a while? You could stay at our Salt Box in the Cape," she suggested.

"The Cape? That's a nice place, but too far away, and there aren't enough people who look like us."

"Oak Bluffs, maybe? The Vineyard?"

"That's more to my liking. My aunt has a house there, somewhere on the bluffs."

"Go visit then," Mamie said soothingly. "Take those broken pieces of your life, girl, and try and remember how to put them back together."

They went to the front door where Annie was waiting, purse in hand, ready to leave and wanting to be paid.

Turning back, face amber under the soft lighting, Jemma gripped Mamie's hands.

"Thank you," she said with a smile. "You've been very firm and straight with me. But I can forgive my dear friend for that."

7

Later that Evening

Mamie drove home on sparsely lit Pennsylvania roads that were canopied on either side by thickly wooded trees. As moonlight cut into the blackened forest, a feeling of unease set in, and she gripped the leather-bound steering wheel more tightly. She thought about Carlton, who had about as much control over his existence as Annie had over hers. Both were victims; both were vulnerable to the cruel and casual harshness of life.

"You don't burn bridges," her mother had always said. "You never know if that's a bridge you may one day have to cross."

Initially, she'd felt good about standing up to Jemma and calling her out on her unkind and unwarranted humiliation of the girl. It had to be said. But then she worried about the effect that it would have on their friendship. Perhaps, like a stack of dominoes, their relationship would come crashing down. *That would be sad*, she thought, *but let the dominoes tumble where they may. We can always try to stack them up again.*

She was glad to have had some practice at speaking her mind that evening. It was now time to do the same with her husband.

* * *

Mamie poured herself a glass of water as soon as she arrived home. She added ice to the glass, vigorously stirred the contents and then turned toward Theodore.

"How was the party?" he asked. He had been up waiting for her and sat at the kitchen table.

Rather than answer his question, Mamie simply shrugged her shoulders. She looked at him again, turned around and walked upstairs.

"That bad, was it?" Theodore said as he followed her.

Mamie went into the bedroom, strode to the windows, and opened them wide to allow the cigar smoke to seep out. She then turned back toward him.

"You've got to give to get," she said sharply.

"What's that?" Theodore asked, confused. "I don't know what the hell you mean."

He looked around the room. He couldn't conceal from her that he had been drinking that evening. The bottle and the shot glass were right there on the night table to prove it, and he didn't give a damn.

"I said…" she said, pausing for emphasis, "You've got to give to get."

Then, without another word, she went into the bathroom to shower and put on her periwinkle blue nightdress. When she returned, she was surprised to see Theodore standing in the same place. She flopped down on the bed and looked thoughtfully at him.

"What I mean, dear, is that you've got to give up that board membership of Colsol. I don't know how you can stay on there after Bettie's husband was killed."

Mamie could see Theodore's jaw harden.

"Oh, is that what this is all about?" he asked, voice rising. "How many times have I told you that I'm waiting to see the investigation report, and then I'll be in a position to force the company to adopt better safety rules? And if they don't…"

"And if they don't?" she asked, the back of her head flat against her pillow. "What happens then?"

"If they don't then I will resign."

"I'll hold you to that," Mamie said. "Now, please come to bed, Teddy. And put the glass down. Remember what the doctor said. You need to be mindful of your heart."

"And you…" he said, voice rising suddenly again, "need to be more mindful of your tongue."

Theodore was already dressed for bed in his black and white Brooks Brothers pinstriped pajamas with the pant legs that were too long. Mamie had misjudged her husband's height when she'd bought them at John Wanamaker's.

"Teddy, what was it again that you called whisky?" she asked. "Wasn't it the *Black man's gallows*?"

"I've never said that. That's a bunch of horseshit," he said, his back to her. "By the way, when was the last time I asked you to do something that you actually did?"

The room fell quiet.

For some reason, the memory of Lawrence's baptism and its aftermath—when the two boys fought—came back to her. She could not erase from her mind the sight of Theodore hovering over Lawrence's forlorn and frightened figure.

"You know, it was Robert, not Lawrence, who was in the wrong the day of Lawrence's baptism," she said softly. "I don't know why you had to pick on him, especially on a day like that. Out of all days in the year, why chose the say of his baptism? A sacred day…"

She looked over at Theodore with tears in her eyes.

"I always thought that one of the qualities of a good judge was that he displays judicial temperament. It was your temper that was on display when you hit Lawrence, not your temperament."

Theodore said nothing in reply. Nonetheless, she knew the effect that she'd had on him. Her words had struck him viciously, like a bludgeon. But she'd stood by too many times in the past as their son had been mercilessly cowed by his father. She was anxious for sleep, so she lay back on her pillow and closed her eyes. But Theodore had more to say.

"Oh," he said. "I nearly forgot. Someone by the name of Paige called you the other day."

His smile was wide and sardonic as a gleesome Cheshire cat.

"It was last Sunday, in fact. You'd stayed back at the church for one of those phony church women meetings that helps you feel sanctified. So, I picked up the message when we got home."

"Why didn't you tell me then?" she asked.

"Does it matter?" he said. "I'm telling you now."

She stared wide eyed at her husband, all light seemingly extinguished from his hazel-colored eyes.

"I gather from the message that Paige is Clarence's wife. Remember Clarence? Your erstwhile lover? The one you had an affair with after Robert was born? The man who is Lawrence's real father? Well, she seems to be under the impression that you intend to see him again and she made it very plain that she'd rather you didn't. That's the gist of the message, although as you can imagine she expressed it rather more forcefully."

Theodore waited for a reaction, ticking off the seconds in his head. Mamie remained silent but, just as he was about to speak again, she suddenly pushed the cover off her with an exasperated sigh.

"Theodore, first of all I have no intention whatsoever of seeing Clarence again," she said, her voice rising. "And secondly, if you cast your mind back, you'll remember that I had the decency to tell you about it and apologize. I begged for your forgiveness, which is something you have never done after the affair you had with that piece of trash who posed as your assistant! Why haven't you apologized to me about Jackie Alexander?"

The bedroom air conditioner unit whirred in the background as Theodore walked slowly to the bed, his pant legs trailing on the carpet. It was cranked up high because, although Theodore could tolerate the cold, for the life of him he could not withstand the hot and humid Philadelphia nights. He sat down on the bed facing her. Mamie bundled her knees in her arms with her back to the headboard.

"You have the wrong end of the stick about Jackie Alexander, Mamie," he eventually said.

"You think you know," he added, pointing to the side of his head. "But you don't know a damned thing, my love. Jackie and I never had an affair, I'm afraid. She accompanied me and my colleagues to a few retreats to take down minutes and that's all."

Mamie took a hard, cold look at him. Theodore turned his head, not wanting to give her the satisfaction of seeing the truth spread out on his face. He could feel the white-hot rage emanating from her as she lay less than a foot from where he sat.

"I might believe you," she said. "But your red face and your inability to look me in the eye tells me something different."

"Only you, Mamie, my love," he shouted as he turned back to look at her. "Only you and your vague, stupid imaginings…"

She was about to say that her accusation wasn't vague, and even less imagined, when she heard a quiet, insistent knocking at the door. Instinctively she knew which son it was. She had no doubt.

"Is everything alright, Mom?"

"Yes, Robert," Mamie said wearily. "Everything is fine. Please go back to bed."

"It's just your mom and dad having a go at life," Theodore added ruefully. "Don't worry. If we live long enough, we all get the hang of it."

"You sure everything's OK?"

"Yes, Robert. Go back to bed."

About a minute later, they heard Robert's bedroom door slam shut. Theodore got into bed and looked at Mamie contritely.

"Let's put all this behind us, shall we? I have to live with the fact that I'm not Lawrence's biological father, and you have to live with your suspicions about Jackie Alexander. Let's put the whole, sorrowful show behind us and live for the present. It's only you, Mamie," he said, his voice breaking. "It's always been only you."

He turned toward Mamie to gently kiss her tear-stained face.

"We have the boys and each other," she said. "Let that be enough."

8

July 1967

When Mamie first met Bettie, she initially determined that she was not the right girl for her. "Girl" was what white employers called their Black and Hispanic maids. And while Mamie was far from white, she herself had almost involuntarily used the word, albeit only in private conversations with her Bridge partners. That, she determined after calling out Jemma, had to end. She remembered how Bettie had dressed for the interview, as though she were being considered for an executive job. She wore a well-fitted gray suit, albeit with scuffed black pumps that had seen some wear. She wondered if Bettie would be too proud for the heavier cleaning duties, like scrubbing kitchen floors and window washing. But she had been wrong, and on the very first day of work, Bettie had not only scrubbed the floors but had helped Mamie lug a heavy box of apples from the yard into the garage.

The memory of Jemma's treatment of Annie persisted in her mind, and as the argument with Theodore faded to the background, Mamie began to focus on how she could help Bettie. There was Jimmy's death, and then of course, there was Georgia. The child had witnessed a senseless act of violence against a poor defenseless girl in the bus station washroom. Hard troubles just seemed to come right after another to the good-hearted Smythe family.

On that Monday afternoon, Bettie was in the kitchen, having her lunch and reading her *Jet* magazine. She was nibbling at a homemade corn beef sandwich that she'd taken out of a brown lunch bag. Mamie took a plate of tuna fish salad out of the refrigerator and made herself a sandwich with white Wonder bread. She switched on the radio before sitting down. Although they knew and respected each other, both women knew their boundaries and music eased things for them.

Aretha Franklin's new song "Respect" came on the radio, and within a minute, their sorrows were laid aside. Radiating in each other's warm smiles as wide as a Southern horizon, they were getting it all straightened out with a little help from Aretha Franklin. There was not a shred of doubt who they were. They were both Black American women—the fighting, formidable, forlorn band of survivors of a rich culture, quick to be spat upon but just as quick to rebound and flourish.

"Now I want you to put your feet up Bettie!" Mamie said as the song ended, her soft Southern inflection suddenly appearing and coloring her diction. "Why don't you take it easy while I spend some time with Georgia."

With Bettie's consent, Mamie had made it a ritual to have what she called her and Georgia's "Morning Book Club" on Saturdays.

"Fine ma'am," Bettie replied as she lifted her mug of hot Constant Comment tea to her lips. "I'd appreciate that and so would Georgia."

Mamie closed the kitchen door as she quietly walked out and made her way to the living room where Georgia sat cross legged on the carpet. Mamie grabbed a hardback book from a side table and went to sit in front of her on a carved Ashanti stool that she'd fiercely bargained for on a trip to market during a sun speckled trip to Accra. She opened the book to the first chapter.

"This is *I Know Why the Caged Bird Sings* by Maya Angelou," she announced.

She watched as Georgia flopped her legs on top of one another, her toes able to touch the seams of her bright peach-colored culottes.

"My, you're flexible," she said.

Mamie put on her horn-rimmed bifocals, tipped her head down, and began to read.

"Where's Lawrence and Robert?" Georgia interrupted.

"They're at a friend's house down the street."

"Are they…?" Georgia looked mischievously at Mrs. Whitman, as though trying to determine how she'd respond to the question she just had to ask.

"White kids?" Georgia said with a smile.

"Does it matter?" Mamie inquired, a quiet reflective note in her voice. She knew, though, that the answer to her question was already clear to the intelligent child.

"But since you asked, yes, they are," she replied firmly before Georgia could respond.

Bettie had told her that Georgia's teachers said that, although she was a gifted writer, she had taken to daydreaming and, at times, had become openly defiant toward her teachers. They said that she had pig headily refused to remove a navy knit cap from her head. One, she'd insisted to them that it was the only way from preventing the white kids in her class from touching her braids. Her black and white speck-led composition journal, once overflowing with words and colorful drawings, was now reduced to a series of blank white pages—save for one page. And it was that one page that spurred a telephone call to Bettie from Georgia's fourth grade teacher.

"She has not written one word in her journal since the crisis," her daughter's English teacher told her. "I am concerned, however, about a drawing on the first page."

"What was on the page?" Mamie asked when Bettie told her about the call.

"A drawing," Bettie said faintly, her back to Mamie. She was leisurely emptying a few dirty dishes from the sink and placing them in the dishwasher.

"A little girl is kneeling in front of the toilet. The drawing shows the back of the girl's sweater and her legs. Her shoes were colored pink. The head's not visible."

"What?!"

Mamie decided that she had to do something to help. So, every weekend Mamie read to Georgia as she sat on the floor. She'd given her a latch hook picture kit with a Black Beauty horse theme to work on while she read. Georgia had quietly worked on the picture for a few Saturdays, but this week there was an unexpected breakthrough.

Mamie was in the middle of reading the chapter when Georgia sunk her head into her hands and started crying. Her small, doll-sized tears became big, rollicking sobs.

Bettie popped her head out of the kitchen. "Is everything OK?"

"Everything's fine," Mamie said.

After her mother had walked back into the kitchen, Georgia asked, "Does Jesus love little girls who've had their head shoved down the toilet?"

"Do you mean the little girl who you saw at the bus station?"

Georgia nodded.

Mamie took off her horn-rimmed reading glasses and laid them gently on the oriental rug that Teddy had bought for a song on South Street in Philly.

"Jesus loves everyone and then some," she said.

"What about the big white girl who put her head in there? Does Jesus love her, too?"

Mamie paused for a moment. She got off the stool and sat herself, crossed legged, in front of Georgia and watched her pensive little face.

"That girl called her a little nigger. Called me the same."

Mamie held her breath as she considered how to answer Georgia's question. Then she finally exhaled.

"Yes, he loves her, too," she said in a small whisper. They both paused as though to listen to the faint ticking of the Whitmans' grandfather clock in the corner.

"But here's what to know, Georgia. Bad things can happen. Bad things do happen. Take, for instance, what happened to that little girl."

Georgia put the hook kit picture down and looked trustingly into Mrs. Whitman's eyes.

"Those bad things don't change Jesus's love for you. They just make it sweeter. Please remember that."

Without announcing herself, Bettie walked into the living room and straight up to her daughter. "It's time for us to go," she told Mamie while dabbing at Georgia's eyes with a tissue.

"Can I use your bathroom before I go?" Georgia asked.

Mamie nodded in agreement and in the meantime, Mamie motioned for Bettie to follow her into the kitchen.

Bettie looked at Mamie questioningly, waiting to hear what had triggered the tears.

Mamie sighed wearily. "All I got to say is, this country got some work to do. It's like Dr. King said. My guess is that all the man ever really hoped for—died for—was that the color of folks' skin wouldn't stop people from treating folks with decency. And to think…he died for that."

Mamie turned up the radio as she explained the cathartic break through. Then, just as she finished, a mutually favorite single came on the radio. And it was like a clear, cool, spate of wind had entered the room. Rapturous smiles spread across their faces as they listened to "Uptight (Everything's Alright)." They felt the music pulse through their veins, erasing the minutia that made up their respective lives of privilege and strife. At that moment, their newfound sisterhood didn't need any fixing.

It just was.

9

June 1968

Bettie had never begrudged Mamie for having more money and a nicer home than her. Never did and never would. But few people in her circle thought that way. Rich folk, any half-witted fourth grader could tell you, don't get rich on their own account. They climb on the backs of others to get there, and it was no mystery at all about on whose backs they trod: poor folk, especially poor Black folk. Mamie had never asked her, but if she ever had Bettie would have told her the truth. She wouldn't mind having a nice home and pretty things, but at the end of the day, her quiet life in a row home in North Philly was enough. But she did worry about Georgia. The yawning gap between what she could afford for Georgia and what the Whitmans were able to provide for Lawrence and Robert was sometimes difficult for her swallow. But at the same time, she was grateful for what Mamie did for Georgia.

Bettie chuckled to herself as she drove to Georgia's school to pick her up on her last day before the summer break. She recalled Mamie's heroic efforts to help Georgia, going even so far as to attempt to emulate her daughter by contorting her body into a pretzel as she sat with Georgia on the Whitmans' living room floor. Mamie had been insistent on doing whatever needed to be done to help Bettie's child. Whether it was from feelings of guilt or a compulsion to do good, she didn't know and didn't care. The lady was doing what she could to help, and that's all that mattered.

She smiled as she thought about what Jimmy would say if he were there. "Bettie," he'd say with a wink, "now ain't that mighty white of her."

* * *

School was finally out for the summer, and from the moment Georgia's teacher had told the class it was time to hand back their well-thumbed textbooks and remove all of the leftover apple cores and rechewed gum from their lockers, she'd fallen into a state of bliss. She'd wiped down her locker with abandon and carted her folders and possessions home with a smile pasted on her face. It was summer and she was free for a sweet slice of time.

Mamie had invited Bettie and Georgia to join them for the long country ride to drop off Lawrence at his summer camp in Pottstown, and Georgia was more than happy to tag along. She'd seen pictures of the camp only the week before in the Whitmans' kitchen. Her mother had allowed her to wear shorts for the first time since school had ended and she was seated on the high stool that Mamie called her designated perch. She allowed the heels of her white summer sandals that her mother had bought for her to hang off her feet and dangle. She picked up a brochure left in the middle of the kitchen counter and showed it to her mother.

"What's this?" she asked.

"That's where Lawrence will be going to camp," Bettie replied.

"Why's it soggy?" she asked, wagging the wet leaflet in front of her eyes.

"He got it wet. He spilled orange juice on it this morning before his soccer match."

Georgia examined the brochure. On the front was a photograph of a huge red oak that canopied a creek below, and by it a brown cabin doused in sunlight. Blond laughing children were splashing in water in their swimsuits. She turned the pages, fascinated to see pictures of the activities available: drama, craft, ballet, music, swimming, and so many more that she lost count.

"Will Robert be going to camp with Lawrence?" she asked.

"No, Georgia. He's not going this year."

"Why not?"

"Miss Mamie said he's decided to go to Daily Vacation Bible School."

Georgia grinned excitedly back at her mother. With Robert not going, she would get to sit in the back of the Whitmans' new station wagon alone with Lawrence.

* * *

Groggy from being awakened so early, Georgia got herself showered, walked slowly down the stairs of their row home so that they wouldn't creak—a sound her momma always told her made the house poor. She wore a new navy and white striped matching short outfit from Artie's, a secondhand store in Conshohocken, an hour's drive from Philly, where her mother bought all of their gently used clothes.

As they got settled into the car for the drive, Georgia and Lawrence sat in the rear-facing seat of Mamie's spanking new six-seater, two-toned station wagon. Lulled by the early morning ride, no words were spoken between the two for a while. It wasn't until Mamie had to stop the car in the middle of the road for a passing herd of sheep that Georgia used the opportunity to lean over and pull out a book that she had pushed underneath the car seat.

"What's your book?" Lawrence asked.

"Nancy Drew."

"May I see?"

"Yes," she said, flashing Lawrence a warm, toothy smile as he gently took the book out of her hands.

Mamie and Bettie found themselves listening idly to the children's conversation with half an ear, the other half focused on the talk radio's discussion on the state of crime in Philadelphia.

During a lull in the conversation Bettie shouted back, "You'd better watch out, Lawrence! Georgia is a bookworm!"

They played "I spy with my little eye," peering intently out the back window at layer upon layer of shimmering cornfields stretched out yellow and green for miles under a hazy, hot sun. They took cat naps, Lawrence's head—oblivious to him but starkly noticeable to her—falling heavily onto Georgia's shoulder as he slept. She let it rest there, his cheeks warm against her bare arms. They drove off an exit ramp from the highway to find a place to have a picnic lunch. Mamie opened the tailgate. She and Bettie carried a white Styrofoam ice chest to one of the picnic tables on a shaded spot of ground. The children were given two dollars each to buy soda pop and some treats from the nearby store.

Georgia walked in first with Lawrence trailing her. She looked around, zeroing in on the crisp white and red striped box that said "candy cigarettes" on the outside. On the shelf below were shiny plastic bags containing yellow and white swirled saltwater taffy. She pursed her lips, mulling happily over how to spend her allotted dollars when her eyes happened to fall on a package of red licorice.

"Come over here you two!"

Georgia's hand had begun to reach for the licorice, but the store-keeper's rough voice held her back. She was surprised to look down and see her fingers tremble as she touched the bag.

"You children from around here?" the storekeeper demanded.

"We're from Philadelphia," Lawrence pronounced.

"You forgot your manners. You forgot to say sir!" the man insisted.

Lawrence stole a sidelong, bewildered glance at Georgia. "Philadelphia...sir."

"Where are your folks?"

Georgia stared at the man in front of them. He was tall and wore work overalls, just as her father used to wear when he'd go to his work in the mines, and there was a gruff heaviness to his voice, as if he was struggling to push the words out of his mouth. She was nervous and moved to stand behind Lawrence for protection. The man's eyes followed her, and their eyes locked for a second. Suddenly, the image came back to her of the little girl in the bathroom of the bus station, her head dunked in the filthy toilet water. She blinked hard and moved nervously to stand behind Lawrence for protection.

"Where are your folks?" the man asked again.

"Uh, they're right outside…sir," Lawrence said.

"That your sister?" he asked.

"No, she's my friend, Georgia. We, her mom, and my mom, we stopped to have a picnic 'cause we saw the table across from your store."

"Where you all heading to?"

"We're on our way to summer camp."

The man rubbed his chin thoughtfully. "Sir!" he demanded.

But Lawrence did not respond this time as the man's eyes bore into his.

"Where did you say you children are from again?"

"Philadelphia," Georgia said, answering for Lawrence, who was looking down at his shoes. She moved to stand by Lawrence, shoulder to shoulder.

"OK," the man finally said as he glared at them. "You two go and get what you need and be quick about it. I'll check you out over here, and then I want you colored children to get the hell out my store. You hear me?" he said, his voice rising by degrees.

"Yes, sir. We hear you," Lawrence said.

Georgia put a packet of candy cigarettes and the wrapped package of red licorice on the glass counter by the cash register.

"Would you like to buy some rolling papers, too?" the storekeeper asked derisively as he rang up the candy cigarettes.

Georgia didn't answer. She knew when people were making jokes at her expense. Lawrence had only had time to pick a Fresca soda pop out of the refrigerator before he'd been accosted by the man. He put down his soda, the top of the can as dusty as the glass counter where it stood next to Georgia's candy.

"That will be three dollars and seventy-five cents."

They both handed the storekeeper their dollar bills, placing them neatly in a pile on the counter.

The man's smile vanished. Georgia could see that he was now sizing them up and looking closely at Lawrence's watch. She knew the watch was an expensive one because she had heard Mrs. Whitman tell Lawrence to be careful not to lose it at camp.

"We would like our change, sir," Georgia said timidly. "Then we will go."

"What did you say?" the man demanded.

Georgia looked into his eyes. They were so narrow, she thought, that they looked like the slits she had carved into her Jack O'Lantern pumpkin last Halloween.

"She said," Lawrence said loudly, "that we need our change back." After a long pause, he added, "Sir."

The man breathed hard, and his face turned a deeper shade of red. Eyes wide and menacing, he put his big hands on the counter and gripped the edge.

"Boy, I don't care where you come from. You hear me," he shouted. "You can come from Philadelphia or the moon as far as I'm concerned. Makes no difference to me. But boy, don't you *ever* talk to a white man like that again."

He hoisted himself over the counter's edge just enough so that Lawrence could see the full expanse of his barrel-like chest, which was only partially covered by his white t-shirt. Then, seemingly content with the result of the fright he had inflicted on them, the man stood upright and smiled. He used one of his beefy hands to lightly dust off the top of the glass counter, as if cheerily tidying up things.

Just behind him was a crowded display of cigarettes including Camels and Newports, Marlboros and Parliaments. Below those shelves were small bottles of whisky. Georgia stared at the rows and rows of cigarettes, all lined up neatly on the shelves. She recognized the Camel brand with the picture of the animal and what looked like a pyramid in the background. Her father used to smoke them, she remembered, Camel unfiltered.

"That your girlfriend?" the man asked Lawrence, pointing to Georgia.

"No, sir. She ain't my girlfriend," Lawrence said, and reached out to hold her hand. "She's just a friend."

It was the first time Lawrence had held Georgia's hand, and it gave her warm feelings of reassurance and happiness. The whirr of the overhead fan in the small country store seemed to make the aroma of coffee and tobacco more pungent as the scents mingled in the air.

"Look here, I'm just doing you a favor, boy," the man said. "You need to know how things are in this neck of the woods."

He slammed the change on the counter and watched as Lawrence winced, then quickly shooed the coins off the counter and into his palm.

"Just take this as a practice run, boy. Because me, I'm generally as harmless as they come," the storekeeper said, chuckling as his eyes darted between the two children. "But you find yourself in other rural parts of this country, say south of Norfolk, it would be a grave mistake to speak to a white man like you just spoke to me. Any white man, rich or poor. In fact, it could cost you your life."

The man's graveled voice caused the back of Georgia's hair to stand on edge and she held onto Lawrence's hand tightly.

"Let me tell you about a boy named Emmett…" the storekeeper began to say, but the children didn't wait for him to finish.

Lawrence and Georgia bolted to the screen door. They looked behind and could see that the storekeeper had begun to walk around the counter toward them. They charged through the door, a small bell tinkling softly as it opened and fell shut.

"Just hold my hand, Georgia, and don't let go," Lawrence said as they ran.

* * *

As they saw the children running toward them, Mamie and Bettie turned in the direction of the store. Mamie shielded her eyes with her hand to get a good look at the hulking man standing in the doorway and staring at them.

"Hey you two!" Bettie called out, smiling and waving to them as she finished sponging down the top of the picnic table. "I hope you're hungry!"

She placed a red and white checkered plastic tablecloth on the table. Bettie was glad that she and Mamie were on good terms, and happy that Georgia had been able to get out of the house, even if it was only for a day's drive to the country. But as she looked toward the children again, she saw that Lawrence was walking ahead of Georgia, having dropped her hand now that they were a safe distance from the store. Bettie's eagle eyes picked up on something she saw in Lawrence's face. She could see that something was amiss.

"What's wrong, Lawrence?" she asked as they came closer. "You all look like a couple of ghosts!"

Both children had lost their smiles since coming back from the country store and Bettie wondered if anything untoward had happened in there. Something about the deer-in-the-headlights look in the children's eyes triggered her concern.

"Something happen back there?" she asked.

"No, Bettie!" Lawrence replied forcefully as he looked sidelong at Georgia, as though signaling her to say the same. He stared down at his new docker shoes, now filthy from kicking up mounds of dirt on the path from the store to the grassy picnic area.

"We're fine Bettie," he added, as Mamie walked up to them.

"Miss Bettie," she said, correcting her son.

"I'm sorry, Mom. Miss Bettie, everything was fine back there. Can we eat now?" Lawrence added brightly, flashing a disarming smile.

He was anxious to put the situation in the store behind him. It had frightened him so much that he didn't know how to put into words what had just happened. He would try to put the puzzle pieces together later when he had time to think.

"Yes, let's eat, y'all," Georgia said good-naturedly.

Bettie could see through it all. She looked past the children at the storekeeper, who was still outside and staring at them. Their eyes met in mutual disdain for a few seconds before he turned and went back inside, slamming the door shut.

Meanwhile, in response to the children's request for food, Mamie laid out four place mats on the tablecloth and asked Georgia and Lawrence to help bring the food over from the station wagon. Meanwhile, Mamie poured everyone a cup of sweet Sassafras tea that had been kept chilled in the cooler.

"Lawrence," Bettie asked again, "did that white man in the store have words with you and Georgia?"

Lawrence knew that he couldn't completely evade the question, so with a quick warning glance at Georgia he said, "No, not really, although he wasn't very nice to us. We were just about to leave the store when the man said that he was going to tell us the story about Emmett. We wanted to get back to you, so we didn't stay to hear it."

"Momma, who's Emmett?" he asked, as Georgia bit into her salami sandwich.

Mamie's and Bettie's mouths dropped open. The white plastic fork that Mamie had been using to scoop up yellow-colored potato salad fell to the ground and was immediately descended upon by ants. The heads of both Black mothers turned toward their children.

"Emmett was a Black boy from the city, several years older than you," Mamie said, levelly. "It all happened a long, long time ago when he went to visit his family in the country. Nobody knows for sure what happened, but he probably stepped out of line, and, and…"

Mamie's voice broke and she was unable to finish her sentence.

"What happened to him?" Lawrence asked.

"He got killed for it, whatever it was," Bettie said, finishing Mamie's sentence.

"Well, that couldn't happen to me," Lawrence said bluntly. "Because this isn't the country. We live in Pennsylvania, not the south. Dad says people got better sense here."

"I wouldn't be too sure of that," Bettie said thoughtfully. "Some things have changed for the better since poor Emmitt's life was taken from him. But in some parts of the country, Black folk like us still need to be careful."

Lawrence looked thoughtfully at her, and her heart went out to this shy boy who devoted his life to trying to make his father love him. And the insight came to her that adversity had started to refine the Whitman boy, like fire chastened metal. She glanced at him again as he dug into an ear of sweet corn, smiling brightly.

"Mmmm, mmm! This has got to be your corn, Miss Bettie, not my momma's, right?" he asked, laughing.

"That's right," Bettie proudly replied.

Mamie frowned in mock dismay, causing Georgia to giggle, which set the whole table laughing.

They say that Robert is the one who will walk in Judge Whitman's footsteps, Bettie thought as she swatted away a mosquito that was bothering her. *But this one here? He's a chip off the old block, too. He's gonna be just fine. Just fine, so long as the judge lays off the boy's neck.*

10

Dropping Lawrence off at the camp in Pottstown, PA, was going to be a straightforward affair, Bettie imagined. They would assist him in moving his trunk to his cabin, introduce him to his counselor, and get back on the road in search of an A&W for shakes and cheeseburgers, a promise made to Georgia that Bettie intended to keep.

From Bettie's vantage point, the trip was an opportunity for Georgia to get a little fresh air into her lungs and get an eyeful of Pennsylvania beyond the narrow confines of their Philadelphian row home. It was a healthy change from reading her summer books on the back porch of the Whitman home while she worked, and her daily after-supper ritual of playing Jacks on the front stoop with a constantly changing constellation of friends. Georgia had asked if she could go to camp with Lawrence, and Bettie had told her—in the plain and direct manner of working Black mothers who don't have time for foolishness—that she most certainly could not. Black children had to know just what was what, as the old folks said. It made the challenges they were certain to face in the future much easier to cope with. She wished with all her heart that she could afford to give Georgia the same experience as Lawrence, but she could only dream of sending her daughter to camp.

* * *

The crunch of luxury car wheels on pebbles could be heard as they pulled into the parking lot. It was the first day of camp and the place was a horde of counselors, children, and parents, the latter dragging luggage behind them. As they filed out of the car, Bettie could see that Camp Victory was even more beautiful in real life than portrayed in its brochure. It was set in a forested inlet of pines, river birches, and dogwood trees and, from where they stood, a vast azure lake could be seen peeking out from the green hills. Rugged wooden cabins and quaint, clapboard arts halls, were nestled within the forest of trees.

A girl with long floppy hair and kind, green eyes that almost exactly matched the color of her bandana, walked vigorously up to the group.

"Is this the Whitman family?" she asked jovially.

When this was confirmed, she proceeded, without being asked, to help Bettie and Mamie hoist Lawrence's trunk across the field. Bettie carried a small fan and Georgia held Lawrence's flashlight and a Disney backpack across her shoulders.

"I'm Beverly," the girl said, turning around to make sure that everyone felt welcome as she walked with them toward Lawrence's cabin.

"How did she know that we were the Whitman family?" Georgia asked her mother quietly.

"Color, baby," Bettie said. "The counselors have lists. They must have known that the Whitman family was Black. How many Black folk do you see around here?

"Now hush," Bettie added, as Georgia began to pepper her with more questions.

On the way, Beverly paused to point out the camp amphitheater and an array of music practice rooms, all freshly painted white with arched wooden windows, all lined up in rows like obedient soldiers.

"You're a musician, aren't you?" Beverley asked Lawrence. "You play the guitar, right?"

Lawrence looked at the counselor from over the expanse of the trunk. He seemed to pause a second before gently nodding his head to indicate that she was correct. Turning to Georgia, Beverley got down on her knees so that she could see Georgia, eyeball to eyeball.

"What bunk did they assign you to?" she asked. "I only see one Whitman child."

"Oh, no, miss. I won't be going to camp this summer."

Noting the counselor's confusion and sensing her mother's distress, Georgia added, "I'm not sure that this camp is for me anyway. I don't play an instrument and I'm allergic to trees."

Bettie and Georgia followed as Mamie and Beverley carried Lawrence's trunk up the steep hill to a cabin that was shaded by a cluster of green pine trees. Lawrence turned around to speak to Georgia, who was trudging behind him.

"Can you carry this up for me?" he asked.

"Yes. What is it?"

"It's a metronome. It makes a tick-tock sound like a clock, and it helps me to play in time. Please don't drop it. If it breaks, I'll be playing all my pieces at the wrong speed."

Georgia smiled and hugged the metronome to her.

Girls were not allowed in the boy's cabins, so Bettie directed her to wait on a nearby bench while she went with Mamie to help Lawrence. She sat down under the shade of a dogwood with her book and listened to the softly rippling creek water coursing over river stones. But the calming sound of the water was soon eclipsed by girlish laughter. Three little girls, two white and one Black, had just strolled out of the cabin to the east, clutching their towels to their chest. They sat next to each other on a nearby bench as they waited for their counselor to take them down to the dock for a swim before supper. Georgia's eyes narrowed as she scrutinized the three girls to confirm that there definitely *was* a brown-skinned girl there, just like her, seated on the bench.

"Do all of you go to this camp? It seems really nice," Georgia called over.

The tallest of the trio wore her curly auburn hair in a ponytail tied back with a white ribbon. She looked over at Georgia and then turned back to her bunkmates on either side of her.

"What do you think, stupid?" she said. "Are you blind? Can't you see that we've got our swimming suits on?"

"We're about to go swimming in the lake!" the other white girl said. "Of course we're staying here."

A camp counselor strode over with three head garlands fashioned with white lilies and ignored Georgia seated just a few yards away.

"You may put these on after your swim, I promise," she told the three girls as they admired the garlands. "I just wanted to give you a glimpse of the kind of arts and crafts activities that you can expect at Victory!"

As the girls oohed and aahed, Georgia gazed longingly at the garlands of white flowers, and wished with all her heart that she could wear one. She stared at the little Black girl, whose hair was braided in two plaits, just like hers, although hers lay flat on her back like two good sleeping children. She waited for the little girl to say something. Anything that might ease the pain that she was feeling. The Black camper somberly held Georgia's gaze for a few seconds, then cheerfully returned to the kind of conversation that little girls who live in big houses and have nice wardrobed have.

The three laughed as Georgia looked on. Then, to her absolute mortification, the mischievous girl pulled out a package of chocolate tootsie rolls, her number one favorite candy. She watched as the candy was shared between the girls. I hope it makes them sick, she thought as she looked at the giggling huddle of heads only just a few yards away.

The sun was hot and, rather than try to escape it by moving into the shade, Georgia allowed the sunlight to soak into her face. While keeping her eyes shut, she thought about what kind of bathing suit she would be wearing right now if she were seated next to the trio of girls. It would not, she decided, be the babyish Snoopy bathing suit that her mother had bought for her to wear when the city got unbearably hot and the fire hydrant was opened. That was when all of the neighborhood children came running out of their sweltering houses and jumped and laughed in the cooling spray.

* * *

"Georgia! Georgia!"

Georgia opened her eyes when she heard her mother calling her name. She looked around and saw more campers arriving with their parents, eager to unpack their neatly folded clothes from their trunks. The children breathed in the mouthwatering smell that the junior camp counselors in the know told them was homemade meatloaf and French fries. Those who had already unpacked their trunks were loitering on the stoops of their cabins, just waiting for the sound of the bell which, they were told, was the signal that they could begin to line up and walk down the hill to the camp dining hall.

She looked around for Lawrence and saw him sitting down outside his cabin blowing bubbles with a purple plastic bottle of liquid in his hand. Mrs. Lawrence and her mother were standing in front of him, and she went over to join them. It was time, she heard Mrs. Whitman tell Lawrence, for them to head back to Philly.

"What, already?" Lawrence asked, smiling, preoccupied with blowing his bubbles.

"Yes, I'm afraid so," Mamie said, raising her hand to her forehead to shield her eyes from the late afternoon sun.

Georgia's eyes seemed to be glued to the ground. She was busy using the toe of her shoe to make a circle the size of a basketball in the sand where she stood. She was edging the circle deeper until Bettie nudged her shoulder.

"Stop that," Bettie said. "Your shoes will get filthy."

Georgia looked at Lawrence's brand-new brown docksider shoes and then back to her own.

"There're not my shoes anyway. They're Rebecca's niece's shoes that she sent to me. So they're hand-me-downs."

Before Bettie had a chance to reply, Georgia walked over to Lawrence and sat down beside him. Startled, he put his bubble mixture to one side and looked up at her.

"I hope that you have a good time at camp, Lawrence," she whispered. "But please be careful who you make friends with. There are some not very nice people here."

Lawrence just stared at her, so Georgia stood up and walked back to her mother. Mrs. Whitman gave her son a hug, telling him to be good, enjoy himself, and above all not to disobey the camp counselors. They then said goodbye to Lawrence and the three of them walked slowly back to the car, amidst happy screams and laughter. As before, Georgia sat in the back of the station wagon and watched as a billowing brown swirl of dust and dirt obstructed her view of the camp where they had left Lawrence for the summer.

* * *

Years later, when Georgia looked back on that summer day, most of the events had been forgotten. Even the stop off at the drive-in A&W restaurant, where the waitress skated to their station wagon and took her special order of a strawberry milkshake with whipped cream and a burger with ketchup.

"Anything you want," her mother had told her, her voice suddenly warm.

But there were two memories that remained. Initially they were both tiny seeds, but they grew in her heart and mind with the passing years. The first was when Lawrence held her hand protectively as he stood up to the bigoted shop owner. She'd never had a boy take her hand and she knew, the very second that she felt his moist hand in hers, that it was something wonderful.

The second was the meaningful glance of the little Black girl with pigtails just like her. At first, she thought it was a look of disdain. Only later did she begin to wonder whether it was actually sheer anxiety. Seated on the bench and sandwiched between the two white girls, perhaps she was afraid that, if she allowed her gaze to rest on Georgia, she might establish a bond between them that would ominously threaten the relationship she was beginning to establish with the two white girls.

11

Two weeks after Lawrence's return from Camp Victory, Mamie was preparing supper. Theodore was having drinks with a colleague and would eat later, so there was just her, the two boys, and a friend that Robert had invited over. She stirred the stewed chicken, wondering what time Theodore would be home and if the chicken would be fit to eat when he did. No matter, she thought as she dipped a spoon into the dish. It was ready now, and it tasted good.

Robert and his friend appeared immediately when she called, but Lawrence took his time. He came down from his room when she called a second time and ambled over to the dinner table, shrugging off his mother's angry stare. The others had already began eating.

On the other side of Robert sat a boy Lawrence recognized. He attended Oak Street Church, as well, and was in the children's choir practice with him and Robert.

"What's your name again?" Lawrence asked.

"Mind your manners," Mamie said sharply.

Lawrence ignored his mother's admonition and, without waiting for an answer, brought a fork full of chicken to his mouth with rapturous delight.

"He told you before, but you've forgotten already…haven't you?" Robert said, exasperatedly, jabbing his fork toward his brother.

Lawrence glanced quickly over to the boy and then back to his brother.

"Can't he speak for himself?" he inquired. "I know you from church, right?"

"Lemuel is my name, but I'm called just Lem," Robert's friend replied, and then fell silent.

"Lem attended daily Vacation Bible School with your brother," Mamie said, filling the gap in the conversation. "His father is a painter. He paints houses. Inside and out."

She paused and turned to look at Lemuel, who was seated rigidly in his chair.

"And his mother…his mother…"

"My mother doesn't live with Dad and me," Lemuel said in a hollow voice.

"Where does she live?" Lawrence asked.

"She lives in LA," he said. Then, breathing in and out slowly in a studied way, as though taught once to practice this, he continued. "Where…where she is—is—living life on her own."

Mamie deftly changed the subject by standing up and pushing her chair back.

"Since you've all finished, I'd like you boys to clean up now," she said to all three, but with her eyes fixed on Lawrence. "All of you."

She looked over at Lawrence's plate. He'd eaten everything save for a wishbone left over from his devoured chicken. He flashed a perfectly white grin toward his mother then, and as she watched, he held one end of the wishbone out to his brother.

"Make a wish!" he said, bowing his head theatrically and closing his eyes tightly.

They pulled and Lawrence ended up with the larger piece. He stared mischievously from Robert and then over to Lem, who had politely stacked Robert's plate onto his.

96

"What'd you wish?" Robert asked.

"That I'd one day be lucky enough to have a friend like yours. That's what I wished for."

Something about her son's answer didn't set right with her, so Mamie relegated all of the remaining kitchen duties to Lawrence.

"Now you sound like Dad! Always jumping on me for never being good enough."

But his protests fell on deaf ears. After finishing his last chore of wiping the kitchen counters he ran upstairs to grab his guitar. He then went outside and began walking toward his favorite tree, but he stopped before reaching it.

To his left, by the hedge that was the boundary between the Whitmans' and the neighbor's property, Robert and Lemuel were seated side by side on a pile of logs. Music streamed from a radio placed at their feet. Lawrence changed direction and began walking closer to them. The boys, he could see from just a few yards away, were unaware that he was watching them. They were whittling, immersed in the practice of stripping off brown bark from sticks with the penknives and scraping the remainder until the sticks were pale and green, the color of avocado flesh.

Their complete contentment was mirrored in each other's faces as they whittled, and, as Lawrence stood quietly watching their deft handling of their red handled pocketknives, he felt an unexpected stirring. As he stared at them, he realized that these two—his brother and his friend—had something good between them, something like a gift that he didn't have, and it disturbed him. He looked down at his shoes. Chicken grease had spilled on them as he was cleaning up, all because he didn't get any help. He thought of his father and how Robert would always be the favorite, for no good reason that he could see. So, he stood and stared and chose his moment.

The second Lem's head bent over to lean on Robert's, Lawrence called out in a pitch perfect impression of his father's voice, "Hey! What's going on here!"

PART TWO

12

June 1972

In the summer of '72, Lawrence realized that Bettie's daughter had gotten a hold on him in a way he understood about as much as the way the gangly limbs of his body seemed to have a mind all their own. But something about the tender way Robert looked at Lemuel allowed him to recognize his feelings toward Georgia. So, when she appeared at the back door right next to him—just as her mother was finishing up in the kitchen and probably wanted to get home—he didn't ask her why she was standing there looking at him.

"Hey!" he said when he saw her.

Her long hair was in heavy plaited cornrows that reached below her shoulders. At the ends of the braids were tiny golden beads that clinked against each other like tiny bells whenever she moved. She wore cut-off jean overalls and in her front pocket was a sprig of holly, which he found unusual since it was nowhere near Christmas.

"Hey, back!" she replied cheerily.

He didn't say a thing when she followed him as he walked out of the house with his book, *Black Boy*, nestled under his arm. And he didn't respond when she said, "I'm going with you," as the door slammed shut with a thud.

A hot yellow sun baked their shoulders as they walked down a well-trodden narrow dirt path from the top of the hill to a small bank of grass. Lawrence sat down first, put his book down, then patted the spot next to him indicating where she should sit. A sweet scent billowed from her as she sat down.

"You smell good. What's that perfume called?" he asked, thinking of the fact that every Christmas his father bought his mother the same perfume. It was called Estée.

"Ivory soap," she said. "Momma won't let me wear perfume yet."

She was thinner, more fragile and yet more beautiful than ever before. She was looking straight ahead as he looked at her long neck. It reminded him of a picture of a Nubian princess that he'd seen in a *National Geographic* magazine. He thought her beautiful, seated next to him, cross legged and lithe as a dancer.

He was thirteen now, just like her, and from somewhere deep inside him, he felt the urge to kiss her. He was about to ask her whether that would be OK with her when, before he had a chance to speak, she turned toward him, brown eyes shimmering, and lightly brushed her full lips against his.

"You smell like your house," she said, after a prolonged silence. "Rich," she added.

Then, before he could reply, she said, "I have to go. Momma will be waiting for me."

As she scrambled to her feet, he saw that she had one shoe off and one shoe on, like the time she'd come with Bettie to his guitar lesson to pick him up when they were children.

"Do you ever wear both shoes, Georgia?" he asked, laughing and looking up at her.

She looked down at him. He was holding *Black Boy* in his lap.

"Only when they both fit," she said turning to run off. She rushed up the hill, then called back, "And they never do!"

Lawrence sat and read his book, as the afternoon sun sauntered to the side. The sound of a sole bluebird's call could be heard behind him in the branches of an oak. He sat and read as the sky turned to a dusky blue with faint swirls of lavender, content to be a spectator to the ending of the day.

13

Enjoying the taste of salt on his tongue, Teddy stood tall on his summer property under the bluest of skies. To the east was the bone-colored ribbon of sand that swanked around Bank Street Beach in Harwich Port. The air infused his lungs, making him feel young and rejuvenated in a way not even a stiff Scotch on a dismal day could. He turned toward Mamie and smiled.

They were waiting for their guests, the Scott family, to arrive from the long commute from Pennsylvania.

He'd bought the Cape Cod house on a whim four years ago. With the loss of the Kennedys and Dr. King, the country had begun a precipitous descent into a thick brew of fear, apathy, and racial division and Theodore intended it to be a cool haven, far from the maddening crowds. Mamie agreed with the idea but had originally baulked at the thought of a vacation home so far from Philadelphia. "Why not Cape May?" she had asked. But she had come around, recognizing that the Cape had more of a social cachet and a more traditional feel than her friend Jemma's chosen stomping ground, Martha's Vineyard.

Mamie knew that it was important for the family to get out of Philly from time to time, given the deteriorating state of racial

104

relationships that had gone from bad to worse. Frank Rizzo, the paunchy, brutal, and racially motivated former police commissioner, was in his first term as mayor of the city. While commissioner, relations between the police and the Black community had deteriorated to an all-time low, and now as mayor he opposed the desegregation of Philadelphia's schools and argued against the construction of public housing in majority-white neighborhoods. Mamie recognized the difficult position her husband was in, caught between the racially oriented politics of the mayor and the demand for fair and equitable treatment by Philadelphia's Black community.

She was grateful that Theodore had purchased the vacation home and she had encouraged him to carve out time so that they, as a family, could put the problems of the city behind them for a few weeks each summer. Didn't they deserve that?

* * *

All was good on the eve of Independence Day, as the couple stood, arm in arm on the doorstep, waiting for their guests to arrive for a long weekend. As they waited, their eyes were languidly drawn toward the east where a patient half-moon waited for the sun to set. Theodore sighed. It had been some years now since his precious Mamie had confessed to having an affair, but it was all in the wake now, he told himself. They were still together, side by side with arms locked, watching a brilliant russet sunset.

Theodore closed his eyes and breathed in deeply, allowing the cool, salty fresh sea breeze to rejuvenate him. And it was at that precise moment he heard a car lumber slowly down the street and park in front of the Whitmans' picket fence.

Shirley Scott rolled down the window of the car. "We're here!" she called out ebulliently.

Her smile, Theodore noticed, was as lustrously white as the picket fence that he had just applied a fresh coat of paint to only two days before. Meanwhile, Mamie took note that Shirley's hair looked freshly washed and styled as if she had just stepped out of a salon.

How did she achieve that miracle? she wondered. *When did she find the time for a roller set during the journey from Philly?*

Theodore and Mamie walked over to the car together, hand in hand.

"Welcome!" Mamie said as they disembarked from the car. "I hope that you had a good journey."

Theodore helped Sherman Scott retrieve the suitcases from the car, while Mamie walked with Shirley and her daughter, Claire, up to the house. She couldn't help but notice how Claire had grown. She was becoming, as the old folk said, a beaut. Thin and long limbed, she offered a shy, quiet smile as she passed through the front door.

"The boys are upstairs somewhere, Claire," Mamie said, gesturing with her hand. "Why don't you see if you can find them?"

"What a beautiful little home!" Shirley exclaimed.

Theodore flinched, having overheard the word "little." *Should have sprung another ten grand for a something a bit larger*, he thought.

She was one of Mamie's bridge partners and a member with her of the elite Black social group, the Links, while Sherman Scott was Theodore's friend and a tenured sociology professor at the University of Pennsylvania.

"Well. This is a sight for sore eyes, Teddy!" Sherman pronounced as he bounded into the house with two of the suitcases. "And I'm going to change my opinion of your tastes," he joked. "You've chosen a quintessential Cape house for your summer home, and I couldn't be more envious. You've done good, brother."

Whether by good luck or sound judgment, Theodore had chosen their summer home well. It was an 18th century wood-shingled Cape Cod Saltbox home on a quiet neighborhood street in Harwich Port, only a few miles from Banks Street Beach on the Atlantic. The house was a showstopper, at least by the quiet standards of the modest residential street. It was wood shingled and in the shape of a birthday cake with sloping sides, and on an acre of land. Theodore loved looking at the abundant grass on the property. He admired how it shined like cut glass by day, only, chameleon-like, to shimmer like a carpet of green fire under the moonlight.

Once the suitcases had been taken to the rooms and unpacked, they settled down to a feast of fried clams, and potatoes with chives, butter, and sour cream. Over dinner, Shirley and Sherman brought Mamie and Theodore up to date with the latest news and scandal from Philadelphia while both boys tried to engage Claire in conversation. They couldn't help but stare at her, as if she were some kind of exotic bird in a zoo.

Just after 10:00 p.m., Shirley and Sherman declared that they were pooped from their long drive and so, with apologies, they went upstairs to bed. Theodore and Mamie were also exhausted so, not long after the Scotts retired, they did, too—leaving Robert, Lawrence, and Claire to chat among themselves. Their eyelids closed almost as soon as they were in bed and, holding each other close, they fell asleep, lulled by the fresh ocean breezes that tumbled through the open bedroom window.

* * *

At just after 7:00 a.m. the next day, Robert was quietly taking a shower upstairs while Theodore was already dressed in khaki shorts and a white Ralph Lauren polo shirt. He stood by the kitchen counter, looking out the window at a tiny ruby-throated hummingbird hovering outside. The bird darted away in search of nectar, so Theodore walked into the living room, where Robert and Lawrence had spent the night—having given up their room to Claire. Lawrence was curled up on the couch bed with his eyes closed.

"Lawrence, please get up and put the couch back," Theodore said.

"Dad, could you give me a chance to wake up?"

"Before the Scotts come downstairs," Theodore added insistently.

"Good morning to you, too," Lawrence grumbled in a half whisper.

"What was that, boy?"

"Nothing," Lawrence said, admitting defeat. "I'll get up."

The Fourth of July holiday had always resonated with Lawrence, mainly because of the thrill of seeing colored bursts of fireworks in the black night. Any new and bright thing that disrupted life's monotony—a gadget, a car, a sound—had always enticed him. The Cape suited him just fine, with weeks of summer spread out liberally, like thick jam on bread. Still, he wouldn't regret going back to the city, with its faster pace and distractions.

He stood up, rubbing the sleep out of his eyes, and dutifully put his and Robert's pillows from either side of the fold-out couch on the side chair, took off the sheets and blanket, then folded them and put them away.

When Robert came downstairs from his shower, Lawrence went upstairs to take his.

"Don't wake the Scotts up," Theodore called after him as Lawrence walked up the narrow staircase, the old wooden boards creaking as he did.

Once everyone was showered and dressed, the two families sat down together at Mamie's brown country table in the kitchen nook of the summer home. Over fried eggs and long strips of Taylor's pork roll, Claire, Lawrence, and Robert decided that they'd prefer to skip Banks Street Beach and walk instead to the boys' favorite swimming hole at Sand Pond.

"It's only a fifteen-minute walk from here," Lawrence said, trying to sound reassuring. He was the first to notice Sherman Scott's raised eyebrows.

"It's fine," Mamie said with a smile. "Sand Pond is very safe, and they have a lifeguard on duty. He's fully trained, and his name is Sam. He's a young colored man and his family is from the Cape Verdean islands. So please don't worry, Sherman. Robert and Lawrence will take good care of your daughter."

"And unlike Philly," she added, looking around the table, "nothing much ever happens around here. That is, unless you count the heated arguments over the cost of summer beach parking tickets."

Mamie looked over at Claire, who seemed preoccupied with taking bird-like sips of the chilled orange juice. Looking at her now, with shreds of orange pulp clinging to her lips, she reminded Mamie of a fawn deer, all big eyes and long legs.

After breakfast, everyone contributed to washing up the dishes. There was no dishwasher appliance in the home since Mamie and Theodore had agreed not to install one, preferring instead to retain as much as they could of the 18th century house's historical bones.

"Now be gentlemen, boys. You hear me?" Theodore said, as the trio got up to get ready to walk to the pond.

"If you don't, there'll be trouble from me!" Sherman added.

"You all be back by three p.m. for our cookout," Mamie said. "If you come back before us, the key will be under the doormat."

She watched as her sons and Claire walked single file out of the door, the boys in their swimming shorts and t-shirts and Claire in her jean skirt and a pink shirt that demurely covered a one-piece red and white checked swimsuit, the spaghetti straps prettily exposed on her long, swan like neck. Each carried a beach towel under their arms as they left the house.

"Bye, Mom!" Lawrence called, consciously omitting his father's name. "We'll be back on time. I promise!"

Watching them depart, Mamie kept her eyes on the fawn-like Claire. She'd had a chance to view the market and size up the daughters of her friends. Claire would make a great match for Robert when the time comes, she thought with a smile. Their babies would be beautiful.

After the children had left, the adults piled into Theodore's rented blue Nova and drove to Banks Street Beach. When they arrived, the foursome had difficulty in finding a parking spot since it was a holiday. Vehicles were parked everywhere in both legal and illegal spots.

But then, just as Theodore's exasperation was about to boil over, a car helpfully pulled out of a space in front of them. He immediately claimed it, explaining to Sherman as he maneuvered into the space how it made sense to buy a beach parking decal at the very start of the season.

"It's a lot less expensive that way," he said.

They grabbed their towels, beach umbrellas, and folding chairs and walked the short distance to the beach.

"It's a beautiful day," Shirley said, looking up at the luminous blue sky.

She noticed that none of the white bathers seemed to pay any mind to these four brown bodies maneuvering amidst their umbrellas and beach towels in search of the perfect spot.

"They're definitely not color struck around here," Shirley mouthed to her husband as Theodore indicated the spot that they should take on the sun drenched, ivory-colored sand.

The men pitched two long-poled blue and white striped umbrellas into the sand while the ladies unfolded the chairs. Everyone then laid back and relaxed, allowing the sun to bake them into a calm stupor. Everyone that is, apart from Theodore, who kept his eyes wide open, blinking hard like an owl against the Eastern seaboard sun.

After a while, he stood up and volunteered to trudge in his Dr. Scholl's sandals over to an ice cream stand that was set between the parking lot and the beach. He bought four of the same, ice cream cones topped with chopped nuts and hardened dipped chocolate sauce. He was grateful for the cardboard tray into which the four cones neatly fit, that enabled him to carry them without mishap.

He trekked back to the group and distributed the treats, receiving grateful thanks in return. But as he sat down to enjoy his own ice cream, his thoughts turned to the intractable problems of the city, in particular, the demands of youth justice groups to curb police brutality that was spiraling out of control.

I should be there, he thought as he closed his eyes and pondered what could be done and what role the justice system ought to play. But before any answers came, the fresh ocean breezes had lulled him to sleep.

14

The three young teens wandered aimlessly down the dirt road to the pond that was a favorite of the locals. Robert was in front, followed by Claire and then Lawrence. Along the way, Robert took it upon himself to point out the local attractions to Claire.

"They say that house is haunted," he said, indicating a dilapidated house on the corner.

They walked a little further and Robert picked up a long stick to use as a pointer.

"Someone from that house died," he said, drawing Claire's attention to a small salt box home with a rose-colored front door. "He fell into quicksand, and no one helped him."

"And just over there," Robert continued, "that's where Lawrence was supposed to pick fresh berries for a blueberry pie that our mom had planned for last night. Instead, you got scones. Sorry about that! You still with us Laurie?"

"You know I hate it when you call me that!" Lawrence called back, increasing his pace to keep up so that he could walk alongside Claire. Her sparkling laughter heralded his arrival.

When they reached the pond both boys immediately dove into the water, racing each other from the dock to the shore and back.

"Stop splashing!" Claire called out as Lawrence swam by.

She was seated on the white sun-bleached, weathered dock and had taken off her shirt to reveal her swimming suit. She kept her jean skirt on and held a boat hat with a wide black sash in place over her long, pulled-back hair.

"Why aren't you swimming?" Lawrence asked politely, intermittently dipping his head into the water and then raising it out again.

"I don't want to get my hair wet," she replied, sticking her tongue out at him.

"Suit yourself," Lawrence said, taking his wet forearms away from the edge of the deck and allowing his body to slowly sink and then disappear into the water only to pop up again within seconds.

Nonplussed, Claire unrolled her beach towel, lay down on the dock, and attempted to doze. But her peace was disturbed by Robert, who climbed onto the dock and stood at its edge. She sat upright as he executed a perfect dive into the pond, keeping his long, lean back ramrod straight as he entered the water.

"Wow!" she said, excitedly. "That was a great dive."

He grabbed the side of the dock but, as he hoisted himself out, he grazed his arm and it started to bleed. Claire rushed over to him. She took her cloth belt out of its loops and improvised a tourniquet.

"Don't know why you're doing that," Robert said, mystified. "It's only a scratch and it's just going to get wet again."

"Mom says that if I want to be a nurse, I have to start early," she said, smiling as she wrapped the cloth tightly around his arm.

When it was Lawrence's turn, he waited until he caught Claire's eye and then executed a flawless dive, back and head aligned, cutting through the water like a polished blade.

"How'd I do?" he asked her, after surfacing and shaking the water out of his hair.

Claire just smiled coquettishly. Her eyes roved from one brother to the other.

"What, no accolades for me?" He had just learned the word accolades and thought he'd try it on for size.

Lawrence looked over at Claire, whose mind seemed elsewhere. He then glanced at Robert, who was busy hoisting himself onto the dock, allowing water to drip from his fit body onto the sun-beaten slats. He also seemed to be in a world all his own, so Lawrence dove back into the water and began a leisurely swim. As time went by, other groups—white, Black, Portuguese, and mixed race—joined him in the water. By noon, under a piercingly warm sun, the small sandy shore beside the pool became overrun with screaming children and their sunbathing mothers. It was not until their stomachs started to rumble that the three decided it was time to return to the Whitman cottage.

* * *

Robert and Claire were the first to arrive, and they both went upstairs to change. Lawrence then walked in, allowing the heavy wet towel that had been on his shoulder to dangle from his hand.

"Pick up your towel, Lawrence. Don't let it drag on the ground!" Theodore yelled. "Your mother and I didn't raise you to be slovenly."

"Give the boy a break, man!" Sherman said as Theodore gave him a beer and ushered him outside to the patio barbecue. "I feel sorry for the kid. I'm sure he does the best that he can, but he seems to have acquired an uncanny knack for upsetting you. I hear you hollering at him all the time."

Theodore fired up the barbecue and soon the aroma of grilled burgers, steaks, and hot sausage links began to fill the air. Mamie and Shirley joined them on the patio, each carrying a glass of sweet iced tea. The women chatted amicably amongst themselves about the quaintness of Harwich Port, while Teddy decided that the men would have a discussion about the respective merits of W.E.B. Du Bois and his intellectual rival, Booker T. Washington. It was a cocktail party favorite of Theodore's, and he was anxious to put Sherman to the test.

"I don't care what you say, Washington was a step and fetch it Negro," Theodore said. "Let's tell it like it is. Du Bois, on the other hand, understood what we needed most. Education. His talented tenth idea was conceived to uplift the masses by establishing models among people like us. That's what Du Bois preached. He believed in the talented tenth. And guess what?"

He put his drink down on the table and peered over at Mamie, Shirley, and Sherman.

"We *are* the talented tenth."

As he spoke, Theodore had in mind his own father, who had migrated to Baltimore from the South with little more than a twenty-dollar bill. But through pluck and hard work, and no scarcity of prayer, he built a shoe and jewelry repair business in West Philly from scratch and saved all his money so that Theodore could attend school.

Sherman laughed, and as he did, an edgy sarcasm came into his voice that was detected by Mamie. She turned and looked over at him.

"W.E.B.'s talented tenth never did anything to solve crime on the streets, did it?" Sherman shot back. He stopped for a moment as though gathering his thoughts. He glanced intently at Shirley and then turned his attention back to Theodore.

"Never did a blessed thing to put food in the mouths of the hungry, did it? These days, the elite Black who were supposed to comprise the talented tenth all belong to private clubs like you, Theodore, and do nothing to ease the suffering of those who haven't had the same advantage."

"Well, Sherman, you don't look too miserable to me," Theodore deadpanned.

"And neither do you, Teddy, truth be told," Sherman replied.

Theodore looked down at the back of his hands, which had been hardened from outdoor summer jobs as a teen long before he became a judge. Sherman took a sip of his beer and looked sheepishly over at his wife. She would not be amused, he knew. But something inside compelled him toward one last salvo.

"Well, I'll just say this, Teddy. That board membership of the mining company you're sitting on ain't making you any poorer."

Theodore decided not to take the bait. He knew that Sherman was simply trying to get him all jawed up. He was probably even a little jealous. Prompted by Mamie, Theodore had given considerable thought over the past three years as to whether it was time for him to leave the board. After the board had decided not to upgrade its safety regulations following Jimmy Smythe's tragic death, he had decided to resign.

"Guess word doesn't get around too fast. I've resigned," he said, staring into Sherman's eyes and relishing the feeling of one-upping his friend.

Fresh from his shower, Lawrence came out onto the patio and looked at the stacks of burgers piled to the side of the barbecue. Hot oil was oozing out of the charred meat.

"Can I have one?" he asked his father.

Theodore turned toward him angrily, waving his spatula in his hand as if it were a weapon.

"Goddamn it, Lawrence," he said. "Can't you see that I'm speaking with Dr. Scott? Don't you have the common sense and courtesy not to interrupt?"

Lawrence thought of telling his father that he and Dr. Scott seemed to have finished their conversation before he'd asked for a burger, but thought better of it.

"That boy reminds me of the saying… 'you can't put a ten-dollar hat on a ten-cent head,'" Theodore said, just loud enough for all to hear.

"He's just a boy, Teddy," Mamie said, coming to Lawrence's defense. "Couldn't you leave him alone for once?"

"He'll be a man soon enough," Theodore retorted.

Lawrence felt heat rising to his face. These small battles were becoming an everyday occurrence. Before matters became even worse, Mamie decided that she had better try to deflect the approaching storm.

"Lawrence, could you please go and pick up the apples from Mr. Peterson next door? Our neighbor has been kind enough to give us two bags from his tree and I want to make a pie tomorrow morning."

"Why me? Why can't you ask Robert?" he asked. "It's the Fourth... can't we fetch them tomorrow?"

Riled, Whitman instantly pounced. "Do as your mother asks you, boy, if you know what's good for you," he said, and walked over to where Lawrence stood.

"We don't want a trip to the woodshed, do we boy?" he said in a near whisper.

Mamie walked over to the grill and lightly touched Theodore on the arm.

"Leave the boy alone," she said, her voice quiet yet strong. She then indicated that Lawrence should follow her inside.

"You know, these verbal jibes your father loves," she said. "You know what I think? I think that they just come naturally to him from his years of arguing cases in court. He's good at that, and that's why he became a judge. Please try and understand and forgive."

She looked at her son, now thirteen, eyes searing with teenage righteousness.

"Forgive, Mom? I'll try, but it happens every day. He can't stop picking on me," Lawrence said as he went to retrieve the apples.

When he returned through the back gate a few minutes later he could see that Robert and Claire were in the small grassy area playing the croquet game that Mamie and Shirley had set up for the teens. Claire had a yellow rabbit's foot poking out of the back of her blue jeans. He had one, too, except it was colored blue.

Now that Lawrence was back from his errand, Theodore banged his spatula against the grill.

"Time to chow down!" he announced.

A stack of sizzling burgers, steaks, and some charbroiled hot links were deposited on one of the tables, along with all the fixings.

Lawrence's attention was firmly fixed on Claire as the three young people sat at the card table that had been set up for them.

"Hey, what's up?" Robert asked, sensing that something was wrong.

Lawrence ignored him.

Robert, athletic, brooding, and yet effusive when called for, was in many respects an anomaly in their family. Slow to anger, he was both sensitive and physically gifted. While he also excelled in school, it was Lawrence who was the voracious reader. The Collected Poems of Langston Hughes was on his nightstand, under well-thumbed sheets of guitar music. Robert was the jock, a natural sportsman who was fearless on the field.

"What happened back there?" Robert asked his brother.

"Oh, nothing," Lawrence mumbled, glancing over at Claire, who was obliviously tucking into her hamburger. "You know Dad…what can I say? He's like a dog with a bone."

He couldn't peel his eyes away from Claire's face as she put a spoon of yellow-colored potato salad in her mouth. He examined each of her movements, unconsciously trying to find safe harbor from the onslaught of his father's abuse. He thought of Georgia, who was different than Claire. Not better or worse, just different.

Claire smiled back at him, and as she did, the ear of corn he was holding dropped to his plate, splattering butter everywhere.

"Now I've done it," he said.

She laughed without opening her mouth. "Don't blame yourself," she said, just under her breath. "We all do that."

Even you? he thought.

* * *

That evening, the boys stayed up to roast marshmallows under the stars. Lawrence moved his marshmallow stick in and out of the flames until the marshmallow became charred on the outside. His mouth watered thinking about the sweet gooiness inside. He was about to let it cool and take a bite when he looked over at Robert, whose head was beginning to droop from tiredness.

"Claire is cute," Lawrence said, but it was more to himself than to Robert.

It was clear that Claire only had eyes for Robert, and he could feel a wave of jealousy rise within him. He held his marshmallow stick again to the flame,

"You didn't ask Claire for her phone number," Lawrence finally said.

"I didn't want it," Robert replied.

"You didn't even look at her. Why not?" Lawrence said, his stick animatedly pulsing the flames.

Robert didn't answer but was now fully awake. He took his stick and shoved it into the hot, red fire alongside Lawrence's.

"Huh? Robert? What's up with you?"

Robert calmly took his stick out of the fire, let it cool, and then bit into the blackened, sweet and charred marshmallow.

"That's good," he said, licking his lips. Then, turning toward his brother after a moment's hesitation, he added, "I'm not sure. I don't think I'm geared up that way, man."

In the crisp night air, all Lawrence could see were Robert's two shining eyes drilling into him, along with a sadness there that worried him. He looked toward the house and saw the broad silhouette of his father, helping his mother with the dishes.

"Please don't say anything to Dad," Robert implored, taking his eyes away from Lawrence and staring into the fire. "I plan to tell him…. I'll be seventeen next year and…"

Robert paused, unable to finish his sentence.

"OK," Lawrence said. "It's cool, man. I ain't telling."

His marshmallow fell from the stick and fell flat on the ground. He picked it up and wiped it on his shorts before popping it in his mouth.

"I'm not sure what I'd say anyway. What the hell does it mean when you say that you're not geared up that way?"

Robert's toned body leaned forward toward the diminishing fire. His face was close enough to kiss the brilliant, orange flame.

"Trust me," he said. "You don't want to know. You really don't want to know."

* * *

That evening, Sherman tried to go to sleep in the Whitmans' guest bedroom, but his wife reached out her hand and gently shook his shoulder.

"Are you awake, Sherman?" she asked insistently.

"I am now," he grunted. "What's on your mind?"

"I know Teddy is your friend, just as Mamie is mine, but I worry about this family, Sherman. Something's just not right," she whispered.

"Well, given this evening's exchange perhaps Teddy's not such a great friend after all…. But what's your concern?"

"I worry about Teddy's relationship with his sons and the way that poor Mamie seems to be caught in the middle. It's obvious that Robert is Teddy's favorite and that he treats Lawrence with contempt."

Sherman watched as Shirley raised herself into a sitting position and looked apprehensively toward the bedroom door, as though frightened by what she might find if she opened it.

She continued, "I don't know why he does that but that can't be a good thing for Lawrence to bear, and it can't do much for his relationship with his brother. I wouldn't be surprised if Lawrence and Robert didn't seriously hurt each other. I have a nasty feeling that's going to happen before they're much older."

"You may be right, honey," he said after a few moments.

He yawned deeply, the fresh ocean breeze calling him to sleep. "I tried to call Teddy out just today on the way he treats that boy. But that's the Whitman family's business, not ours. I'm not sure that there's anything we can or should do.

"I suggest we leave it alone," he added firmly.

"But I will say this," he said, voice simmering with emotion. "Where there's smoke there's fire."

Shirley tittered. "I thought you were above clichés," she said, waiting for his reply.

But in response all she got was the sound of her husband's loud snores.

15

Every April, Robert and Lemuel, representing their respective schools, competed in the celebrated Penn Relays at Franklin Field. Fortunately for the runners, the day of the relays turned out to be dry and sunny, in contrast to the day before which had been a classic Philadelphia maelstrom of wind and relentless, torrential rain.

Robert had become something of a minor celebrity in their private Quaker school, having carried his team to victory the previous year. Lem also excelled in track, and his school—West Philadelphia High—was also hoping for victory. Lawrence had a feeling that Lem's predominantly Black school would put his and Robert's school to shame this year, but his hopes were still pinned on his brother's team.

Lemuel had become a Saturday evening fixture at the Whitman house these days. Lawrence wasn't sure if it was the traditional hot dogs and beans that enticed him to join the family around their dining room table, or whether it was his evident adoration of Robert. Either way it didn't matter. Lemuel, with his intelligent high forehead and mannerly ways, brought welcomed laughter to the table, and that was something Lawrence could use these days. It took his father's focus away from him for a blessed while.

Lemuel was born and lived in West Philly. With its wide streets and narrow homes piled close to each other, his father had told him and Robert that it was a place that would either make you or break you. It was, Theodore admitted, a place where he himself might have lived if he had not managed to gain an education and escape his roots. Lemuel's home, Lawrence knew, was on Master Street. There was a crab and shrimp po boy shop on one end of the street and a Chinese convenience store on the other.

Robert had invited Lawrence to join him and Lemuel after the meet for a post-competition picnic at Cobb's Creek Park, and since Lemuel and Robert had carpooled together in a mutual friend's car to the relays, Lawrence drove himself, having just gotten his license. He parked as close as he could to the pedestrian bridge at Cobb's Creek—the spot indicated by Robert where they had planned to hang out—and then leisurely made his way to the bridge. As he approached it, he admired the way in which it arched over the creek. Like the neck of a woman, he thought. Long and elegant…like Claire's neck, he decided, remembering her reluctance to swim at the pond.

He recalled Robert's directions.

"When you walk over the pedestrian bridge, turn left by the picnic tables that'll be about ten yards from where you're standing. You'll know you're heading the right way if you pass the swing set on your left. When you near the riverbed, you'll see an oak tree leaning over the creek. That's where we'll be, at the nearby picnic table."

Usually, the park was crowded on Penn Relay Day with sightseers and scores of athletes from around the city with their friends and families shooting the breeze on their staked-out patches of grass under a hazy sun. It was also a place where couples met up, streaks of grass stains smearing bare limbs and faces, and where bottles of beer, wine, and liquor appeared out of nowhere, tipping over on the picnic blankets. There was also the ubiquitous earthy smell of premium pot flaunting itself everywhere you walked. But the crowds thinned out as Lawrence followed the trail to where Robert said they would be. A soft breeze jingled the chains on a holstered child swing and the noise distracted him for a second. When he turned to walk on, he saw his brother and Lemuel in an embrace.

They sat side by side on the riverbank, which overlooked the creek several feet below, and were in front of the long wooden picnic table that Robert had given him as the meeting point. As he approached, he picked up a stone and threw it in their direction to announce his arrival, but it didn't distract them. Robert's finely shaped head, like the bust of a Grecian statue, was leaning heavily on Lemuel's shoulder.

"Hey!" Lawrence said, several feet away, reluctant to embarrass them.

Robert and Lemuel immediately drew back from one another. Lawrence smiled awkwardly as he approached. He could see that Robert had a long stick in one hand and a small pocketknife in the other.

"Whittling again?" Lawrence asked, remembering the two of them at his house.

Robert turned. "So what?" he asked defensively.

Lawrence noticed that his brother's face flushed deeply, but beyond that Lawrence saw not a trace of rancor. He then watched as his long-legged brother walked over to the picnic table, opened up a lunch pail and plucked out wrinkled paper napkins, three salami sandwiches, a bag of Fritos, and three cans of Mountain Dew.

"There you go," he said. "Instant picnic."

Lawrence noticed that Lemuel had not lifted his eyes from peeling the bark off a long branch with his Army Navy pocket knife. He noticed how the blade flashed silver under the bright sun, which was now beating down on them.

"Start eating now, if you like," Robert said. "We'll be over in a minute." He turned and sauntered back to Lemuel and, as he sat down this time, Lawrence noticed that he'd put more space between them.

Lawrence sat down at the picnic table and took a bite out of the sandwich, allowing his eyes to lazily trace the branches of the old oak tree that partially shaded his brother from his view. He was just about to take a second bite when something rustled by the knot of green trees, which was just north of the picnic table. Suddenly, two young men appeared out of the blue. Lawrence immediately knew who they were.

One was Carlton Lavington, Jemma Lavington's son. The other was called Myron. He didn't know his surname, but he attended the same church as Robert and Lawrence and, like Lemuel, he went to West Philly High. He was short and compactly built, like a bulldozer. Limp, silky hair framed his square pit bull face. Both boys trained their hardboiled eyes on Lawrence.

"See that brother of yours over there?" Carlton demanded, pointing toward Robert. "Such a big guy on campus. A track star, Momma says."

Robert and Lemuel swung their heads around in surprise.

"Word on the street…" Carlton began.

"That your brother is a…" Myron continued.

"Don't say another word!" Lawrence heard himself shout, but Carlton ignored him and began to advance toward Robert.

"Don't you know about these two?" Carlton yelled, looking back at Lawrence.

He was now within a few yards of where his brother and Lemuel sat.

"What do you think, Myron?" he asked, as Myron appeared alongside him.

Carlton spat on the ground and now directed his conversation toward Robert, who had just now stood up to face him.

"We saw what was going on before your brother got here," he said, staring into Robert's terrified eyes. "We saw you kiss that faggot."

Lemuel stood up and started to join Robert, but he told him to sit down. "I can handle this," he said.

"That's not what you saw," Robert said to Carlton, his voice cool and calm.

"Shit," Carlton said, spitting on the ground again. "I know what I saw—two faggots kissing."

Lawrence's stomach began to churn with the recognition that the situation was quickly getting out of control. He looked around for help. The only movement was the sight of a little girl on the swing, soaring higher and higher with each push from her mother.

"I'll ask you one more time, white boy," Carlton yelled to Lawrence. "Did you know about your brother and lover boy?"

"I ain't white," Lawrence replied coolly. "I'm just as Black as you are, dude."

"Well, you may not look white, but you act it," Carlton shot back. "You must be some kind of Oreo."

Before Lawrence could speak, Lemuel stepped forward in front of Carlton.

"Just leave us alone," he said. "We don't want any trouble. But we can give you some if that's what you want."

"No, Lem!" Lawrence shouted. "Just leave it. These thugs aren't worth it."

Just then, Carlton moved in like a snake on Lemuel, grabbed him and threw him to the ground. He had him in a choke hold and Robert stood over them, trying to pull him away from Lemuel.

"The more you do that, the more lover boy is going to be short of air to breathe," Carlton said as he squeezed his fingers more tightly around Lemuel's neck.

Lemuel started to cough.

"Help!" Robert cried, but his voice was eclipsed by the sound of thunder. "Stop! Oh my God! Please don't kill him!"

As rain began to fall and wind pummeled the trees, Lawrence walked toward the base of the oak and picked up a large, heavy stick. He came back and threatened Carlton with it.

"Move back! Don't get any nearer," Myron commanded, spewing out his words like shattered glass. "If you do, you're dead meat."

Robert came to Lawrence's side and then charged at Myron as Lawrence clubbed Carlton with the stick. He fell back, leaving Lemuel gasping for air. The next few minutes became a blur. Myron was nowhere to be seen. He had disappeared into the watery green landscape like a forest dryad. In the time that it took Lawrence to realize what he'd done, Carlton had recovered from the blow and was now dragging Lemuel to the creek's edge. Robert fell on top of him, but Carlton, flushed with adrenaline, kicked him off.

"Stay back," Carlton barked, his eyes corroded slits. "This little faggot is going to be given a chance to prove how brave he is. How long do you think he'll be able to hold his breath?"

As Robert tried to make Carlton release his iron grip on Lemuel, Lawrence spotted Lemuel's pen knife on the ground. He quickly retrieved it and, maneuvering behind his brother, shoved it into Carlton's thigh without hesitation.

Carlton squealed, instantaneously releasing his grip on Lemuel, who was able to squirm away from over the edge of the creek and tumble onto the soaked ground.

"We'd better get help!" Lawrence said.

The rain was pouring down fast and hard as bullets.

Lemuel, shaken badly but now sitting up, cupped either side of his neck in his hands, trying to recover from the attempted strangulation. They stared down at Carlton, each trying to summon up a little remorse, but it was hard to come by. Robert went over to Lemuel and gently helped him to his feet. He sat him down at the picnic table, said a few words to him, and then walked back to Lawrence.

Carlton was squirming and holding his leg. Blood oozed from his wound, the color of crushed beets. They looked at him suffering for a few seconds, and then Robert broke the spell. He ripped off part of his shirt to fashion a tourniquet and stem the flow.

* * *

By evening the rain had abated, and the brothers had managed to put the events of the day behind them. They had showered, changed into clean clothes, and now sat at the dinner table, waiting for Mamie to serve them. As if to punctuate the end of the heavy April thunderstorms, the dining room was suffused in an intense orange glow as the sun began to set.

"It was a superficial wound," Theodore said perfunctorily, as they sat around the dining room table.

Lawrence picked at his corn beef and cabbage, which was Robert's favorite, not his. He had just excitedly recounted a blow-by-blow account of what had transpired at Cobb's Creek Park earlier that day and had been careful to omit any hint of the relationship that existed between Robert and Lemuel. He glanced over at Robert, who smiled back appreciatively.

"I phoned the hospital and they told me that Carlton will be fine," Theodore said sternly. "And thank God for that."

He paused and glared at Lawrence.

"But don't you ever try that again," he said. "You're not Rocky, boy, don't forget that."

He shrugged and looked over at Mamie.

"They were thugs, Dad," Robert said, reaching for his ice water.

Theodore ignored him, choosing instead to focus on his youngest son.

"I said don't try that again because, believe me, next time you may not be so lucky!"

"Yes, suh!" Lawrence said, even before Whitman had a chance to finish his sentence.

"Are you trying to sass me?" Theodore shot back angrily. "Because if you are…"

The smell of cruelty, like charred meat, was in the air and Mamie sought to dispel it.

"Leave him alone please, Teddy," she pleaded. "He saved Lemuel's life and probably Robert's, too!"

Apart from a few short shreds of desultory conversation, the rest of the meal passed in sullen silence. After desert, Lawrence and Robert both announced that they were tired and going to bed. As they climbed the stairs, Lawrence looked at his brother.

"This is your fault, you know," he said. "I got in trouble, yet again, for your lie."

"And what lie is that?"

"You're not who they think you are," Lawrence said.

"And what excuse do you have?"

"What do you mean?"

"You're not who you think you are either. You're not Dad's son. I heard them arguing about it."

"Go to hell! You're lying. I don't believe you," Lawrence said as he ran to his room and slammed the door

"Goodnight boys!" he heard his father say a few minutes later, his thick-as-steak voice echoing down the hallway.

Screw you, Robert, he thought as he turned over, hugging his pillow to him.

16

Grievances are like dried flowers in that, if looked after and nurtured, they can last forever. Carlton Lavington knew that he was that type of person whose mind nursed past grievances long after their shelf life has expired.

Almost preternaturally self-reflective, he ruminated on that fact as he, along with his family, watched at a distance the seared pain etched on the faces of the Whitman family as they stood rigidly in a half moon around the fresh flower strewn casket. As it was slowly lowered into the cold ground, he thrust his hands deeply into the pockets of his black formal slacks and bowed his head.

* * *

Two weeks before the funeral, Carlton had been watching *M*A*S*H* with his parents in the den of their home. On the wall was a photograph of his second-grade class in the Quaker school that he attended. As an only child, every significant event in his life was etched into his mother's heart and she lined the walls of their home with photographs that commemorated those occasions. Many of them, Carlton would have preferred to forget.

In the photograph, Carlton was standing next to Robert Whitman, who attended the same school. The shorter pupils sat in the front row, while the remaining boys and girls were arranged by height in successive rows. But on that particular day it must have been like herding cats for the photographer to get the children in order, because Carlton ended up standing glumly in the middle of the third row from the front with the tallest children in the class. To make matters worse, he was next to a smiling Robert Whitman, the tallest boy in class.

When the show was over and they had all stood up to go to bed, Joshua Lavington stopped at the wall to look at the picture.

"Now why they'd have to do that is beyond me," he said, frowning.

"What?" Carlton asked.

"Well, you would have thought that the photographer would have more tact," he said, "putting Robert Whitman, tall as that boy is, right next to you."

Carlton had little interest in his school pictures, so had no idea what his father was talking about. He walked over to the photograph to peer at it. It did not bring back happy memories. He'd been bullied at his previous school and had transferred to Robert and Lawrence's school in the hope that it would stop. It did not. The intimidation continued at his new school, mostly perpetrated by kids in his class who mocked his short stature.

He stared intently at the picture and noticed that he was wearing a light blue short-sleeved shirt. Just the sight of him wearing that shirt brought back painful memories; he had been wearing the same shirt the following week when one of the white kids tripped him as he was walking down the hallway. He'd landed with a thud, but no one—including Robert—had stopped to help.

Carlton looked from the photograph to his father, wondering why he could not have been more sensitive. Pointing out the difference between him and Robert had only made things worse.

He was still seething at the comparison the day after, when his mother summoned him to the phone.

"Hey, man," an angry, almost desperate voice said.

"Who's this?"

"Lawrence."

"Lawrence Whitman?"

"Yeah."

"What d'ya want?"

There wasn't any bad blood between him and Lawrence right now, but the last thing Carlton needed was to revisit the fight he'd provoked at the park that had landed him in the hospital. Since then, he'd started doing weight training at the local Y. He was determined never to allow his height to dictate his future again. Next time he was in a fight, he was going to win.

"I just thought you'd like to know," Lawrence said.

"Know what?"

There was a long, uncomfortable pause before Lawrence replied and, like a squirrel harvesting nuts, Carlton's sharp mind stored that fact away in case it proved useful later. Lawrence's hesitancy piqued his interest. There was something going on here that Carlton intuitively knew would require him to make a decision one way or another.

"I'm sorry about knifing you in the leg the other day," Lawrence said, tentatively changing course. "I overreacted and I apologize for putting you in the hospital. I wouldn't blame you if you felt compelled to get back at me for that."

"Don't sweat it," Carlton replied. "It hurt like hell for a while, but it's all good now. In any case, I've no beef with you. You were only defending that no good brother of yours and his faggot friend."

"So, would you like to get back at...at..."

Carlton pressed his phone to his ear. Lawrence seemed unable to spit the word out, so he waited until his patience ran out.

"Would I like to get back at your brother? Is that what you're trying to say?" he asked, switching the phone to his other ear.

As he waited for Lawrence's reply, he carried the phone with him to the window, allowing the long white cord to stretch across his room. He'd heard a noise outside in the front yard and wondered what it was. Pushing the curtains aside he looked down to see his father, dressed in his robe and slippers, pulling in the trash can.

"I'm not going to go so far as to say that," Lawrence said.

"Then what are you saying?" Carlton said, exhaustedly.

"Next Friday evening, around 8:00 p.m., Robert will be at the Church Road entrance of the park." After a moment's pause, he added, "To jog."

The phone clicked and Carlton was left holding it, perplexity etched on his forehead. What was he supposed to do with that information? Lie in wait for Robert and attack him? He didn't think so. After all, he'd been there and done that and had nearly killed him and Lemuel in the process. He really didn't have the stomach for more. Lawrence could damn well fight his own battles with his brother, not expect him to do it for him.

* * *

And it would have been left there, but for a chance encounter.

Two days after the phone call from Lawrence, Carlton was fulfilling one of the items on his to do list—buying some weed. At sunset, he parked his Nova at Ranstead and walked over to Market and 15th Street. Then he stood at the corner of the street and waited, looking up at a rare blood orange sunset that flooded the cold city corner with color and warmth.

Lost in thought, he was startled when his tried-and-true dealer of nearly three years appeared suddenly in front of him. Carlton looked to his right and left, wondering how he could have snuck up on him unseen.

The dealer was tall and skinny, with a broad forehead that seemed to dominate his round face. His gentle bearing gave him the appearance of someone who had courted patience throughout his life, either a result of tough times or by choice. That evening he was wearing a conservative white oxford shirt, smart blue jeans, and plain, understated canvas shoes. He dressed well for a dealer, which is one of the reasons why he was Carlton's dealer of choice. His neat appearance made him inconspicuous and lessened the chance of either of them being arrested by any cops who happened to be staked out nearby.

At the very moment that the fast-as-lightning exchange took place—Carlton pressing a crisp ten-dollar bill into one of the dealer's hands while accepting a small brown envelope stuffed with pot in the other—he heard his name being called.

Turning in the direction of the voice, Carlton saw a silver Audi slow down and stop at the light. He recognized the face behind the wheel.

"Hey, Short Stuff! I see you still haven't grown much since I last saw you," Robert called out to him.

"Short Stuff" was the hated nickname of Carlton's childhood and it brought back bitter memories. For a moment, he froze; then, sharply mindful of the drug exchange, he quickly thrust the bag of dope into his pocket. He then turned around to give Robert a piece of his mind, but when he turned his head in the direction of the stop light, Robert and the Audi were gone.

* * *

At 8:00 p.m. on Friday evening, Carlton stood quietly at the entrance to the jogging path at the Church Street entrance to Valley Green Park. He held a large, carefully selected stick in his hand. The park was deserted and all he could hear was the sound of his own heavy breathing.

He waited for what seemed an eternity, but was in reality ten minutes, wondering if the information that Lawrence had given him was accurate. But then, a few minutes later, he saw a figure running along the hilly jogging path. As the figure drew closer, he could see that it was Robert. So, he made his move in the dark toward the shadowy figure.

Robert stopped at the steep wooden stairs that connected the dirt jogging path to the shrubbery gated entrance to the park. He was considering whether to call it a day and head on home when he suddenly saw Carlton standing in front of him with a heavy stick raised in his hands.

"Carlton, what the hell are you…" he began to say, before instinctively taking a step backward and falling down the stairs.

He landed prostrate and unmoving at the base of the stairs. Carlton gingerly walked down and looked at Robert. He lay there, his head at an awkward angle.

"Robert," Carlton hissed, careful not to attract attention in the unlikely chance that someone was around. "Robert, are you OK? Get up, man."

There was no answer. Frightened, he panicked and ran.

* * *

The next morning, Carlton awoke to the memory of a dream that he had been arrested, screaming his innocence, in Valley Green Park. Relieved that he was not in a cell and in handcuffs, he got up and, wearing only his pajama bottoms, strolled to the bathroom that adjoined his room.

He thought of life's little incongruities. If Robert hadn't happened to drive by Market and 15th Street, none of what took place last night would have happened. And if he hadn't called him Short Stuff, he'd still be alive. He splashed cold water onto his face and peered, menacingly, at himself in the mirror. He interrogated himself silently, but there was no response, not even a glimmer of admission of guilt.

17

It had taken Chief "Stud" Polanski of the Philadelphia Police Department two and a half nervous hours to make the decision to drive out to upscale Chestnut Hill to deliver the devastating news to Judge Whitman and his wife himself, rather than dispatch one of his lower ranked detectives. It was the least that he could to for a judge who was well respected among the white people, even if he was a Negro. Polanski liked him because he didn't make him feel uncomfortable, unlike the Black preachers with whom he often came into contact.

What he would never understand to his dying day was the way in which the news he had to deliver was received. He had primed himself for the kind of overly wrought emotion he knew could be expected from a Negro family when there had been a loss of this kind. He religiously watched the sitcoms *Good Times* and *The Jeffersons*, and even though they were only TV shows, he felt certain that there had to be certain elements of truth in them. And one of those truths was the fact that crushing news of the kind he was about to deliver would trigger an onslaught of emotions that he could only described as primitive. That's what he anticipated, but his belief proved to be unfounded.

When he rang the bell, Mamie appeared at the door fully made up and dressed in a tailored pant suit, a stylish auburn shade. As she opened the door, the chief noticed the distracted, harried look in her eyes. She was obviously irritated that someone was preventing her from getting to wherever she needed to be—a meeting of some kind, it looked like.

He was momentarily taken aback that his presence at her door, in full uniform and with cap in hand, didn't ring alarm bells for her. And then he realized, as she stared back at him with a forced smile, that she had misinterpreted the reason for his visit.

"You want to see Theodore, I take it. I'll go get him," she said, her long hair swishing vigorously to the right as she turned.

"Wait," he said firmly, but anxious to be on time for her bridge game, she didn't hear him.

However, when she came back with Judge Whitman, he could see that his presence had begun to concern both her and the judge.

"What's this about, Chief Polanski?" Theodore asked. "To what do we owe the pleasure of your visit?"

"I only wish it was a pleasure, Judge and Mrs. Whitman," the Chief began, "but I'm afraid I bring bad news about your son Robert."

"Bad news? What kind of bad news could that be? He's upstairs in his bedroom fast asleep."

Theodore went to the bottom of the stairs and yelled, "Robert!"

There was no answer, so he shouted his name again as Lawrence appeared sleepily on the landing.

"Did Robert come home last night?" he shouted to Lawrence, who was now seated cross legged and barefoot in his pajamas on the landing. "I said, did Robert come home last night?" he asked again when there was no answer.

"How should I *know*?" Lawrence shouted back as a sense of foreboding began to overcome him. "He's not in his bedroom and I've no idea where he is."

Chief Polanski had patiently waited during this exchange, but now attempted to step in and take control of the situation.

"I'm so sorry for your loss," he began.

"What? What did you say?" Theodore demanded, returning from the bottom of the stairs to confront the chief. "Whose loss? Are you sure you've got your facts straight, man?"

"Yes, Judge and Mrs. Whitman, I'm afraid that we do have our facts straight. We'll need you to identify the body, of course, but I'm so sorry to inform you that your son Robert has been found dead."

The Chief paused, waiting for the dreadful news to sink in. He'd had to deliver the same bad news to other families many times during his career, and it was never easy. He'd found over the years that in these tense situations it was better to talk straight, be firm, and show empathy. The difficult thing to do was to get the balance straight, because if you didn't, you made a bad situation even worse.

"What happened?" Theodore asked the officer, bewildered as he cradled a weeping Mamie in his arms and caressed her hair.

"We got a call at 6:00 a.m. from a jogger who was in Valley Green Park, Judge. We found Robert dead at the foot of the stairs that lead from the jogging path to the Church Street entrance to the park. He was in his jogging gear, and it appears that he must have tripped and fallen down the stairs. As far as we can tell at this stage, there are no signs of foul play. It appears to be a tragic accident."

"What time did it happen?" Theodore asked with little show of emotion.

The Chief watched as Judge Whitman's hand stroked his wife's back over and over again as she whimpered, nestled in his arms.

"I can't say precisely, sir, until I receive the report. But the indications are it was around eight or nine o'clock yesterday evening."

"Thank you, Chief Polanski. I appreciate you coming to tell us yourself," Theodore said firmly and in control of his emotions. Almost too much in control, Polanski thought. "But before you go I want you to assure me about one thing. Despite Robert's death seeming at face value to be an accident, you will nevertheless conduct a full and thorough investigation. I expect nothing less from you."

"Of course, Judge Whitman," Polanski replied. "I'll be in touch with any further developments."

* * *

That night when Chief Polanski returned to his neat three-story row home on East Passyunk Avenue, a street that contained people who were just like him—white, hardworking folks who kept their nose clean and their opinions to themselves—he did something that he rarely did, which was to talk to his wife Mary about his day.

"This Judge Whitman…" he said, as he sat down for supper at their kitchen table.

"You mean the Negro judge?" Mary asked, his back to her as she brought over a platter containing a beef roast surrounded by roasted potatoes.

"Yeah, that's the one," he said. "Their son died in Valley Green Park last night. He was jogging and fell down some stairs. He broke his neck."

"My, that's so sad for the family," she said, as she sat down and folded her hands together to say grace.

Mary glanced at the empty chair beside them. Since their seventeen-year-old son Peter had died of an overdose five years before, she always kept a table setting for him. It wasn't as if she expected him to miraculously appear for supper, she reassured her husband when she began doing so. It was just that she wanted to make sure that they thought of Peter at least once every day.

"Was it an accident?" she asked, her eyes cast down.

"Uh-huh," he said. "That's the way it looks. But we'll need to do a thorough investigation. Otherwise, the judge will have my hide for a doormat."

They ate in silence for a while.

"Nice house they have there, up on Chestnut Hill," he said, taking a sip of sweet iced tea.

Mary had no comment to that, so he watched as she slowly chewed her food, neither happy nor unhappy but somewhere in between. She'd been like that since Peter had died and he'd become accustomed to it.

"Well, two things I noticed," he said, feeling as though he were talking to himself. "First is that the Judge and his wife must have nerves of steel. I've never seen a couple take the loss of a son so resolutely. I guess it comes from being a judge, but Judge Whitman can sure keep his emotions in check."

He stopped to compliment his wife on the dinner and put a forkful of beef into his mouth.

"What was the other thing?" she asked.

"It was their other son. I only caught a glimpse of him, and he looks nothing like his father."

* * *

Theodore smiled ruefully. It was just his luck, a few days after his son's death, to read about the accident in the Bulletin under the fold. The headline read, *Judge's Son Dies from Fall in Valley Green Park.*

Time, he thought regrettably as he sat in the back of the polished black limousine, was not on his side and never would be. He had always prided himself on his ability to invest his daily God-given waking hours wisely, with every precious minute accounted for like a child saving pennies in a piggy bank. Time invested with purpose and with an eye to the future. But this day—the day before Good Friday—presaged a future he had never envisioned.

He took in the smell of new leather and death and felt nauseous. Like a hapless sock puppet, he let Mamie squeeze his hand tightly. The slow, mournful drive to the church was almost unbearable to him, a primitive form of torture. He could not erase from his mind that the car he was seated in with Mamie on the way to Oak Street Baptist was following another car and that car was the one that cradled his precious son, Robert.

140

Eyes swathed in a fresh layer of tears, Theodore turned toward the window. Yesterday, the temperature had dipped considerably for May, and it had been in the low sixties. But today was near eighty and all he could think was that Robert would have loved this—would have been out in it, milking every sunny second of the day for what it was worth.

He looked out the window and up at a palette of pure, blue, cloudless sky. Turning his head to stare straight ahead, he felt himself shiver. Then Mamie planted a soft, dry kiss on his cheek.

"We will get through this," she said, pulling a wad of Kleenex out of her purse.

She handed one to Theodore, who had begun to cry the soft, muffled, plaintive cry of a small child.

"Blessed are those who mourn," Mamie said. "For they will be comforted."

Theodore drew in his breath sharply.

"I can't take it," he said, nonchalantly but chillingly cold, in the way desperate people do.

The black car pulled up at the Whitmans' church as slowly as an ocean liner pulling up at the dock. Lawrence was in the front passenger seat and opened his door as two male ushers in black suits and white gloves went to open the rear doors for Theodore and Mamie. Theodore quietly thanked them as he was helped from the car.

As an usher went around the car to help Mamie out—who for a moment sat rigidly in the back clinging to a wad of Kleenex in her hand—Theodore's eyes were drawn to the face of a white police officer sitting on a motorcycle with red taillights flashing in the morning sun. He had been at the head of funeral procession escort down Germantown Avenue to the church. His young face looked somber.

"I am deeply sorry for your loss," he told Theodore.

The judge nodded gravely in reply and reached out for Mamie's hand.

As the family walked in together, Whitman looked from side to side, not knowing how else to behave on the day that you have been

141

asked to bury your eldest son. For a moment, his eyes locked onto the sight of Mamie's great aunt decked out in a topaz blue dress suit, who he was mildly surprised to see was still roaming the earth. Then, just by happenstance, his eyes rested on an individual who was seated in a pew on the right side of the church, seven rows from the back. It was Jackie, his former assistant who he had been forced to let go after Mamie had accused him of having an affair with her. She looked good, he thought, as he glanced quickly at her and hoped that Mamie didn't notice she was there.

It was not until the family was sandwiched tightly in the reserved front row of the church and he was forced to look at the casket that it finally became real to Theodore that his beloved son Robert had died. A cruel tidal wave of grief overcame him. He looked over at Mamie, who had begun sobbing volubly into her Kleenex. An usher all dressed in black—from the little cap on her head to her opaque stockings and serviceable shoes—suddenly appeared next to Theodore. She knelt in the aisle and reached across Theodore to hand Mamie a fresh wad of tissues.

It was then that he began to flounder. While praying with him the previous night, the minister had advised him that, should this happen, he should focus on one spot in front of him. He did this now by focusing on a single petal of one of the white flowers among the dozens draped on the casket. He squirmed in his seat and struggled to keep the composure that the minister told him he must do, since so many would be counting on him to show strength. The thought of Robert's smile came to him, and he began to feel faint.

In these situations, every need of every grieving family member is attended to, from an endless supply of Kleenex, to smelling salts—*and just in the nick of time*, he thought—to the offer of a small silver flask containing a few sips of brandy. It was discretely pressed into his palm by Deacon Williams, the head of the ushers' board. His kind, penetrating eyes looked as though he and the Bible had not missed one day spent together.

"Thank you, sir," Theodore said humbly as he took the flask and watched as the man disappeared down the aisle.

If it had not been for this gentle man's kind gift, Whitman would have collapsed in anguish that morning, and would have done so before this blessed commune of friends and family. He held onto the flask tightly as if it were a sacred relic and found to his surprise that it gave him consolation. He considered unscrewing the cap and taking a discrete sip of the brandy, but decided he had no need to do so. Just gripping the flask gave him the strength to continue.

Theodore had always been a believer in light—or at least a dwindling fog—at the end of the tunnel. Due to the nature of his job, he'd been moved by countless poignant stories of human fallibility, and he firmly believed that the considered and thoughtful process in his court more often than not led to outcomes that shed helpful light on perpetrators and victims alike. He thought of this now, as he sat listening to one of the most noted Black tenors in the city sing "Precious Lord."

The judge knew that folks thought that a long black robe and a big chair propped a few feet higher than ordinary people was enough to insulate him from the outpourings of poor folks down on their luck. But they were wrong. Over the years, all the tears and sobs had had an effect on him. But at the end of the day, however you cut it, life is a contact sport and champions are made, not born. All you can do is get out there and give it your best.

Robert, his beloved Robert. He'd played a good game.

Theodore listened to the pastor's pitch-perfect eulogy, and then his call for family members to come to speak from the pulpit.

Mamie and Theodore had had the conversation about who would speak the night before. Theodore knew that he would be overcome by emotion, so Mamie reluctantly volunteered. But in the early hours of the morning, she changed her mind. She explained to Theodore that—like him—the emotional burden would be too great and so, against his will, Lawrence was deputized.

Theodore watched his youngest son walk slowly to the pulpit in his creased black suit and scuffed sneakers. *He could have shown some respect by wearing a decent pair of shoes,* he thought as he coughed nervously in his hand, concerned about what Lawrence might say. But it was not until his son looked out calmly at the crowd of some seventy family and friends that the judge's heart truly began to beat hard. Its beat increased when Lawrence proceeded to recite the words of Robert's favorite song, Steely Dan's "Rikki Don't Lose That Number."

Theodore sat frozen. Without moving his head an iota, he felt the rustling of bulletins and polite whispers all around the sanctuary. Somewhere, to his embarrassment, there was a muffled chuckle. He wanted to stand up, stride to the pulpit and put his hand on Lawrence's shoulder to make him stop. But then he thought better of it as Mamie gently tapped his leg. That was their code since the very first days of their courtship. Cease and desist, the code meant. The remainder of the service passed in a blessed blur.

* * *

Lawrence's eyes were on a huge, sliced country ham dotted with cloves, that Bettie had set up on the buffet table. He stood in line behind Lemuel and waited his turn.

"I'm sorry for your loss," Lemuel mumbled, his eyes red from incessant crying.

The ham wasn't the only item on the table that he craved. It was everything on the table, from the Baked Alaska that one of his mother's bridge members had brought over to the jambalaya and the baked oysters. Grief had built a scaffold that could only be dismantled by food.

He sat down next to Bettie under a shade tree at one of the little tables covered with white tablecloths that dotted their backyard. She was seated alone with a plate that contained only potato greens, the name he knew only because his mother told him that there would be one African-inspired dish and it would be from Bettie. They ate in silence.

He turned, hearing his father's voice.

"Why would you humiliate me?" Theodore sternly demanded.

"I didn't want to humiliate you," Lawrence replied. "That was his favorite song. I didn't want to humiliate *him*." For the first time since he had learned of his brother's death, tears streamed down his face.

"I wanted to honor him," he sputtered through his tears.

Mamie came over to them and looked as though she were about to say something to her husband. But instead, she pursed her mouth shut and handed Lawrence a tissue. She was searching for a way to defuse the situation when her eyes alighted on Georgia sitting on her own at the rear of their backyard where her boys used to play.

"Georgia is sitting down there…just on the other side of the hill," she said. "Why don't you go and say hello to her."

"Yes, do," Bettie added with a smile. "I'm sure she'd be glad to see you."

He'd devoured the food on his plate, but he still felt hungry and had never felt so empty before. Scowling, he left the table, turning to look at his father. But his father's mind was now elsewhere, so he walked toward the path down the hill to speak to Georgia. Then something made him stop. He heard laughter and the incongruity of it, the sheer inappropriateness of it, sickened him.

His mother's friend Jemma Lavington was hugging his mother tightly as they stood next to one of the small folding tables. Seated at the table was a little girl he didn't know who had just shoved a spoonful of Bettie's potato greens into her mouth, only to immediately spew it out. Carlton, dressed in his neatly pressed black suit, was doubled over, laughing at the child. It was the first time he had seen him since the fateful phone call and Lawrence couldn't pry his eyes away from him. He stopped laughing the minute Jemma chastised him and now his eyes were fixed on Lawrence. The eyes that drilled into him on that improbably beautiful day were of the hunter, and they left him chilled to the bone.

Lawrence began to feel faint, so he averted his eyes and turned away. The last thing he needed on this day of all days was an angry confrontation with Carlton, so he turned away and walked toward Georgia.

He found her propped against a tree, sitting on her coat that was the color of tobacco and had brown, leathery buttons. Her corduroy pants were out of place in spring. A yearning for her, for her fragile, huddled body, surged within him as he drew closer to her.

"Hi," she said. "You found me."

He looked at her face and smiled, her smooth skin made even more lustrous by the shimmer of the green leaves and bark and wide, green space. She looked at him as he stood before her, undecided as to whether to sit beside her or not.

"Where are your shoes?" he said, pointing to her bare feet.

She shrugged off the question.

What he did not know is that she had longed for his presence. And when he finally did appear, her eyes feasted on him and lapped him up as though a cat with milk. There was no end to her young desire for him, although he did not know it and she did not tell him. As he walked toward her she watched his clumsy gait, his black shiny lace up shoes navigating each of the rectangular wooden steps. She examined his head as he walked. He still held his head high, and his dusky, prominent chin jutted out like the prow of a ship. It had been that way since childhood when she used to sit in his mother's kitchen on the high stool.

Hi, Georgia…. Bye, Georgia. That had been his crisp and clipped greeting for years, with the exception of the few times they'd met for PB & Js by the tree. And on those occasions when he was rushed, she'd nonetheless humbly taken whatever bone he had on offer, usually one gleaming smile tossed in her direction as he ran, backpack and guitar case in hand to leave the house, the sound of a slammed door heard resoundingly in his wake.

"Hey! Are you OK Georgia?' he asked as he sat down. "Earth to Georgia!"

He playfully pulled on a long plait that sat flat and intricately braided on her back. She smiled at the small, gentle gesture but then thought of her mother's recent recrimination when she'd worn her heart on her sleeve and disclosed her feelings for Lawrence.

They live in a different world than we do. Best not to get designs on him," Bettie had said. *"They already have the boy pegged for another girl, the one that they hoped Robert would marry. Her name is Claire."* She'd hid her devastation from her mother by mumbling something about having to finish some work from school.

"You don't look well," he said, bringing her out of her reverie.

"Neither do you," she said, scrutinizing his face.

"Well, I'm not supposed to. It is a funeral after all."

But today was different. Today was remarkably sunny and that's all that mattered. Against her mother's advice she was wearing red corduroy pants and her favorite pink cap-sleeved knit shirt.

"I asked, where are your shoes?"

"I left them in your kitchen," she said. "By the way, I'm sorry for your loss. I know that you two didn't always get along, but you must miss him."

"Thank you," he mumbled. She watched as he started digging up a mound of moist black soil with the tips of his sneakers until both the grass where he sat and his shoes were covered in dirt.

"Look, I'll be straight with you," he said. "Since he died, Robert's face has been haunting me and its always the same. It's him in front of the fire, holding a roasted marshmallow on the end of a stick. He's angry. He's trying to tell me something, but I don't know what it is."

The sincerity of his words touched her, especially after her mother's constant deluge of reprimands.

"Now it's your turn," he said, looking up to see if, as promised by the weather forecasters, there was any sign of rain.

147

"For me, it's the little girl in the bathroom and the flushing sound. I can't get that image and that sound out of my mind."

He turned to her and lay his hands on her skinny shoulders, turning her toward him, forcing her to look in his eyes. She could see that they were glistening and wet. It made him forget about the sorrow of his brother's fate and he dug into the moment for all that it was worth, dying to break the grip that his brother's death had had on him.

He breathed in the sweet, clean cottony smell of her clothes. He held her chin in his hands and brought her face to his face and touched his lips lightly to hers, surprised that she permitted him to do so. Encouraged, he felt that gave him license to kiss her harder, forcing her lips open and thrusting his tongue in her mouth. He reached under her shirt to grope her small breasts.

Suddenly, he felt her very cold hand fitted snuggly like a glove over his.

"No," she said.

"You like it, too," he said, staring pleadingly into her brown eyes.

"Even if I did, today is Robert's funeral. What we would be doing is probably a sin of some kind," she replied as she moved away from him.

Lawrence smiled and then looked longingly into her eyes.

"Birth is a sin," he said and as he spoke, she was taken aback by the hard edge in his voice. "It's life threatening."

She leaned backward, her head resting gently against the tree.

"Robert, my brother, was my hero. Did you know that?"

"I didn't know that, Lawrence," she said as she reached for his hand. "Momma said you got a girl."

"That's not true."

"No, that's true. Momma heard that she's a rich Black girl."

"Well, I'm afraid your mother heard wrong."

"Are you calling my mother a liar?" Georgia asked, playfully laughing.

Suddenly, they could hear their names being called.

"Georgia! Lawrence! Come back here now. Bettie wants to go home."

By now, one of Georgia's legs, the color of toasted walnut, had inched its way back beside Lawrence's. They ignored the calls for them to return for a few minutes, but then acknowledged that it was time for Georgia to go back. She stood up and Lawrence brushed the grass from her pants.

They walked back to the house holding hands, but Lawrence dropped her hand the minute he saw Bettie scowling at them from the back door.

"Where were you both?" Bettie called to them, her eyes drilling into Georgia's. "And where are your shoes, girl?"

Suddenly, Georgia felt badly. Her mother was still wearing her white apron over her dress. Even on a day like this, Robert's funeral, her mother was compelled to work. Georgia rushed in front of Lawrence to retrieve her scuffed brown loafers from where she had left them in the kitchen. She'd felt embarrassed to wear them, big as boats and cheap as a water ice, but she had few others and none that remotely matched her outfit. As she ran, little twigs and stones on the ground dug into her bare soles. Then, turning to look behind her, she saw Lawrence trailing leisurely behind.

What would her beloved author Toni Morrison think, she asked herself. She felt confident that she would stand by Georgia's belief that dreams were not only for good little white girls. She'd stand with her on that fundamental truth, and she'd support her determination to brush aside any obstacles in her way. Of that, she was sure.

18

Eskimo Bars had always been Robert's favorite treat, Lawrence recalled as he stood numbly by the refrigerator while his mother arranged flowers on the kitchen table.

He reached into the freezer and, sure enough, there was a pack of them in there. Even though Robert had died in the accident nearly two years ago, his mother still obstinately continued to buy packs of Robert's favorite ice cream bars as though he was still around to eat them.

"Lawrence," his mother said, interrupting his thoughts, "I'd like you to please go and get me a shoofly pie from the Amish people down at Farmer's Market in Reading Terminal. And while you're there, you could buy me some scrapple, too."

"What? Are you serious?"

Lawrence knew that his father's birthday was the next day, but that was no excuse for his mother to make him take all that time out of his day just to buy a pie.

"Now, come on now, Lawrence. You know it's your father's favorite pie."

"Yeah, how could I forget that," he said. "And it was Robert's favorite pie, too."

150

"Lawrence, how many times do I have to tell you?" she said with evident exhaustion in her voice. "Grudges are for children. It's time you grew up and let them go."

"But my car, or should I say Dad's car, is in the shop. I don't have any wheels today."

Lawrence was allowed to use his father's old navy BMW and thought that it was about time for his father to gift him his own car. But despite his repeated requests, his father had not been inclined to do so.

"That's no problem," his mother said firmly. "It's a nice day and the walk to St. Martins train station will do you good."

* * *

Lawrence walked out of Reading Terminal Station, carrying a pound of scrapple wrapped in cellophane under one arm and the shoofly pie contained in a cardboard box under the other. In his back pocket he had two dime bags of pot. He figured that if he dropped either the scrapple or the pie, at least he'd have the pot to smoke to tamp down the bad vibes that were sure to come from his parents.

He started to cross the street at Broad and Market to take the subway for the quick ride from Reading to 30th Street Station for the commute home to Chestnut Hill. As he stepped off from the curb he saw a familiar figure waving to him. Lemuel had spotted him, and he found that unsettling. He had no wish to talk to Robert's former lover.

"Hey, Lawrence, got a minute?" Lem called across the street.

Lawrence gestured toward the subway, but felt compelled to walk toward him, nonetheless.

"You're the last person I thought I'd see taking the subway," Lem said.

"I'm taking the subway to 30th Street Station."

"Where's your wheels?" He saw Lawrence's frown as he came nearer, and added, "Hey man! I was just kidding!"

Lem looked tired and anxious, but Lawrence wasn't sure what was the cause. *Drugs, possibly*, he thought, although as far as he knew Lem wasn't a user. So perhaps it was just the shock of seeing his dead lover's brother.

"Yeah, well my car's in the shop," Lawrence said in response to Lem's question.

He felt ashamed for telling a lie. It was his father's car, not his. It wasn't a huge lie, he said to himself, only a little white lie. So why was his heart racing?

Each young man stood facing the other while the aroma of fry bread and stench of exhaust fumes surrounded them. For a minute, Lawrence was caught up in a time warp that revolved around Robert. As he looked at Lem, his thoughts went back to the evening that his brother died, and he felt an immediate and vicarious need to leave and get away.

"I lived for Robert," Lemuel finally said, breaking the silence and allowing the muggy August air to whisk the words from his mouth. It made little difference whether or not Lawrence heard or understood. None of it mattered because Robert was gone.

Standing beside them was a Black boy around the age of thirteen who was wearing a black t-shirt and a red and white Phillies baseball cap backward on his head. He was talking insistently and incoherently, and for a minute Lawrence wondered if the kid was under the influence of something. Pot couldn't do that, he thought, but speed might. And he obviously couldn't afford coke. The sweltering, humid air clung to Lawrence. The kid was singing now, and all he wanted was for him to stop.

Lawrence's arms began to ache from the awkward way he was carrying the pie and the scrapple. He could see that Lemuel had not recovered from Robert's passing. Not nearly…you could tell from his eyes.

"You OK?" Lemuel asked, blinking.

"Yeah," Lawrence said, pointing with his thumb toward the kid. "I just wish that he'd shut up."

"Hey, can I help you carry one of those?" Lem asked, gesturing toward the packages that Lawrence was carrying.

"Nah, Lem," Lawrence said. "I'm fine."

They looked east on Market Street, both desperate for the bus to arrive. As one came toward them, Lawrence was relieved to see that it was Lemuel's bus, the one that would take him into the hollow of the city where he lived. As it pulled up, Lemuel looked straight into Lawrence's eyes and rubbed his chin.

"Look man, I was in love with your brother. Dig?"

He waited, but Lawrence had no reaction for him.

"If you don't want to talk about that night, that's perfectly cool with me."

Lem turned to look at the boy who had been standing beside them. He'd stopped his continual talking and was about to board the Septa bus.

"Look Lawrence," he said, as he was about to board the bus himself, "I know I owe you one for saving my life that time at the park. I'll never forget it."

As he was speaking, Lawrence saw something in Lemuel's eyes that frightened him. It was a look, under those heavy lids, that screamed regret and unfathomably deep pain. It chilled him to the core.

"But I know that it's harder for you than it ever will be for me," Lem called out to him as he got on the bus. "Much harder."

"Wait a minute, Lem! What did you mean by that? What are you talking about?"

Lem paused, turning swirling his head back toward Lawrence.

"That night," he said crisply. "I'm talking about *that* night. The night he died."

Lawrence watched as Lem turned his neck stiffly and walked glumly to the bus and mounted the steps without turning. Lawrence watched in silence as the bus pulled away and lumbered down Market Street.

19

It had been six years since Robert's death, and it had taken some time for Lawrence to become adjusted to the fact that he had become the basket into which his father was now determinedly placing all of his eggs. Shouldering that responsibility was both an honor and a profound burden.

As he stirred from sleep, he could feel the warm sunlight stream through the oblong windows that overlooked the backyard and onto his bare shoulders. It was dawn and the sky was carrot colored at the horizon. He reached, aimlessly, for his nightstand and the ashtray that was on it. His hands grasped at something.

Ah, he remembered now. He had left a roach there on the night table. It was just a tiny thing, but it was still ripe to smoke. All that mattered was that it was weed. That's all that mattered. It was life-giving pot. He had dabbled in drugs a lot more since the loss of brother and it helped diminish the hot, burning shame that he'd nursed for years. His mother had her way, her faith. He had his own way. He'd come to recognize over time that the only option for his survival was to suppress the memory of the role he'd inadvertently played in Robert's death. He fashioned himself like the narrator in *The Invisible*

Man. He lived underground, yet not a physical structure. An underground cavern in his mind.

The drugs that he had tried since '79 all had their qualities, each one different but good in their own way. He could not deny that cocaine went damned straight to the point, made him feel like a new man even on those days that had hit him hard, but it was grossly unaffordable on the meager paid legal internship that his father had secured for him in a swank, ivy-covered brownstone on Lombard Street. Quaaludes were truly calming, but he didn't like the feeling of living underwater and the mind-squashing effect they had. And then there was crack, which he had smoked, but was just too damned smelly and sticky and ultra-addictive.

No. There was only one.

Pot—green, mossy, and fragrant; Colombian preferably.

Lawrence sat upright in bed, still under sheets that smelled of Ivory soap and the first days of summer. He took the roach and smoked it, placing the tiny white bud between his lips and closing his lips around it. He took it and inhaled deeply, allowing the weed to seep into any portal within his lungs that it could find.

He put on his slippers and walked by the life-sized John Coltrane poster on the wall to his adjoining bathroom to take a steaming-hot shower. A cluster of white oak trees was in full view through the casement window and a few gray, rough, branches brushed it. After his shower, and while still dripping wet, he cracked open the window using its shiny brass handle and reached out to touch the branches. His eyes were transfixed by the sight of a leaf—as wide as his palm—sealed by water against the open window.

Just the sight of that leaf, velvety and fragile, like an elegant lady's delicate green-stained glove, enthralled him. He could see every glossy vein of it. He hoisted his body—toned from the fifty sit ups he imposed on himself each day—on top of the slate-gray marble vanity to open the window wider and get a closer look. A light summer breeze rustled a pile of white rolling papers that sat on the ledge. The faint tinkling sound of wind chimes could be heard in the distance.

He carefully peeled off the top paper and then began to roll himself a thick joint packed with ganja. For some folks, it was tea. For him, the ritual of rolling the weed was almost as satisfying as the smoking itself.

Lawrence allowed his mind to rest on Georgia. He thought of the chasm that lay between her life and his. Of the fact that if he were to look at her situation with an unjaundiced eye, she was just one of the millions of Black girls who passed through life, unseen and barely noticed. The world, he felt sure, bestowed its bounties only on the strong ones. People like Georgia, and Bettie for that matter, were more familiar with the backhand of God's grace. And, if he were to be entirely honest, people like Robert, too.

It had been Georgia who had hooked him up with the Colombian dope. He surmised that paying top dollar had helped buy Georgia's new shoes—those sky-high platform heels, bright and shiny, the color of candy apple. Georgia shared that she'd taken drugs, too, but—just like him—she'd settled on pot to help ease the pains of daily living.

He stood by the open window of the bathroom, blowing smoke out and looking at the swing set on the east side of the house that he and Robert used to play on. It was curious that his parents had never bothered to dismantle it, he thought. Perhaps they were leaving it up for any grandchildren that might come along.

His thoughts turned back to Georgia and how she never seemed to be without that damned little pink Walkman cassette player, little white earphone cord dangling from her right ear. One day he asked her what she was listening to, and she gave him her earphones. Out of them came a woman's voice he didn't recognize. One thing he knew from the whiny voice he heard was that she wasn't a sister.

"What's that?" he asked her.

Georgia was sitting at the kitchen table with her back to him. Bettie was washing up and suds were flying every which way from the sink.

"You mean who's that," she said, correcting him with a little laugh. "She's Joni Mitchell, and I love her music. Now leave me alone. I've got work to do."

"What's that?" he'd asked.

"Paperwork."

"What kind of paperwork?"

"An application to Hampton University," she said dryly, her eyes not wavering from the forms in front of her.

"I thought you said you'd decided you weren't going to college."

"That was then," she said.

Bettie was still at the sink, strong brown arms layered with a coating of white suds.

"Don't pay that girl any mind," she said, turning around to look at Georgia first and then Lawrence. "We don't have the money…. But she can still window shop. Ain't nothing wrong with that."

He pulled up a chair and sat next to her, leaning over to inspect the papers.

"No, you don't!" Georgia said, covering the folder containing photographs of the school and application form with her hands.

"Oh, you're Mr. Big Stuff now, aren't you?" she said, raising her large doe eyes to look him straight in the eye. "Now that you're about to graduate, nobody but you and your fake friend Miss Claire can say who can and who can't do what."

"Who?" he said, reddening.

"Your damned girlfriend!" Georgia said forcefully.

"Georgia!" Bettie's voice resounded in Mamie's kitchen. "You better watch what comes out of your mouth!"

Ignoring her mother, Georgia continued. "Just because you're finished with college and starting law school doesn't mean that other people can't do something with their lives, too."

157

When Bettie left the kitchen to go upstairs to clean, it was then that he'd asked her about the weed.

There was that smile again, her lopsided, crackerjack sweet smile. As he leaned in closer, he could smell her scent. She smelled of bubblegum and Ivory soap.

"It just so happens that I know where you can get some fine Colombian," she said. "I'll hook you up. But he's a careful guy, and he might want to deal with me rather than you."

* * *

"Forget it!" he heard his mother yell, exasperatedly from the kitchen. "I've called you twice for breakfast and you've been a no show. These biscuits I made for you are going in the trash!"

Lawrence rested his joint on his nightstand and got dressed hurriedly. He'd taken his LSAT in December and had passed. Commencement was in two weeks, after that he would be out of there and bound for law school, fulfilling his father's expectation that had always been there but had been accentuated even more since Robert's passing. And although a career in the law had not been his personal choice, Lawrence secretly reveled in the fact that he had finally done something to earn his father's praise.

He went downstairs, taking the steps two at a time, the aroma of the hot, buttery biscuits accelerating his pace. Every morning Mamie made homemade cream biscuits from an Antebellum Essex County family recipe.

"Dad at court already?"

"Yes, he left hours ago."

He'd been on a rollercoaster ride with his father since '79 but things were finally beginning to improve. While Robert was alive, Lawrence had grown to accept his scapegoat role, had come to accept it and wear it, like a too-big suit that's the only one you have. But now, he felt compelled to succeed, just like his father wanted him to. Just like Robert.

"Laurie, do you remember how those girls would flock to soccer practice on Saturdays just to see Robert?" his mother asked.

Things hadn't changed much for her since Robert's passing, he though. Not really. She still adored his late brother. He'd become her favorite, the golden boy.

"Mom, you know I hate it when you call me Laurie," Lawrence said, wincing.

"I'm sorry, Lawrence," she said.

"It's OK," he said. "Yeah, he was a real jock, wasn't he?"

He opened his mouth, as if to add something, and then closed it.

"So true," Mamie said, shutting her eyes.

Lawrence picked up the knife that he had just used to smooth butter onto his biscuit. He licked it clean with his tongue. Just those two words, *so true*, jabbed at him.

The effect of the pot kicked in and he asked, "Funny that Robert was the jock, huh, Mom? Especially when it was me, and not Robert, who nailed the girls. But you forgot that part."

"Lawrence," Mamie shot back. "Are you still jealous of your brother? Please don't be so sensitive. It was just an observation.... That's all. With Claire doting on you and Georgia still pining, I don't need any convincing."

Lawrence persisted. "Mom, listen to me please. What was wrong with Robert?"

"What do you mean...wrong with Robert? Don't go down that track, son," Mamie said sternly.

"Lawrence," she said, changing the subject. "Would you mind picking up Georgia from her work at seven this evening and then taking her back home to Bettie's? She'll wait for you outside of the childcare center where she works."

"But it's Claire's party this evening, Mom. Did you forget?"

"Yes, I know that Lawrence," she said tiredly. "That's why I want you to drop her off home before the party."

"But I won't have time, Mom. The party starts at 7:30 and Claire wants me there on time. Why do I have to pick her up? Why can't her mother do it?"

"Don't be short with me, son! Bettie's car is in the shop. That's why she won't be coming in to clean for us today, and that's why she can't pick Georgia up.

"What's wrong with you this morning?" she added. "Have you been smoking that dope again?"

"No, Mom, I haven't," he said, lying. "So, what are your plans for the day?"

"Not chauffeuring Black folk back and forth across the city, if that's what you're asking," she deadpanned. "So, could you do this for me, Laurie—I mean, Lawrence?"

"OK, Mom, I'll figure something out. I'll pick her up."

Lawrence went upstairs to his room, and Mamie sat down at the kitchen table. *He's worked hard and done well for himself,* she thought. Lawrence would graduate with an English and Philosophy degree from Coleridge College, and he had been on the Dean's list for consecutive semesters. Whip smart, he'd pleased his father by finishing a law internship with flying colors and he'd already submitted his law school applications. *Yes,* Mamie said to herself, *he's got a bright future ahead of him. And, who knows, perhaps that future might be shared with Claire, the Scotts' daughter. And, from there,* she thought wistfully—looking outside of the kitchen window that Bettie had cleaned only the week before, inside and out, at the delicate purple and yellow crocuses that had suddenly overpopulated the flowerbed below—*a houseful of healthy, bright, beautiful, and brown chortling babies.* That's all she wanted.

20

In the opinion of the Philadelphia Black elite, Claire Scott had become a beaut. No two ways about it, the old folk said.

Unfortunately, the word had reached her finely shaped ears and her expectation of compliments had become second nature. Possessing a French sense of style—brightly hued silk scarves an essential—she had already begun to fit into the Black elite circles like the narrow stockinged foot of a lady into a Ferragamo shoe.

Her parents were pleased that Claire had done well enough at Coleridge to have been accepted into the nursing school at the University of Pennsylvania where she planned to begin in the fall. They would have preferred medical school, but nursing was acceptable because trained colored nurses were few and far between. Since she was an only child, all their hopes and dreams were pinned on her, and Sherman, her father, still secretly hoped that in time she would decide to apply for medical school.

In her mother Shirley's view, Claire had gone a long way to compensate for deciding on nursing school by attracting the interest of Judge Whitman's son, Lawrence. He had grown from an ornery reed of a boy to one who was decidedly a catch. He was tall, handsome and—as rumor had it—apparently brilliant.

The news that Claire was dating Lawrence was greeted by her parents with unvarnished glee. Being that the families had known each other for years, the fact that their matchmaking had worked was like having a good nightcap at the end of a long workday. As the younger son of Judge Whitman, they couldn't have wished for a better prospect for their daughter. But after several months in, and with no word from Claire about any talk of engagement, they decided that it was time for a family chat. One bright Saturday morning they sat Claire down in the sunny breakfast nook of their home and, over freshly ground Brazilian coffee and chilled, just-squeezed orange juice, they gave her "the talk."

Mrs. Scott began. "You need a plan."

"What kind of plan?" Claire asked, perplexed.

"Some kind of plan so that you can avoid your relationship with Lawrence being drawn out excessively. We need to know his intentions."

"We? What about me? And we're not having sex, in case you were wondering."

"Exactly the point," Mr. Scott interjected, reaching over the table to grab a donut that had been sprinkled with confectioners' sugar.

"Your plan should be to get engaged, without going to bed with him first," he said. "An engagement should be on offer first."

Claire now realized that her parents thought of the party as an investment toward getting her engaged to Lawrence, rather than a celebration marking the end of her college days. Her father had laughed when he'd casually remarked that morning, "If it takes two DJs and five dozen bottles of wine spritzer to bring that boy to the table, well, that's money well spent."

She recognized the fact that, for her parents, Lawrence was someone who if her mother was asked during a Bridge evening, "Who's Claire seeing?" she could proudly announce that it was Lawrence J. Whitman. The Whitman name carried cachet in Black Philadelphia circles, especially among the select club of Blacks who sojourned in Cape May every summer to escape the oppressive heat.

* * *

Claire whiled away the early evening on Friday prior to the party, fulfilling her hostess duties. She checked against her list of invitees to make sure that there were enough comfortable chairs in the living room and bottles of Coke in the fridge. She'd also made sure that the guest bathroom was stocked with fresh white linen hand towels and that the vanities were immaculately clean.

The Scotts lived in a three-story stone house on Wayne Avenue in West Mount Airy. It was an ideal party home with its narrow window seats for trysts and a backyard of carefully tended lawns, lush flower beds, and manicured green hedges. Her father had bought it cheaply from his father, who in turn had inherited it from his father, one of the first Black math teachers in the Philadelphia school district.

Claire fingered the Egyptian cotton fabric of the delicately embroidered black and red Indian handmade blouse that she'd decided to wear this evening. She heard her stomach rumble but ignored it. She was not motivated to eat anyway. She was cruising on pure adrenaline, anxious to get the party started. She decided to calm herself by racing around the house on her coltish legs, hurriedly placing little bouquets of forget-me-nots in tiny vases throughout the living areas.

She knew that there was no question that Lawrence would want sex that evening. Not only want it, but probably demand it. Earlier, the two had discussed the possibility after everyone had left and Mrs. Scott was asleep. Twirling the end of a shiny, black lock of hair with her right hand, she decided that she'd know the right course when it happened. And that decision could be hers and not his, she'd staunchly determined.

Claire, like other girls in her set, had been schooled in the stoic, puritanical African Episcopalian Church school of thought during youth Sunday School. She was a part of a group that had moved up with each other from class to class since Sunday nursery school. The more conservative girls—those who arrived at church with their black King James Bibles pressed up against their front like bullet proof vests, schooled the others about the dangers of premarital sex. Claire had weighed the Bible teachings carefully. Her and Lawrence had recently made out furiously on a damp patch of grass behind her mother's garden shed, and they'd come tantalizingly close to sex. She didn't think he would take no for an answer, so she lied to him and said that she heard her mother approaching. Just the memory of his piquant mouth on her swelling breasts had nearly convinced her to risk damnation.

An hour before the party Mrs. Scott sat her daughter down in the kitchen for the Black mother and child ritual of western conformance to the time-honored Anglo standards of beauty. Mrs. Scott was secretly pleased that no one knew that Claire's long, luscious locks were not natural, but rather the courtesy of painstaking, longsuffering appointments with a sizzling hot comb and a skinny black comb.

Claire had just showered and had dabbed a little Chanel Number 5 into her décolletage. Her hand trembled as she put on her Coty makeup, almost poking out her eye with the thin Kohl black eyeliner she had bought at the mall. She'd brought the radio into the kitchen and had put on an old smock over her slip. She would change immediately afterward.

When an obscure jazz single, "Please Don't Talk About Me," came on, she hummed along, as her mother draped a large, white towel over her shoulders.

"Do I really need it pressed for tonight?" she asked, craning her neck to make eye contact with her mother. "I mean, is it absolutely imperative that I look like a white girl for Lawrence to like me?"

Her mother's fine boned hand stopped midair as the steaming hot comb hissed.

"Maybe not Lawrence, but certainly his folks," she said without an inflection of emotion in her voice.

"And by the way," she added. "Let me let you in on a little secret, sweetie."

She thought suddenly of the day she had happened to stop by the Whitman house and had seen Lawrence looking at the maid's daughter, Georgia. Healthy was an apt descriptor and well-endowed only barely getting to the heart of things.

"Frankly, God has not endowed you…there," Mrs. Scott said cruelly, pointing to Claire's chest. "But He did give you some seriously thick hair. It's your best feature, next to your face. So please don't argue with me."

Then Shirley gently took her daughter's perfectly shaped oval head in her hands, twisted it to face forward, as though she were an expensive mannequin.

That explains it, Claire thought.

From the age of fourteen, she'd determined to revolt against her mother's expectation for her, which was to become a replica of herself. But lock, stock and barrel, her mother was solely dependent upon her father for all of the frivolities and non-frivolities of life. She'd have a husband, yes. But that wasn't all.

Claire kept her head rigid as the hot comb moved firmly through her hair, at times coming daringly close to her scalp. Neither mother nor daughter said a word, content to allow the ritual to be spun out. The silence was disrupted only by the crackle and sizzle of hair against hot steel in pursuit of an elusive straightness of hair. Both the elder and younger had no illusions. They knew that hair straightening was, at its essence, a sleight of hand. One good thunder shower could send those straightened locks back to their natural state.

After Claire's hair had been straightened to her mother's satisfaction, Mrs. Scott went upstairs and cloistered herself in the master bedroom, nonplussed that her husband was away on yet another trip. After picking up the phone to call Mamie so that they could relish in the beauty of their well laid plans, she would hunker down on the duvet with a bag of Fritos and Johnny Carson on the TV.

When the doorbell rang, Claire's heart jumped. She trotted through her parents' tastefully illuminated hallway. She somehow sensed, with the precision of a bloodhound, that Lawrence was behind the door.

21

Georgia was tapping her heels waiting outside on the front porch when Lawrence drove up that summer evening to pick her up from the child center. She waved at him, and the first thing he noticed as she walked to the car were her ankle boots that were the color of the cranberry bog that he and Robert used to visit in the Cape over summers. He couldn't explain why his heart started racing at the sight of the boots, but they did. When he parked and opened the car door for her, she smiled.

"What a gentleman," she said as she climbed in. "Look, I'm sorry about this."

"Sorry about what?"

"Sorry that you're having to take me to your girlfriend's party. Momma told me."

"Yeah, but it will be cool with Claire."

"What about you? After all, I ain't up to being nobody's charity case you know. I don't want any trouble between you and Claire."

Lawrence kept his eyes glued to the road, both hands firmly gripping the wheel.

"Yes, it is, and no, you're not," was his curt response.

"Well, that's cool, too. I was worried there for a moment."

"But behave yourself, OK? Otherwise, I'll have to take you home," he joked.

"Got it, big stuff."

She smiled at him as he glanced at her. She wore a short black jean skirt that showcased her legs and a crisp, white button-down blouse that he noticed—as she bent down to crank up the volume on the radio—had several buttons undone.

At a stop sign he took a minute to look at her braids, which dangled below her shoulders and were capped with tiny, shimmering golden beads. He remembered the day when she allowed him to feel her up by the tree. He'd never met a girl quite like her. It was she and not him who had stepped nearer, close enough for him to smell her. She, not him, who had edged closer. What was it about her that aroused him so?

He was both besotted by her while also feeling a twinge of guilt. How did he get himself in this predicament of driving Georgia to the event where he and Claire had preplanned to finally go all the way? And what happened to the little girl in bobby socks that used to sit like a statue on a stool in his mother's kitchen?

* * *

They arrived at the Scotts' home and walked to the front door, Lawrence ahead of Georgia. He rang the doorbell and Claire opened the door. She was wearing a tasteful Indian handmade blouse with balloon sleeves, paired with black silk pants with a draw tie.

"Hi Claire," Lawrence said sheepishly. He leaned in to kiss her on her lips, but he missed when she abruptly turned her face to glare at the person standing next to him.

"This is Georgia Smythe. Bettie's daughter."

Claire, looking past Georgia, whispered, "Bettie…your mother's maid?"

Before Lawrence could answer, Georgia stepped forward, smiling.

"Love your hair, girl," she said, reaching out to touch Claire's tresses.

Claire, stunned, pushed Georgia's hand away and took a step backward. She glared at the petite girl with the big cornrows standing in close proximity to her boyfriend. Lawrence tried to referee.

"You remember that I called you, Claire. You said that it would be fine. She'd be welcome to join the party."

Claire looked trustingly into Lawrence's eyes and politely turned back toward Georgia.

"You're welcome Georgia," she said.

She extended a wan hand for Georgia to shake, which she did.

"Gorgeous crib!" Georgia said as she walked in.

"Lawrence says that you work at a childcare center," Claire said. "I think that's really great. Parents need good places to drop off their kids," she said, looking sidelong at Lawrence.

"That's the truth. Especially poor mothers who have to work two and three jobs," Georgia replied, as Claire coolly eyed the girl from head to toe. "Like most Black folk," she added, surveying the wide, breezy kitchen where the three of them now stood.

Claire couldn't help but observe that Georgia had left the top three buttons of her white top undone and saw that her attractive cleavage had not gone unnoticed by Lawrence. Seeing that Georgia had noticed her looking at her cleavage, she became a little unnerved and transferred her gaze to Georgia's hair.

"Mom's legacy," Georgia said with a disarming smile. "She does braids in her spare time. Charges by the hour, if you're interested."

There was then a long, awkward pause as the two girls sized each other up.

"You guys should get to know each other better anyway," Lawrence finally said, in an attempt to end the standoff. He made it a point to move toward Claire and stand side by side with her.

"Two gorgeous sisters," he added, magnanimously, "both with a love of red."

He looked down at Georgia's red boots and then, before she had time to react, reached out to touch one of Claire's earlobes which were dressed in tiny red garnet earrings. They were a gift that he had chosen but were a graduation present from the entire Whitman family.

She relaxed and smiled, lightly touching both lobes. "Your mother dropped them off earlier today. They're beautiful," she said, looking up at Lawrence.

She forgot that Georgia was there for a moment until she saw her take a step toward Lawrence. In the tasteful lighting of her home's foyer, she saw that Georgia was taller than her.

She looked down at Georgia's boots.

"Where'd you buy those?" she asked.

"They're Goodwill's finest," Georgia said, then suddenly asked, "Hey, what's this Killer Queen bullshit we're listening to? Girl, ain't you got anything with a little more soul?"

"What sort of music appeals to you?" Claire said, defensively.

"How about Honey Cone's 'Want Ads'?" Georgia replied and began to sing the first few lines

Lawrence's strained face grew more so as Georgia suddenly began to dance. But damn that girl can move, he thought as he went over to Georgia and grasped her elbow.

"I thought I told you in the car," he whispered in her ear. "No mischief or I'll take you home."

"Where's the bathroom?" Georgia asked, ignoring him and shaking his hand away.

"You mean the powder room?" Claire sneered. "It's over there and to the right."

Claire started to walk after her, but Lawrence grabbed her hand.

"I'm sorry about this," he said, "about her."

"My mother insisted," he added, grumbling.

He caressed her shoulders. She opened her mouth to speak, but before she could utter a word, he drew her to him and kissed her.

"I'm sorry if I overreacted," she said, staring at his mouth that was now stained the color of her pinkish brown Clinique lipstick.

"Don't blame yourself," Lawrence whispered to her. "You've every right to be annoyed. But if there's anyone to blame it's my mother. She insisted I pick up Georgia from work."

That seemed to smooth things out so, when the doorbell rang and more guests arrived and claimed Claire's attention, he went to search for Georgia. He found her alone in the Scott family study, seated crossed legged in the dark.

"You're welcome to join the party, you know," he said as he flipped on the light, "just don't irritate Claire. It's her party and her house."

Georgia looked down at the plate of food that she had collected. Hot spicy tomato sauce oozed out from under the wings and onto the frothy macaroni and cheese.

"It's OK," she said pleasantly. She picked up a wing and took a bite. "I'll just sit in here and watch *Gunsmoke*. You go find Claire."

He walked over to her and sat down. He put his hand on her lap and waited for her to push his hand away. When she didn't, he allowed it to stay, the tips of his fingers pressed just under the hem of her jean skirt.

"Do you miss him?" Georgia asked, out of the blue.

"Who?" he asked.

"Robert."

"He was my brother," he said, a pained expression clouding his face. "What do you think? Of course, I do."

But Lawrence's mind was on Georgia's face. He shook his head suddenly, as though arousing himself out of a dream.

"Please act right," he said, his hand still on her thigh. It had not moved.

She turned toward his face. "Lawrence," she said.

He stopped, turning to face her.

"What?" he asked.

171

"You're better than all of them," she said, dark eyes flashing. "And—and you can have me tonight. Because...because...I want you just as much as you want me."

Lawrence took his hand away from her leg and pressed his finger against her lips.

"Don't say it," he said, in a whisper. "Please don't," he said, this time in a near whimper. He stood up again and strode toward the door.

"I'll be ready to drop you off at your house around 11:00 p.m.," he said crisply, as he reached for the doorknob. "Be ready."

* * *

Lawrence found Claire in the kitchen, passing around a plate of hors d'oeuvres to her guests. He snuck up behind her and pecked her on her long, swan like neck while she was talking with her friends.

"Red boots, did you see her? In the middle of July!" she said, laughing to the knot of girls that had gathered around her.

"Hey," Lawrence said, defensively. "Ain't nothing wrong with a little color now."

"Yes, Lawrence, where is she?"

"Who knows?" he answered enigmatically.

This was his girl, he thought as he picked up a bowl of hot buttered popcorn. He looked at Claire, light brown eyes glowing, Indian blouse draped prettily over her slim body. She sensed his admiring glance and looked into his eyes and flushed. He kissed her in front of her friends and then playfully dipped her head back as he popped one piece of hot buttered popcorn after another into her mouth, to her girlfriends' delight. Everyone laughed, apart from one girl who was envious of Claire's relationship with Lawrence and had just entered the room.

This was Eva, who had styled her auburn-colored hair into two French braids that fell like two orange ropes on her back. Her brows were red and thick, above pale blue eyes that seemed perpetually startled. She was a student at Coleridge College and one of Claire's best friends. She was also the only white person invited to the party, which Eva obviously relished. Their common bond was a love for tennis, cultivated since the time they both took Saturday lessons at the Philadelphia Tennis Club. Eva was a year younger than Claire and had fond memories of Lawrence's brother Robert. She had been paired with him for doubles shortly after she began taking lessons as a preteen.

She lived in an impressive house about a mile away from Claire, close enough so that on weekends they spent time at each other's homes for study group sessions, heads buried in their books. When they weren't taking long lunch breaks to listen to endless soundtracks of Bruce Springsteen, they talked about boys.

She didn't trust Lawrence. Whether it was a vibe or her own implicit bias, she didn't know. The dude had always rubbed her the wrong way.

"Hey, I really love that blouse," Eva said, glancing admiringly at her.

Claire looked back at her. "Damn you're as Black as me! Starting early on your tan?"

"Yeah, well you know. Got to keep up with the Joneses!" Eva said jovially, thrusting out her arm and lining it up against Claire's.

Lawrence didn't utter a word. It irked him to no end when white people sporting summer tans compared themselves to Black folks.

Eva sensed that she'd upset him, so she directed her conversation entirely toward Claire, only momentarily glancing at Lawrence from time to time. Every girl on campus knew that he was a consummate flirt, so Eva was a little surprised that there was absolutely nothing about Lawrence's attitude toward her that suggested he had even the remotest interest in her. That had not been her experience with most Black guys. They all seemed to yearn for whatever she had, which she still hadn't figured out. It was most apparent in the cafeteria, where all the Black jocks hung out at the preppie white girl table. She looked at Lawrence, who returned her gaze with indifference.

"Hey, by the way," she said, turning again to Claire. "Who's the girl sitting in your study? I was on my way to the bathroom, and I saw a girl with long corn rows sitting in the dark."

Lawrence opened his mouth to answer her, but Claire interrupted him.

"That's the Whitmans' maid's daughter," Claire said.

"Oh," Eva said, "That's interesting. I didn't know that you had a maid, Lawrence."

Eva's Quaker sensibilities—her family regularly attended the Meeting House on Arch Street and had never thought to hire a maid—suddenly went into overdrive.

"Well, don't you think we should introduce her to everyone? Why is she stuck sitting alone in there?"

"Well, not everyone's sociable like you, Eva," Claire said, anxious to change the subject and stepped toward Eva to tousle her hair.

"You know me. I'm a party animal! Hey, don't touch the hair!" Eva said, laughing while backing away. "If I were you, I wouldn't take my eyes off that one," she added in a whisper, indicating Lawrence.

Claire shrugged, blew a kiss to Lawrence, and walked away.

The party picked up steam as the guests wandered aimlessly through Claire's cavernous house, carrying their pink wine spritzers to whatever corner of the home beckoned. Georgia was nowhere to be found when the DJ put on Superstition, and everyone congregated in the spacious den that Mrs. Scott had transformed into a dance floor.

The room was transformed into a joyful tapestry of moving limbs, sweat and song. Someone called for Grandmaster Flash. Another lit up a bong, and although Claire had made it clear that smoking indoors had been firmly disallowed by her mother, no one seemed to care, least of all Claire, who turned a blind eye.

Couples who had arrived together at the party were now dancing with the partners of their friends, smiling with abandon during the switch offs. Some sauntered outside, the light from the moon illuminating their high cheekbones and the sheen of their bronzed skin against oxford and silk skirts. Anyone who wished to take their ménage á deux outside of the realm of decency would have to do so outside of the hostess's home. And even then, their dalliances must not disturb the neighbors with loud or distasteful noises. They had to show decorum even when smashed, and that was fine with the young, well-heeled set who carried their long-limbed bodies across the lawn and through the house like Nubian royalty.

Within their bubble of private schools and clubs, Claire and her clique of friends had learned since their preteen years when to play within the rules and when to break them. And on this charmed night, boundary setting was made harder for the privileged young women, who wore the earthy scent of cannabis mixed with eau de parfum like a talisman around their long, swan-like necks.

Flat drunk on their charmed, God given beauty, they knew that pot, coke, speed, or anything else they might fancy to heighten and improve an already rapturous night, was theirs for the taking.

And take it they did.

22

Mike the DJ finally took a break. His spinning arm felt like spaghetti dangling from a fork. As he weaved through a cluster of eager, toothy smiles and bodies in crisp oxford shirts, expensive wrist watches as ubiquitous as the tiny bowls of buttered popcorn he'd seen placed on elegant side tables, he thought about how ridiculous the whole tableau appeared.

He had just finished another graduation gig in Bryn Mawr only the week before. The large Tudor house was just as impressive—if not more so—as this Chestnut Hill crib. But somehow, the brusque way in which the white kids acted toward him—one even mistook him as a waiter—didn't rub him the same way as these stick-up-their-butts Negroes.

It wasn't that the host and her guests weren't friendly, he thought as he took a breather, standing with his back pressed against the back wall of the massive stone home, smoking a Camel unfiltered. Oh, they were that if anything. But they were friendly in a clubby *I'm-rich-and-you,-my-dear-fellow,-clearly-are-not,-but-stick-around-for-tea* sort of way. Now that Mike was older and had done the right thing by skipping college and going to work as a delivery driver come DJ in order to be a responsible father, he'd given some thought to his mother's words: *"Never covet the things rich white folks have."*

Well, these weren't rich white folks, these were rich Black folks coveting what the rich white folks had and he didn't want any of it. From their Queen's English diction to their natty boat shoes, when he didn't see a boat—or water, for that matter—in sight.

When Mike walked back inside, he watched discreetly as those guests who had lovers or partners paired off with them, dispersing themselves throughout the home that featured a large oil painting in the living room and a slick, black baby grand piano. One of the couplings included the host, Claire Scott, and who appeared to be her slippery, smooth boyfriend. Someone named Lawrence somebody. He noticed that Lawrence had Claire now ensconced in the study off to the side of the cavernous living room. Lucky fucking devil. She was fine. *I love that sexy, prep school type of girl,* he thought.

Lawrence had guided Claire to the darkly lit study where he had seen Georgia earlier, away from the traffic of guests.

"Something smells funny," Claire said. "Smells like bananas." Thinking about Georgia, Lawrence laughed.

They sat down, she somewhat reluctantly, sharing between them a wide wing chair. He turned his body toward her and kissed her.

"I can't, Lawrence," she said firmly, pulling away.

"But…but last time we were making out at your house, we came close enough to…"

"No, it's not that. I just don't trust that girl."

"What?" He drew back from her.

"That girl. Georgia," she said. "Your maid's daughter."

"What's Georgia got to do with it?" Lawrence's eyes turned toward her, his reddened face and eyes reflecting hurt.

Bettie had been like a second mother to him and Robert for as long as he could remember. And despite himself, his eyes teared up at the memory of how she had grieved along with him, following Robert's passing.

It very well may have been a knee jerk reaction, but he had not appreciated Claire's selection of words—"your maid's daughter."

It upset him viscerally, as though Claire's words had been carefully crafted, like a barb, and directed toward the people he loved.

Claire quietly examined Lawrence's reaction, which seemed strangely cold toward her. She reached up to push back a strand of hair from her face, and as she did she noticed that one of her garnet earrings was missing.

"Must have dropped it on the floor," she said nervously, as Lawrence watched her get down on the floor to look. "Because they were both in a second before."

They both got down on their knees to hunt for the missing earring on the parquet floor.

"Wait, you stay here," she said when they couldn't find it. "I'll go find a flashlight."

She kissed him chastely on the cheek.

"This is not only a gift from you, but it's a gift from your family, and I can't bear to lose it."

As she walked away, Claire swatted a mosquito that had landed on the back of her hand and wondered if she should call the guests who had dribbled outside to come in to keep them from being devoured alive. That thought left her when she heard what the DJ was playing. It was "Want Ads," the song she'd heard Georgia sing when she'd arrived in tow with Lawrence earlier that evening.

Claire went to the kitchen and rummaged through the junk drawer next to the refrigerator. Finally, she found the small plastic red flashlight that her mother occasionally used to walk Dotty—her mother's beloved Kerry Blue Terrier who was holed up with her mother in her room upstairs. She switched it on to check the batteries, only to find that they were dead. Thinking about Eva's cautioning words and desperate to return to Lawrence, she dug her hands deeply into the drawer's accumulated junk, ranging from empty matchboxes, a rabbit's foot, a wad of clean tissue, to her houndstooth barrette.

At last, she found two AA batteries and inserted them into the cylindrical cavity of the flashlight and checked that it worked. It did, so she headed back, and along the way she checked to see that her guests were OK. She air-kissed a friend who was seated cross legged next to the same tall gangly boy with sad eyes whom the friend had been trying to nab since second grade. She looked around and smiled graciously. She'd learned how to be a hostess from her mother, who had perfected what Claire dubbed the "wraparound smile" a smile that was wide and warm enough to be seen by everyone.

Then she spun on her heels and returned to where the earring had fallen. She was immediately stopped in her tracks by the sight before her. All she saw were two figures pressed together and a mass of gold beads perfectly aligned against a white shirt. The beads were blindingly distracting. Then she realized who the two figures were.

"What the hell is going on here?" Claire yelled, face turning crimson and her hands on her narrow hips.

Lawrence immediately broke free from Georgia's embrace, nearly falling over as he stepped backward.

"Where were you?" Lawrence asked, dazed.

Ignoring him, Claire looked scornfully at Georgia.

"What do you think you're doing, Georgia?" she cried.

Furious, she threw the flashlight in her general direction. But instead of hitting her, it dislodged one of her mother's prized jade plants, knocking the flowerpot off the elegant, cherry-wood side table.

"That's my boyfriend you just kissed!"

"Did you say, 'kissed'?" Georgia said calmly in return. "Says who?"

"Says me," Claire replied, then hesitatingly, because she had been schooled since her childhood days not to utter profanities. "You... you bitch."

She glared at Georgia and then strode over to Lawrence. He didn't move away from her but refused to take her hand when she reached for his.

The noise of the party seemed to fade as attention centered on Georgia, who flicked her long cascade of braids behind her back and then slowly and painstakingly buttoned up her blouse.

"Recognize who's singing?" she asked.

Gladys Knight was suddenly in the house, sublimely singing "Midnight Train to Georgia". She started dancing, crouching low, then spinning out in a slow spiral, long neck falling back, face to the sky.

"I don't know what you bourgeois niggers call it," she said searingly. "But I call Gladys soul food."

Claire's face grew redder with each passing second. She opened her mouth, but before she could utter a word, Georgia spoke again.

"Now, I know that there probably ain't no vacancy with that man of yours," she said. "So don't worry your pretty head about me. At least not for now. But if you really want to know why Lawrence just kissed somebody like me, the maid's daughter…" She turned dramatically toward Lawrence. "Ask him. Not me."

Claire stared defiantly at Lawrence, waiting for an answer as Mike, the tall DJ, walked over to her and put his hand on her shoulder.

"Is there a problem here?" he asked, his eyes drilling into Lawrence.

"No, there's no problem," Claire replied calmly and without rancor. "Because he's leaving and taking this sorry whore with him.

"That's right," she added, as she watched Georgia quietly cry. "That's *exactly* what you are," she said, walking away into the Scotts' cavernous living room.

"You heard the lady," Mike said. "She wants you out. You'd better move before I have to make you."

* * *

As Mike walked away to catch up with Claire, Lawrence moved toward Georgia.

"That was wrong," Lawrence he said. "It was straight up wrong. She had no right to call you a name like that."

He looked at Georgia, who, although taller than Claire, seemed diminutive in the Scotts' home. A yearning swelled inside of him, growing with each passing second. He saw her eyes brimming with tears and leaned over, kissing the lids of each eye, tasting her salty tears on his lips. Then he reached out and grabbed a mass of her braids in his right hand, looking down the foyer to make sure no one was looking, and then kissed her long and deeply.

"Time to book," he told her sternly, in command.

23

After the Party

It was near midnight when Lawrence pulled into the parking lot at Valley Green Park, a woody oasis in the middle of the city.

"Valley Green Park was never on our family's radar," Georgia said as Lawrence parked the car. "That was white people territory."

There was no one in the lot but them, and as she looked at the full moon in the sky it seemed for all the world like a splatter of pancake batter on a sizzling black grill.

"We wanted to go, mind you," she said. "But Poppa always said that this park wasn't particularly hospitable to our folks."

She waited for Lawrence to answer, but it was like he was still driving even though they were already parked. His eyes were staring straight ahead, and his hands gripped the steering wheel at ten and two.

"Did you and Robert come here a lot?" she asked. "Is that why you've brought me here?"

"We used to come here after church," Lawrence said, turning his head toward her. "We'd feed popcorn to the ducks. The concession stand was just behind us."

He gestured behind him, but it was so dark that when she looked, she couldn't see if there was even a pond there, let alone a concession stand.

"For some reason Robert always got two bags of popcorn and I got one," he laughed. "One for himself, I guess and one for the mallards. Mom and Dad knew that he had a thing for mallards. Then we'd have an early dinner at the inn just behind us."

"You mean the building behind us as we parked?"

"Yes."

Georgia looked behind her. In the hazy light from the fluorescent bulbs that lit up the stately inn, she could see the vague outline of a statue of a Native American chief. His wide black eyes, set deeply into an artificially painted orange face, seemed to follow her as she moved her head.

"The building is a landmark," Lawrence said. "In 1778, George Washington dined there on his way from Barren Hill. We loved going there in the summertime. The dining room felt so cool, and the wide wooden floors creaked when you walked on them. They brought you ice water in pewter pitchers."

"I don't give a shit about George Washington," Georgia said, abruptly interrupting his thoughts. "He owned slaves. He could have owned your ancestors or mine."

Lawrence opened his door to get out and waited for her to do the same. But she didn't budge. It took a minute for him to realize that she was not going to get out of the car until he opened the door for her.

She wanted him to be a gentleman. Where the hell did she think they were going, anyway? The fucking Academy of Music?

They were going to get laid, he thought.

No ticket needed.

"Penny for your thoughts?" he asked as she suddenly allowed her head to drop. Her long braids fell into her lap.

"Oh, I was just thinking about the party. How they're different from me. People like them—like you—are lucky. No money worries like Momma. Able to get a good education, go on to get a good job. Then cruise through life like a rocket…soaring."

Lawrence sighed. He hadn't bargained on a soliloquy, and he was now beginning have second thoughts about bringing her to Valley Green Park. They sat in the car, both immersed in their own thoughts, shrouded by the night.

"I understand, Georgia," he said eventually, "although it makes me wonder why you're here with me now."

"I don't know exactly," she said, looking up at him. "But I do know that you're not like them. You're more sensitive because you've had a hard life, too, always falling short of your father's expectations. And I like you. I always have. That I can tell you, for certain."

Georgia's heart raced as she heard him open his door. He got out of the car and walked to the passenger side, opening the door for her. As she stepped out into the black night, she could hear the rhythmic hoots of a distant owl. She felt her shoulders tremble, although there was no reason for it. She wasn't cold.

They walked side by side on a heavily trodden dirt path that began a hundred yards or so from the inn and led upward to a hill. He held her hand in his and, as they walked, a wide full moon shone down upon them and on a mass of green pine trees, their long branches stretched over the path like a canopy.

Georgia started when she heard a vigorous rustling sound in the middle of a cluster of bushes.

"Probably a fox…maybe a woodchuck, even," Lawrence reassured her.

After a while, he murmured, "Here's a good spot," and they stopped walking.

It was a secluded grassy area jutting out from a rocky ledge of the hill and within the sound of a nearby creek. The way that the moonlight shone upon the grass seemed to Georgia to be a good sign that this is where they should be. They sat down next to a tree and Georgia reached out her hand to touch and examine the hard, entangled knots of bark. Her fingertips encountered a moist, mossy knob and she reached further and cradled it in her palm. For a fleeting second, as she caressed the gnarled lump, she felt communion with the tree, wedded to it and as closely anchored to it as a shell thrown to the shore, clinging to wet sand. She forgot that Lawrence was with her as she wondered about what things this tree had seen and heard. A minute later, though, she turned toward him and smiled.

"I've always loved that halfway smile of yours," he said. "Those dimples…damn!"

She blushed, grateful that he couldn't see her doing so in the moonlit night.

He took off his coat and laid it on the ground with flourish, as if he were a waiter setting up a table in a Michelin-starred restaurant.

She hesitated. Claire was his girl. Was it right that she should take him away from her? He pulled out a condom.

"That for Claire or me?" she asked.

Choosing not to answer, he gently took her hand and helped ease her onto the coat.

He laid down next to her in silence until the hoot of a night owl graced the night plateau. Lawrence began to shiver, so she shimmied closer to him and looked him in the eye.

"You're here," she said, as though mesmerized. "With me."

"Blackberry girl," he said softly, and she thought that she could hear him quietly chuckle.

A small bottle of Jack Daniels miraculously appeared in his hand as though from nowhere. He offered her the first sip.

"Where did that come from?" Georgia asked.

"I liberated it from the party," he replied, taking a mouthful of the warming liquid. "I thought that we were owed, given the way we were both treated.

"I remember the first day I saw you," he continued. "We were probably both about six years old. I'll never forget you and Miss Bettie walking through the door. She was balancing, holding your hand in

185

one hand and a deep-dish blackberry pie in the other. Those blackberries, your mom said, were picked from her aunt's garden. All I wanted, for months, was to build a treehouse in your aunt's garden."

They laughed lightly in unison.

"That's when I first saw you," he said, looking into her eyes deeply. "I mean, really saw you."

They embraced, and as they did, she smelled the tangy odor of cologne on his neck and the cool tinge of the night air. He cupped her chin in his warm hands, kissed her, and then began to undo the buttons on her shirt.

* * *

After making love, she lay quietly in his arms and watched the quiet rise and fall of his chest. He had fallen asleep. With one outstretched hand, Georgia playfully grabbed a fistful of grass and sprinkled it over his torso and face.

"Man!" he exclaimed, as he rolled to one side and roused himself. "What's this! Some kind of baptism?"

"Baptism by the fire of my love," she said.

He sat up and brushed the grass from his body. Then he began plucking out the blades of grass, one by one, that were caught up in her braids. When he was finished, he embraced her again, even more tightly than before. As tightly, she felt, as if he were gripping the moon in its firmament, lest it come crashing down through the sky. As he hugged her to him his thoughts were of her, of Bettie's daughter, this girl with the crooked smile who needed him as much as he needed her. And he thought of his father, and how his preference for Robert had devastated him and made him feel cut-rate and second best. The difference between that feeling and what he was experiencing now was unbearable, like standing under a storm cloud with rain crashing down on him with every passing minute.

"Do you think it's going to work for us?" she asked him.

"We're going to make it work," he said. "I promise."

As he embraced her, Georgia felt a dam breaking inside of her. And as it did, the tears flowed, cascading from her eyes down her face and neck, bonding her together with Lawrence. Without allowing him to see what she was doing, she reached out with one hand to the tree to brace herself, to steady herself in this new and unfamiliar situation. She looked over at Lawrence as he closed his eyes and dozed. She continued watching as he drifted off to sleep.

* * *

Lawrence woke up to the sound of Georgia singing to herself. *Oh shit,* he thought. He'd fallen asleep and now that he was awake, he couldn't figure out where he was. Blinking fast, he sat up and looked around. He was laying on grass and could hear the sound of water sloshing over river stones. For the life of him he couldn't remember how he got here, but if memory served correctly, it was the same spot that he and Robert used to hang out at on Sunday afternoons. Each had their chosen pastimes—Robert his whittling, a pastime he'd picked up from their father; and Lawrence with whatever book he happened to be reading at the time. They would sit, whittle, and read, smoke a few unfiltered Camels, and talk.

He rubbed his eyes, trying to come to his senses as the details of the evening came back to him. He had been at Claire's party but had left with Georgia. He had to shake his head twice as he looked at where she lay naked next to him on his jacket, which was spread out on the grass. He couldn't remember undressing her, let alone walking with her on the path, but there she was in front of him, her long bejeweled braids covering her bare back. He stared at her for a few minutes, watching the quiet rise and fall of her body with each breath.

He gently caressed her shoulder and she immediately turned to face him, bare breasted and smiling enchantingly, seemingly unaware of her natural allure. She shook her black braids so that they cascaded loosely over her bare nipples. He became aroused again.

187

"Did I undress you?" he asked tentatively. "I…I just can't remember."

"Nope," she replied coolly. "I can do that all by myself."

There it was again, that cockeyed tomboyish grin.

He looked at his watch and gasped at the time. "It's late," he said. "We'd better get moving."

He quickly put on his clothes. The smell of dark, rich soil seemed to be all around him. He looked over at Georgia, who hadn't begun to get dressed. She was looking to her right, transfixed by the sound of cool, gushing water from the creek below. He edged closer to her and touched her hair.

"You need to get dressed now," he said.

He looked at Bettie's daughter, the girl who had not yet put on her shirt, the girl who smelled of honeycrisp apples. He wrapped her in his arms tightly, her bare chest pressed against his shirt.

"What just happened, Georgia?" he asked.

"You loved me," she said simply.

He watched as she closed her mouth tightly, like a purse with a snap closure.

"We'd better go now," he said, and as he did, she looked at him with a puzzled stare. Then she glanced at her watch and silently got dressed.

"I'm cold," she said on the walk back to the car. "Can I wear your coat?"

He looked at her, eyes kind and gentle. "We need to get you back home, Georgia. Bettie will be awake, waiting for you."

"May I wear your coat please, Lawrence?" she repeated.

"Sure," he said, "but it's kind of special," he added, fumbling with his car keys that had a brass Coleridge College fob on them.

"So special that we just made love on it?" she asked, querulously.

"Oh, it was just a gift from…from…"

"From Claire," she said, voice trembling, fishing his sentence for him.

He looked over at her. Georgia's face had turned to stone. Her full, wine-colored lips were the only sign of life in the blank tableau that her face had suddenly become.

When they arrived at the car, he walked over to the passenger side to open the door for her. Once they were both inside, he reached over and kissed her on the cheek before rearranging her braids so that her mass of locks streamed down both sides of her face, giving her a Mona Lisa–like effect. The car, he noticed, still smelled of the perfume she had worn to the party.

They sat in silence for a few seconds as he gripped the steering wheel. Lawrence turned on the ignition.

"Did you know that you're a sleep talker?" she asked.

"Uh, no."

"Well, you are," she stated firmly.

He turned to glance at her while slowly maneuvering the car out of the empty parking lot.

"What'd I say?" he asked, almost as an afterthought, his eyes fully focused on the road.

"Something about Robert's death," she said softly. "You said something about being sorry and not meaning to…"

Lawrence was glad that she couldn't see his reaction. His heart raced. He had no wish to dredge up the past. The past was in his wake now; it could not and must not be conjured up again.

"I'm not sure what that was all about," he said defensively. "I guess I'm still grieving for Robert. He was my brother after all, and I miss him."

Lawrence suddenly felt boxed in within the confines of his car. He took a Kleenex out of the glove compartment and wiped his face, which was glazed in sweat.

"A little hot?" Georgia asked.

"Yeah. Haven't you heard?" he asked, derisively. "You kind of have that effect."

189

"Did she wear your coat?" Georgia asked, changing the subject. Before he could reply, she quickly added, "Remember, Lawrence, she did call me a whore."

"Yes, I know," he said. "And it was wrong and unforgivable. But cut her some slack. Don't be jealous. It's my mom and pop who were desperate for us to be together. The two families have been planning it probably since I was old enough to walk. But...but after tonight, I'd gamble it's probably over. She won't have me back."

"She's very pretty," Georgia said in a near whisper.

"No prettier than you," Lawrence interjected.

"Maybe it's you, though, Lawrence," she said, in a pleading voice, "and not your parents, who is...is...conflicted."

He drove on into the night, eyes affixed to the two yellow lines on the black road that cut in and out like a winding ribbon through the unlit, thickly forested suburb. It wasn't until they drove onto the highway, bound for Georgia's house in North Philadelphia, that he could relax a little. All he knew was that he needed to get Georgia back home to her mother just as soon as he could.

* * *

The following morning, Georgia was still in bed dreaming, hugging her pillow close to her, when across town Mamie got a phone call.

"Do something about it," the voice on the other end said.

"Who is this?" Mamie asked groggily back.

"It's Shirley, and Claire is devastated."

Mamie had to wait for the sobbing to cease to understand what was being said.

"What? I don't understand?" Mamie said, sitting bolt upright in the lavender-colored negligee that Teddy had bought her, to turn on the little lamp on her nightstand.

"It's Lawrence!" Shirley said, in a near shriek. "He humiliated her in front of her friends last night with Bettie's daughter!"

"But...but, yes, Lawrence took her to the party, but Claire agreed."

"She didn't agree for the little hussy to steal her man!" Shirley's uncharacteristic shout was so loud that Mamie had to pull the phone away from her ear.

Theodore was already awake and was in the bathroom shaving. He walked out in his striped pajama bottoms. He saw Mamie, her back pressed flat to the bed's headboard and mouthed the words, "What's wrong?"

Mamie cupped one hand over the receiver and placed her index finger over her mouth, a sign to wait.

"I am so sorry, Shirley," she said. "Yes, yes. Don't you worry about it. Yes, Theodore and I will speak to Lawrence…and yes, to Bettie, too. We will fix it."

24

August 1981

It was a Philadelphian summer evening, as hot and sticky as a benched basketball player, and Bettie Smythe was sitting at a small dimly lit table in a corner of McGillin's Olde Ale House on Drury Street. Judge Theodore Whitman sat stiffly opposite her. They were meeting at Judge Whitman's request, not hers, about what to do about Georgia. They had agreed on McGillin's because few colored people patronized the place. It meant there was a good chance neither one of them, particularly Judge Whitman, would be recognized in this exclusively white neighborhood pub.

Bettie could see that the judge was visibly sweating under the white collar of the shirt she had pressed for him only the week before.

"What? You mean you white boys can't afford better air conditioning than this?" he said to no one in particular. No one bothered to answer the fancily dressed Black man in the corner booth. Whatever he said registered only as background noise.

As Bettie waited to hear him out, she stared at a small red candle that had been placed in the middle of the table. The tiny yellow flame was hypnotizing as it danced and flitted and swirled about. The soft, flickering light imbued a kind of coziness, a kind of deep-dish

192

apple-pie level of comfort in what were otherwise disagreeable surroundings.

Bettie sighed and raised her eyes from the candle to confront Judge Whitman. If he couldn't begin the hard conversation, then she would. She nervously clasped her hands and put them on the table.

"Let me just start off by saying this," she said. "I think that all of our problems would be solved if you just allowed Lawrence to make up his own mind about the two girls."

Theodore had expected Bettie to say this, but he nevertheless hesitated before replying.

"I'm sorry, Bettie, but I just don't think that's a realistic way forward."

Bettie glared back at him.

"What? Ain't Georgia good enough for your son?"

Theodore didn't respond, so she looked up toward ceiling as though hoping for an acknowledgment from the overhead fan. She shrugged as an uncomfortable pause set in.

Bettie had hoped it wouldn't be like this. She had prayed that the conversation between the two of them would be easier. At the very least she'd expected Judge Whitman to show a measure of empathy for all the years she'd worked for him and Mamie. It irritated her that one family could be blessed with so much, while the other struggled for its very existence. And yet her anger was tempered with gratitude for all that he and Mamie had done for her and Georgia. The judge had helped her to secure a lawyer, who, through his pro bono assistance, had enabled her to come to a settlement with Colsol regarding Jimmy's death. And he had been good for his word about quitting its board.

"She's not some kind of two-bit hussy, if that's what you're thinking," she stated firmly to break the uneasy silence.

Theodore put his ice water down and reared back in his chair. He shut his eyes tightly, as though wishing away a bad dream. When he finally opened them, he said, "Bettie, I've never said she was. And never, in all of my days, would I say something so disparaging about your daughter. And frankly, I'm surprised that you could think that of me after all that we have done for you."

"Well," Bettie said, squirming and trying to sit comfortably in the hardbacked chair. "I am grateful to you and Miss Mamie. All I know is that my Georgia is a good girl and she's being berated by you both for no good reason."

"She crashed the party, Bettie, pure and simple. She knew that Claire was Lawrence's girlfriend and despite that, she went ahead and seduced him. She knew exactly what she was doing, I'm afraid."

"With all due respect, sir, she knew no such thing. It takes two to tango."

She paused before continuing, "Look, I know that I've not been able to give Georgia all the advantages that you've been able to provide for Lawrence. I didn't have the money to send her to a smart school or to the Jack and Jill club…and given her background, they probably wouldn't have accepted her even if I could have afforded to pay.

"But just because Georgia didn't have those advantages, that doesn't mean that she's unfit to be with your Lawrence. She's a good girl, and I'm proud of her. As a proud Black mother, it upsets me that you think that her background should prevent her from being with your son."

Bettie realized that she had raised her voice and instinctively looked around to see if anyone had noticed. The bar was not busy. A few men and women—mostly dressed in either their work clothes or uniforms—stood or sat leisurely on the high black leather bar stools, and to her relief none of them seemed to be taking any notice.

Again, Theodore didn't reply so she looked aimlessly past him, toward the kitchen where she could see the dark-skinned face of a girl clothed in white with a full head of hair that she had tried to gather in a ponytail. But it wasn't working—there was just too much of a good thing. The girl—whom she assumed was a member of the kitchen staff and barely older than her daughter—peeked through the window for a second, locking eyes sympathetically with Bettie, then she turned away. The girl reminded Bettie of Georgia, and for some reason she started to cry.

Theodore pulled a clean, white handkerchief out of his pocket and gave it to her. She used it to dab her eyes. Glancing at the pretty Black girl, he—like Bettie—had also thought of Georgia. Drumming his fingers on the table, he waited until Bettie had recovered her composure before asking her if she would like a drink. Then he got up, strode to the bar, and ordered a scotch and soda for him and a Sprite for Bettie. When he returned, he leaned over the table toward her.

"We have both endured losses, Bettie," he said softly. "Great losses. And I'm sure you'll understand that I've got a lot invested in that boy."

"I know that you've suffered a lot, sir. And I, for one, have seen you and Miss Mamie go through the kind of grief no parents should have to go through. But with all due respect, if your son had intended on marrying Miss Sherman, then I find it hard to believe that he would have gone off that night with Georgia. That boy's head is screwed on way too tight for that."

Theodore found himself smiling despite himself.

The drinks were brought by a blue-eyed girl whose blonde hair was tied back with a red ribbon. As she placed the drinks on the table, Theodore noticed that her dangling silver earrings were in the shape of peace signs. After she nervously inquired whether she could bring them anything else, she scooted back to the bar to collect drinks for patrons seated at an adjacent table.

He watched as Bettie drew her purse closely to her. He recognized the bag. It was a worn Dooney & Bourke original that he had bought Mamie many years ago. Mamie had passed it on to Bettie and it was the only bag that Whitman had ever seen her bring to work.

"Yes, I know what you're thinking," Bettie said. "This bag has seen some mileage, hasn't it?"

"Bettie," Theodore said, his eyes kind and gentle. "There are a number of parties who have been hurt in this, not least of all Claire's parents, who have been our good friends for years. I'm sure we can find a way out of this."

He paused and she looked at him quizzically. Encouraged, he carried on.

"Bettie, how would it be if I paid for Georgia to attend Hampton University? I know that she's wanted to go there ever since graduating from high school."

He expected Bettie to be overjoyed at the news. Instead, she stared back at him in annoyance.

"I thought you'd be pleased," he said, bewildered.

"Sir, with all due respect, I know that you and Miss Mamie are good people. You've shown it to me and my daughter through the years. Shown it with kindness and warmth. Shown it in a way that I am truly grateful for."

She stopped for a moment to collect her thoughts and looked for a moment in the direction of the small portal window by the kitchen where she'd seen the face of the Black girl.

"And it's true. Georgia has yearned to attend Hampton University for years. But what you're asking her to do is take your money and leave your son alone so that he can get back together with that Miss Scott. I'm sorry, Judge, but that has to be her decision, not mine or yours."

"Of course," said Theodore, placing his hand on hers. "But Bettie, I simply don't think he loves her."

"He may or may not," she said quickly, as though prepared for the question. "That's for him to decide. But just remember that your family is no better than mine and mine no better than yours. And this situation, it calls for understanding and compassion...not to speak of prayer."

She released her hand from under Theodore's and clasped both hands on the table.

"Look," she said. "I'll put your kind offer of paying for her education at Hampton to Georgia and let you know what she says. That's all I can do."

Bettie sighed deeply and sunk heavily back into her seat. She was dog tired, Theodore thought.

"Let me drive you home, Bettie," he said. "It will be no trouble, and I'd like to do that for you."

"I will take the bus, sir," she said definitively. "The stop is just across the street."

"Are you sure? I'd be happy to drive you."

"No, sir," she said, smoothing the front of her polyester blouse and putting her purse on the table.

Theodore went to the bar to pay for their drinks. When he returned, he noticed that Bettie seemed to be breathing heavily. Her right hand was pressed tight over her chest.

"Are you OK, Bettie?" he asked.

"I'm fine. It's what the physician calls a little hypertension. I need to watch my blood pressure. But I'll be OK," she said as she rose to leave, fumbling nervously in her bag. "I'll see you and Mrs. Whitman tomorrow."

"Well, maybe we could help you with getting a better car—"

"Judge Whitman?"

"Yes, Bettie?"

"You say Lawrence doesn't love Georgia," she said.

"He barely knows her," he said.

"Oh, I think he knows her," she said, laughing quietly. "But did you ever love Lawrence? You never seemed to show it. It's only recently, since Robert died, that you seem to be showing the boy any warmth."

Bettie's words had fallen on his heart like a heavy club. He could do nothing but sit silently in front of this woman, stone-faced and graven. She'd spoken a troublesome truth for which he had no satisfactory reply. And while he was pondering that, a further thought formed in his mind. What was so wrong with Georgia after all? She was Bettie's daughter, a good girl, and salt of the earth. What more was needed than that?

"And I know that I shouldn't say this, Judge," Bettie said, interrupting his thoughts. "But I'm going to say it anyway."

She waited before saying more, to pick up her Kleenex to dab at her mouth. Then, after a few seconds, she looked at him calmly.

"Truth be told, Judge Whitman, I think that that there is more to the story of Robert's so-called accident than you think."

Theodore's hand jerked, knocking a mat off the table and onto the floor. He bent over to pick it up and place it back on the table.

"What? Now wait a minute, Bettie," he said, shaking his head. "You can't just say something like that now and not explain."

"With all due respect sir, why can't I?"

As anger flashed in his eyes, Bettie shrugged. She calmly opened her purse to see if her bus pass was easily to hand and nonchalantly snapped her purse shut.

"So that's it?" Theodore said, his booming voice causing the other patrons to turn their heads.

"Think so," Bettie said. "I'll see you and Mrs. Whitman on Monday. Bright and early."

Theodore remained at the table. His restless hands grabbed for his glass of ice water on the table, but he found that he was unable to pick it up in one hand because it was trembling. He raised the glass to his mouth with both hands, but as he did, the rim of the glass would not stay still against his lips and water splattered from the glass.

"Damn it," he said, as he used a napkin to dab at the water that had spilled onto his shirt.

He stewed in his thoughts, trying to piece together the last few minutes of the conversation, puzzled by her cryptic words. He generously tipped the waitress before taking his leave of the bar. His mind was elsewhere, and he didn't notice that when he politely said goodbye to both the waitress and the bar manager, neither of them returned the pleasantry.

The matter of Lawrence's choice of mate dwindled in comparison to the larger question of Robert's death, he thought. Why did Bettie think that Robert's accident was anything other than just that?

25

The house was blessedly empty of family that Monday morning. Theodore had gotten up at sunrise to get to the court early and Lawrence was off to the law library at Penn to study. There was no need to rush to be on call or at service for others, the age-old hallmark of a good Black woman.

She'd dreaded Teddy's meeting with Bettie and had made him promise to tell her everything immediately after it was over. And he did. He called her from a pay phone down the street from McGillin's to let her know how things had gone.

Mamie looked at the alarm clock and enjoyed a long leisurely stretch under her perfectly white quilt. Then she got up to shower and dress and padded downstairs to the kitchen. She'd given considerable thought to what she wanted to say to Bettie. She'd also given the same amount of thought to what she might hear.

They'd had hundreds of talks in the past, but not like this. Her heart skipped as the insight came that this morning's discussion would be of an entirely different order. Dressed in a Lilly Pulitzer white cotton shift with pink polka dots, Mamie's hands trembled slightly as she took two teacups from the top cupboard and put them on the counter. Then she took out a Tupperware container of her specialty—homemade lemon bars. They were filled with lemony sweetness and layered with a thick rim of confectioner sugar. Bettie loved them, she knew. She'd watched more than once as Bettie devoured half a dozen in a single sitting during one of her coffee breaks.

Mamie and Theodore's lives had reached a kind of angle of repose. Of course, there would always be the dark days when the phantom of their past transgressions reared its ugly head. The days when he refused to wear his wedding ring, the days when she let hers idle in a tiny gold bowl that she left on her polished bureau. But for the most part, they had gotten through those difficult days, surprised by the love that they still harbored for each other.

She hummed as she scooted around the table, placing two red intricately woven placemats that Bettie had gifted them one Christmas, followed by a chilled white creamer with plastic wrap on it—fresh out of the refrigerator—and a tiny sugar bowl and spoon. Her mind then turned to the meeting she would shortly be having with Bettie. One thing puzzled her. Teddy had told Bettie that Lawrence did not want to marry Georgia. However, Mamie had not heard him say that definitively. Whenever she asked, he chose not to answer, gruffly changing the subject. She knew that Teddy was against the marriage, and she wondered if Lawrence was simply toeing the line that his father had established. But whatever the case, Teddy had left her instructions for the sit-down with Bettie. Her job was to convince Bettie that to whatever degree Georgia might love Lawrence, they wanted their only remaining son to stay the course. It was not time for him to take a divergent path, particularly given all that they'd invested in the boy since Robert had died.

* * *

Bettie used the large brass knocker and waited a moment. Then she used her set of house keys to open the door to the Whitman home.

"It's only me!" she said as she entered the house.

She arrived just as Mamie had poured two glasses of ice water and set them on the table. The stifling August heat had spiraled into a torrential downpour, rain cascading down in buckets on the window-panes. Bettie was in her stocking feet when she came into the kitchen, having hung up her raincoat in the foyer closet and peeled off both her galoshes and shoes. She went directly to the cupboard where she kept an extra pair of white running shoes. Then she put her black purse—damp from the rain—in its usual place in the corner of the kitchen counter, next to the large aluminum toaster. She took note of the set table at which Mamie was already seated.

"One of your Bridge ladies coming over for breakfast?"

Mamie didn't answer, and Bettie didn't press. She was occasionally grumpy in the morning, and it had become worse since Robert's passing.

"Care for some coffee, Mrs. W?"

Sometimes, Bettie just didn't feel like calling her Mamie as she'd countlessly requested.

"Yes, I'd love some," Mamie said, turning around.

She noticed that although Bettie was wearing the same black knit knee-length skirt that she always wore, she was wearing a new blouse. It was a pretty floral blouse with tiny pink and blue petals and cap sleeves.

"Please, Bettie, I want to talk to you," Mamie said as Bettie put the coffee on. "Please come sit down with me at the table."

Mamie saw weariness etched into Bettie's face as she grudgingly sat down next to her. There was no mistaking the awkwardness between the two women. They had known each other for more than twenty years and were usually comfortable in each other's company, chatting about whatever came to their minds. But this time was different. It involved their children, and it was intensely personal. It was Mamie and not Bettie who poured both ladies coffee. Black for her, cream and Sweet'N Low for Bettie.

"Thank you," Bettie said after her coffee had been poured. "Now, please, no more meandering around. Can we please just get to it?"

"Get to what?"

"To whatever it is that Judge Whitman has asked you to convince me of," Bettie replied with an uncharacteristic bluntness that took Mamie by surprise. "Because frankly I think that all that needed to be said has already been said between the judge and me."

Mamie watched as Bettie casually picked up one of the home-made lemon bars Mamie had made and bit off a corner. She took a sip of coffee and looked at Mamie across the breakfast table before continuing.

"In case you think it's not true, I am grateful for your and your husband's generous offer of paying for Georgia to attend Hampton University," she said as she used a Kleenex to dab at one eye and then the other. "But, the fact of the matter, ma'am, is I believe I know what was really behind your husband's decision to help. It was to do what-ever he could to put some distance between your son and Georgia."

Both women sat in silence for a few minutes, idly listening to the classical music station that Mamie had on at a low volume. It was scarcely audible above the din of the summer rain that pounded away on the trees and ran down outdoor drainpipes. Mamie clasped her hands tightly on the table, breathing in audibly.

"Please listen to me. I know that this is hard, but Claire Scott—"

"Yes, I know who she is," Bettie interjected.

"Well, she is just…she's just devastated about the matter and…"

She paused for a second to look at Bettie, who peered incredu-lously back at her.

"She's stopped eating."

"Really now?" Bettie asked. She laughed heartily as though she had just heard a good joke. "Now, well ain't that a shame. I hope she survives," she added dryly.

Mamie thought about the carefully selected garnet earrings that she and Theodore had bought for Claire, a graduation gift from the

Whitman family. Claire had beamed when she had dropped off the present. But looking back on the day, she wondered why it was she and not Lawrence who'd brought the gift to Claire. That should have been his role, not hers. Everyone —from the professional-class parishioners of Oak Street church, from Jemma and Sigrid, to their other friends—knew that Lawrence was sweet on the Scott girl. The odds of Lawrence and Georgia having a future together were slim. She knew that, Teddy knew that—why couldn't Bettie accept it?

"Your daughter…Georgia…had no right to intrude on that relationship."

"Just what relationship are you speaking of?" Bettie said, fury swirling in her eyes. After last night, she had not expected to go another round on the matter.

"The relationship between Claire and my son."

Mamie hated doing Theodore's bidding and her voice trembled as she spoke.

"Now, let's not make this any harder than it needs to be," she said. "Theodore and I have discussed this at length. Lawrence is about to start law school, Bettie. Even if he wanted to marry Georgia, now is simply not the right time."

"Now, Mamie," Bettie said. "You and me, we've been through a lot together, haven't we? We've shared things during our little talks over the years."

Mamie—frozen in her seat—didn't reply. Bettie took the opportunity to reach out her hand over the table to the clasped hands of Mamie, in just the same manner that Judge Whitman had done to her only the night before. Mamie felt Bettie's hand softly touch the back of hers and let it stay there.

"I know that in your heart of hearts, Mamie, this is not you. It's not in your nature to drive a wedge between Lawrence and Georgia. You know we're good people."

She paused, unwilling to grovel in front of Mamie.

"The kids have known each other since they were children. Played together since they were children. But your husband has this idea in his head that like should marry like. With all due respect, he should read his Bible more.

"There are those verses in James 2 about a man in fine attire and one in shabby clothing. The good Lord commands us to show no partiality between them. James says, 'Listen, my beloved brothers, has not God chosen those who are poor in the world to be rich in faith and heirs of the kingdom, which he has promised to those who love him?'"

"I know," Mamie said, her eyes red and swollen. "Let me try and explain. He thinks—"

"I already know what he thinks," Bettie interjected sharply. "But what do you think?"

Mamie turned her head away so that only her profile was in view.

"It's a matter of proportion," she said. "After all that we have done for you, for Georgia…"

"We should just be content, accept our lot and shut our mouths. That's it, isn't it?" Bettie said, finishing her sentence. "Don't try and join a world we wouldn't understand. Well, to me, that sounds a lot like white folk talking down to our folk."

Mamie didn't reply and instead closed her eyes.

"That's it, isn't it?" Bettie asked again. When she'd finished speaking, she abruptly picked up her coffee cup and plate. Then—as had been her habit over the years—she reached over to pick up Mamie's.

But Mamie quickly patted her hand over the cup. "I'll do it," she said.

Bettie got up from the table and grabbed a tissue from the Kleenex box that was resting on the windowsill next to a flowering African violet.

"You know, white folks have given us a lot of trouble over the years," she said. "And I don't mean good trouble. I mean bad trouble. But Lord help me with the rich Black folk, with all of your opinions and judgments, trying to tell folk how to live their lives."

She blew her nose hard, threw the Kleenex away, and then went to the closet to grab her raincoat—one of Mamie's cast offs from some years before. "Well, here's my two cents' worth. I may not be an every Sunday type church goer, but God knows that I am an everyday believer. It's like Madame Walker said, I'm not ashamed of my past and I'm damned sure not ashamed of my humble beginnings."

She put on her shoes and galoshes and then checked inside her purse to make sure that her keys were there. Then, with coat on and purse in hand, she turned to confront her employer before opening the kitchen's back door.

"All Georgia's ever wanted while watching your son breeze through college was to have a shot at advancement. No more, no less. I've spoken to her, and for that reason we will graciously accept your and Mr. Whitman's kind offer to pay for her schooling. But I'll let you in on a little secret. Don't think for one minute that it will stop her loving Lawrence, 'cause it most certainly will not."

Before Mamie could reply, Bettie turned her back on her employer.

All she could do was watch as Bettie opened the door and stepped out into the rain, leaving her umbrella forgotten and propped by the door.

* * *

When Lawrence got home from the law library, he found his mother in the kitchen. She was still seated at the kitchen table and had not moved since Bettie had left. He could see from her wet and anguished face that she had been sobbing bitter tears.

"What is it? What's wrong, Mom?" he asked as he walked to the refrigerator, grabbed a coke and filled a glass to the brim with ice from the dispenser on the door.

"Son, can you please tell me this," Mamie said in a voice so low that Lawrence had to lean in to hear her. "Can you tell me if you love her?"

"Who, Mom?"

"Georgia, son."

He gazed unwaveringly into his mother's eyes. "I love her, Mom," he said.

The phone rang and Mamie glanced at her watch. It was 4:00 p.m., the exact time that Shirley Scott had agreed she would call Mamie to get an update on things.

26

Bettie had never missed Jimmy as much as she did on the drive home from the Whitmans' house. With the rain coming down in sheets, she wondered if the engine would give up the ghost in the city where someone might need her car even more than she did. She clenched her teeth and drove.

She parked in front of her row home—as she had done thousands of times before—and calmly got out of her car, taking her purse with her. As she walked the short path from the car to her door, she stopped dead in her tracks and looked at the small huddling of shrubs that were on either side of her doorway. They glistened with tiny beads of rainwater under the emerging sun.

"How do you feel?" Bettie said as she entered the house and saw Georgia.

She was seated at the kitchen table and was just about to put her bologna and mayonnaise sandwich into her mouth when her mother had opened the door. "Better," Georgia said. "I should be able to return to work tomorrow."

She watched as her mother peeled off her coat, took off her galoshes and her shoes and walked wearily in her stockinged feet to the table.

When she sat down, the table lurched to the side. The folded piece of cardboard that had been placed under one of the legs had come away.

"You're home early," Georgia said, taking another bite into her sandwich and putting it down. She opened a snack-sized bag of Fritos that her mother put in front of her.

"Yes, thought I'd come home to check on you…how's the pain?"

"It's OK. My back feels better now. I took the pain reliever the doctor gave me." Eyes wide and anxious for any news about Lawrence, who hadn't bothered to call as promised, Georgia asked, "So, what happened between you and Mrs. Whitman?"

"Well, it's both good news and bad news…. The good news, baby, is that you are going to Hampton University after all. The bad news is that they're still saying that the Whitman boy ain't in the offing… at least for you."

"You don't call the shots, Mom, and neither do they," Georgia said.

"Say that again?"

"You don't get to make decisions for me," Georgia said firmly, and as she spoke Bettie noted how confident and assured her daughter had become.

"Baby," Bettie said, her voice suddenly becoming an oasis of understanding, "let it be, hear me? Just let it be.

"He's not worth the trouble," she added exhaustedly as the mid-afternoon sun poured through the window, lighting up the small room where they sat. "But to tell you the truth, men rarely are. So, when you find a good one, it's best to keep him."

27

Late August 1981

A gathering of vacationing folks were leisurely seated in the lobby on Ivory-colored wicker chairs, sections of the *New York Times* on their laps and cups filled with steaming, dark roast coffee on tiny oval-shaped wooden tables beside them. A few guests were lined up at the reception desk of the Kelley House on the Vineyard. At the head of the queue was a distinguished looking Black man, dressed nattily in a blue tweed blazer and perfectly creased gray pants. He reluctantly approached the counter.

"Good morning, sir. How may I help you?" the young man staffing the desk asked politely.

The man leaned forward and whispered that he was there to make a complaint, which took the young man behind the counter aback. Rarely did patrons report anything other than exceptional service.

"I'm so sorry to hear that, sir. Would you mind telling me the nature of the complaint?"

The man looked hesitantly over at his wife. Her large brown eyes glared back at him, silently indicating that if he didn't complete his report a miserable day was going to follow.

The man coughed, as if a piece of food was caught in his throat.

"It was the noise coming from the room next door, room 204," he finally said.

"And what room did you say you were in, sir?"

"I didn't, but my wife and I were in room 205."

"Would you mind telling me the nature of the noise, sir?"

The man's face reddened as he tried to find a delicate way of saying that a young couple making love had kept him and his wife awake until the early hours.

"Shall we just say that we heard a young couple enjoying each other's company," he eventually said.

"I understand, sir. I'm so sorry to hear that," the young man said. "Would you mind if I went to confer with my manager?"

In less than a minute, he was back. "Again, sir, my manager and I are so sorry that your evening was disturbed. As a recompense for your discomfort, please allow us to deduct ten percent from your bill when you check out."

* * *

In Room 204, a soft blue morning on the Vineyard wafted pleasantly through the window. A gorgeous young woman lay languid and half attired on the bed, next to a gently slumbering man. She was halfway listening to Marvin Gaye's "What's Going On" on the radio.

The man's hand was casually draped across the woman's taut nipples. She lay perfectly still, luxuriating in the touch of the only man she had ever loved. Breeze after breeze gently wafted in through the window that overlooked the Atlantic. The room itself was utter perfection. From where she drowsily lay, she could see a small bank of caramel-colored sand by an expanse of serene water.

A lone tear ambled from the corner of her eye. She bit her lip as it slid down her cheek and onto her lips. She tasted its wet saltiness with her tongue. She should not be here, she thought. Yet here she was.

She felt no shame in giving in to him so freely, and with such abandon the night before, but she blushed to think that their passionate lovemaking might well have been widely heard through the thin walls of the hotel.

As pure morning sunlight streamed into their perfectly appointed hotel room, a shadow from the birch tree just outside their window flickered on the large headboard behind her head. The woman moved, peeling back the soft duvet that matched the airy, beige décor of the room. And before the young man beside her had a chance to open his eyes again and fully adjust to his surroundings, she began kissing him on his lips, which he returned with fresh ardor. Rousing himself from slumber at last, he turned over and hastily enveloped the young woman in his arms.

The intensity with which he made love to her left her breathless.

"Whoa, there," she murmured to him afterward, her lips grazing his long neck. "Babe, you're acting like you better get all that lovemaking in now, before you got to do some serious time."

He smiled back at her.

"So, what's your rap?" she quipped in a feather soft voice.

Lying quietly next to her, looking up at the ceiling fan, he said, "Well, I guess you never really know a person for sure."

"That so?"

"Could be a murderer for all you know."

Georgia laughed in the uncomfortable way people do when they've missed the joke. But then her laughter stopped as she heard the clanking of a trolley come to a stop just outside their room. She was famished, so she grabbed her robe and put it on just before a knock on the door announced that their breakfast had arrived. Smiling back at Lawrence, she opened the door to allow the trolley to be brought in.

* * *

The middle-aged Black couple, seated by the pastry wagon, were finishing up their breakfast of poached eggs, link sausage, and wheat toast, when a young couple leisurely strolled from the hotel foyer into the street outside.

Jemma Lavington was drinking freshly squeezed orange juice that spurted out of her mouth as the couple was taken to their table, which had an unspoiled view of the harbor.

"That's Lawrence Whitman! Mamie's son," she said, turning toward her husband, who quickly put down his *Vineyard Gazette* to get a closer look.

"Yes, I see," he said. "But who is that with him?" he asked, admiring the girl with a mass of long braids with gold beads on the ends.

"I know exactly who she is," Jemma said. "That's Georgia, the daughter of the Whitmans' maid."

28

A sheer, cloudless sky hung like a vast blue canopy above the Petite Café, which was where Lawrence and his father had agreed to meet for an old-fashioned peace talk. The café was an old-world charmer on a red cobblestoned road in the part of the city where the streets were named after trees—Locust, Chestnut, and Pine. Quaint narrow sidewalks were strewn with auburn leaves that had fallen from an abundant array of shade trees.

Lawrence had scarcely had a chance to say hello to his father, whom he'd found tapping his feet impatiently outside the café's front door, when a heavyset white man dressed in a medical orderly outfit touched Theodore on the shoulder.

"There's a line," he said, pointing behind him.

Theodore, in his new seersucker suit and freshly barbered haircut, didn't appreciate the stranger's admonition. He turned, red faced, toward the man, but before he could open his mouth Lawrence intervened, stepping between them.

"It's OK, Pop. Does it really mean so much to you? To be right, even when it's clear that you're in the wrong? And to get yourself all riled up in the process?"

Irritation showed in his father's face, but he allowed Lawrence to guide them to the back of the line. Once there, their eyes were drawn to a scene that was playing out at the entrance to the café.

There were two little girls, one white and one Black, both about eight years old, standing with their mothers in front of a giant gumball machine. The white girl's yellow-colored hair was pulled back into a ponytail and held by a candy-red ribbon. She wore a long University of Pennsylvania sweatshirt that covered her black leggings. She tugged at her mother as the little Black girl watched, standing next to her elderly grandmother.

"Momma, can I have quarter for the machine?" the little girl asked.

The mother reached into her pocket and dug out a quarter, which she gave to the girl and then, distracted, turned to size up the line ahead of them.

The little Black girl also asked her grandmother for a quarter. Her thick, black hair had been neatly brushed and a black-colored band held it in place. She was overdressed for the day, in a woolen, maroon colored coat that had been buttoned all the way up to her neck.

"Don't have a quarter, baby," her grandmother softly replied. "That quarter is going toward my breakfast treat to you."

The other little girl, listening, turned to her mother and said, "That little girl needs a quarter, too. Do you have one for her?"

The grandmother's eyes turned swiftly toward the little girl and stared at her, finally resting on the mother who was digging out another coin from her purse.

"We don't need your charity," the grandmother said sharply.

"And we don't need your ignorance," the white mother declared.

"What did you say?"

The exchanges continued at ever increasing volume until a manager came out and attempted to deal with the problem. Meanwhile, both girls stood aside, and the white girl shared with the Black girl one of the bright yellow and red gumballs she's gotten from the machine.

It was obvious that the manager's entreaties were having no effect, so Lawrence said, "Do something, Dad! You're a judge! Talk to them. Make them understand! Isn't that your job?"

"Since when?" Theodore asked, still eyeing the white orderly who was now at the front of the line. "I only get involved when a crime has been committed. It's not my job to referee bad behavior, son, white or Black."

* * *

Their mood lifted when father and son entered the restaurant. The café had tall sparkling clean windows that brought the sight of bustling commuters into the quaintly decorated space, which had pink marble topped tables dotted around a black and white checkerboard tiled floor. Pert waitresses in gingham aprons with painted-on smiles darted from table to table in white Ked sneakers. The aroma of their specialty hot-buttered cinnamon rolls tantalized within seconds of entering.

The breakfast meeting was timed so that Lawrence could jet off to DC afterward for an interview with his father's former colleague, who was now the Dean of Georgetown Law School. He knew that his father was counting on him to put his best foot forward in the interview, and he was determined to do just that.

More than anything, Lawrence yearned to please his father. He sensed Theodore's newfound interest in him since Robert died and he wanted to fill those shoes. He also wanted to do what his father wanted—extricating himself from Bettie's daughter. But he couldn't. When he went to bed at night it was Georgia, and not Claire, who he saw in his dreams.

After they were ushered to an oval table for two by the window in the back, they sat down and exchanged pleasantries. They were civil to each other, and for a while Lawrence thought that was how the conversation would continue. But it did not.

"Fix your jacket at the collar, Lawrence," Theodore said gruffy.

Lawrence frowned. He'd done exactly what his father had asked him to on the phone that morning. "Dress appropriately son," Theodore had instructed him on the phone. "Please don't embarrass me by coming to the café dressed in your filthy jeans and sneakers."

"Who's going to see us there, Dad?"

"Don't matter. Colored folk are judged differently than white folk. In my day people didn't want to wear jeans out. Jeans were associated with farm work."

"Well, who the hell cares what people think?" Lawrence wanted to say, but thought better of it.

So, Lawrence was dressed as his father had ordered, in gray slacks and a white oxford button-down shirt under a navy-blue blazer. He felt stung by his father's rebuke but tried not to show it as he adjusted the collar of his blazer.

"I have to be perfect, don't I, Dad?" he murmured. "Like Robert," he added quietly.

Theodore ignored him. Lawrence watched him grip the arms of his chair tightly and stare into the distance with a faraway look.

"Damn it, Lawrence," he said eventually. "Why couldn't you have just kept your fly zipped up?"

"What do you mean, Pop? Keep my fly zipped up?"

Whitman sighed heavily.

"The Lavingtons," he said finally. "They saw you at the Kelley House. I know all about it. Seems you and that girl Georgia made your presence known that evening. I'm not sure whether your mother and I could ever show our faces in there again."

Feeling beaten, Lawrence sulked in his chair. Theodore turned from his son and glanced around the sunlit room. He waved down a waitress, who hurried over to them and asked if they were ready to order.

"I'm afraid we're not ready yet. But in the meantime, you can bring us both some coffee," he said perfunctorily, relishing any opportunity to be in charge.

"Yes, sir."

The waitress smiled and walked away as Theodore turned his attention back to his son.

"This is serious business. It's your future we're talking about. You do know that."

"Yes, sir… I'm sorry, Dad," Lawrence mumbled, eyes cast downward.

The waitress came back with their coffee and asked if they were ready to order. Lawrence gestured to his father to go first.

"French toast, maple bacon, and an OJ," Theodore said. "And I could use some cream for my coffee."

"I'm sorry, sir. It will be right over."

"And you?" Whitman asked Lawrence, pursing his lips.

"I'll have the same," Lawrence said meekly.

Both men contemplated their coffee cups as the waitress hurried from the table.

"The thing is," Lawrence said the second the waitress left, "I don't think any of this would have happened if you and Mom hadn't been so fixated on my marrying Claire. I like her very much. Don't get me wrong. She's very pretty, but—"

His father cut him off.

"No, son. Let me stop you right there. Let's cut to the point, shall we?"

Lawrence couldn't help but notice the sweat gathering on his father's forehead and around the edges of the starched, white collar of his shirt. He wondered why his father had to always dress in business attire when he was in the city. Why couldn't he just chill out sometimes and relax?

"I came from Tennessee at a time when opportunities were just opening for Black folk. And I mean *just*. There was still enough bigotry going around that the very simple act of a Negro man coming out of his family home to walk a mile or two down a country road at nighttime to go to the store and buy a box of milk duds for his children was taking his life in his hands. It was an act of courage."

The conversation stopped as the waitress approached and delivered their order.

"Listen here," his father continued, "I have sweated and toiled to build the life that you and your mother now enjoy so that you could have a better start in life than I did. So that you don't have to go shuffling and jiving through life to earn a damned quarter to buy a damned gumball for your child. Do I really deserve more suffering than what I've already gone through?"

"Calm down, Dad!" Lawrence said. He'd noticed that that some of the diners had started to raise their eyes from their cinnamon crusted French toast and stare at them.

"No, I won't calm down!" Theodore yelled. "Fall in line, son, that's all I'm asking. Be a man! A respectable Black man!"

Theodore raised his hand to his chest and grimaced.

"Leave Bettie's daughter alone. Settle for the girl who can give you—and my future grandchildren—a decent future."

He took a long swig from his glass of orange juice as though it were a Manhattan. "What you did, in taking Georgia to the Kelley House...and the spectacle that you made that night...Well, it's...it's unconscionable."

They sat for a moment in numb silence, listening to a Frank Sinatra medley being piped into the room. It had been years since Robert's death and Theodore was still grieving the loss of his favorite son. Lawrence recognized that, and he yearned to fill the void that had been left. He looked across the table and felt as though he could read his father's mind. Robert shared so many attributes with his father—a disciplined approach to life, a fierce drive to succeed, athletic prowess—that it felt natural that he would bestow more attention on Robert than he did on Lawrence. But Robert was gone. It was Lawrence's turn now.

Theodore cleared his throat. He had just devoured his French toast with three strips of crisp, maple-glazed bacon on the side. Lawrence was surprised to see a smile suddenly light up his face.

"About your interview with Dean Chadwick tomorrow, son. You should bear in mind that the Jesuits are fine people. They built Georgetown from the ground up. When you think about the Jesuits, think scholarship. Think advancement."

Bunch of crap, Lawrence thought.

"Attending Georgetown matters—" his father continued.

"Hmmm, I think I remember reading how the Jesuits owned slaves," Lawrence said, interrupting him. "Owned people like us, like pigs in pens."

He watched as his father nodded contemplatively.

"Yes, that's true. But that was then, and this is now. You need to think about your future."

To emphasize his point, Theodore slammed his fist on the table, sending a dinner knife flying. It landed at the feet of an adjacent table where an elderly white couple were just finishing up their meal. Their silent glares were a wordless admonishment. Theodore stared back at the frowning couple until, with a shake of their heads, they continued drinking their coffees.

The elderly white couple, now lingering over their second cup of coffee, their plates long since removed, swiveled their heads sharply toward the Whitmans once more. Lawrence gripped the edge of the table with his hands. He grimaced as he watched his father's eyes focus on his shaking hands.

"OK, Dad," Lawrence said penitently. "I get the message. I'll stop seeing Georgia and I'll do my best to mend things with Claire."

He hesitated, stumbling over his words, before adding with quiet ferocity, "And I'll nail the meeting with your friend, the Georgetown dean, tomorrow. I know how much it meant for you to go there, and how much it would mean to you if I went there, too."

Lawrence moved a white vase holding a single red rose to the side. He wanted his father to get a good look at him.

"I want to make you proud of me, Dad," he said feebly, not bothering to brush tears that meandered down his face.

"I…I may never live up to the promise of Robert. After all, who could? But I promise you that I will do my best to make you and Mom happy so that your struggles were not in vain."

"OK, son…OK," Theodore said hurriedly as his eyes darted here and there, as though searching for something, a wall or a barrier, to hide the raw feelings that had bubbled to the surface.

Theodore was anxious to go. He downed his glass of ice water and placed the glass back down on the table.

"I don't want you to be Robert," he said quietly. "I just want you to get a good degree from Georgetown, join a decent law firm, and marry someone who will add to this family's status. Is that too much to ask?"

Lawrence tried to hold back his anger.

"Dad," he said. "Don't you see? Those are exactly the same things you wanted from Robert. You're just transferring them onto me.

"Don't I have any say in this?" he added, raising his voice and slamming his knife and fork on the table. "How many times do I have to tell you. *I'm not Robert!*"

Theodore looked around the café and saw the elderly white couple once again staring at him and Lawrence in reproof.

"I know," he said quietly, attempting to calm his agitated son. "It's just that your mother and I want the best for you. We don't want you to stumble as so many have before."

"I'm sure you do, Dad," Lawrence replied. "And I want you and Mom to be proud of me. But you have to allow me to make some of my own decisions."

"Fair enough," a wilted and defeated Judge Whitman said stiffly as breakfast wound to an end. "Just make sure you make the right ones. You finish up your meal. I've got to go."

He placed a crisp twenty-dollar bill on the table and smiled wearily at his son.

"One day," he said whimsically, "one day you and me, we're gonna see eye to eye."

"Yes, sir," Lawrence replied crisply, as Theodore pushed his chair back from the table. "Or die trying," he mumbled under his breath.

He watched as his father seamlessly weaved through tables to the exit. Every fiber in Lawrence's body screamed to rush after him and apologize for making the mistake of not being Robert, the favored son.

But it was too late. His father had already left the café, leaving him with an uncomfortable decision that he had to make.

29

September 1981

Twenty-four-year-old Georgia Smythe peered at the street outside her bedroom window. She was lying in the creaky twin bed in her room, which had moved not one inch since her father had moved it there the summer before he'd died. She looked at the sole tree outside her window, its russet-colored leaves stunning in the morning light.

Using her fingers, she rubbed the area of the windowpane that she had fogged up with her breath, hoping to get a better look at the object in her sight that gave her joy.

She heard her mother busying herself in the kitchen.

"I'm going to see him today," she whispered, smiling. "I love him," she added, pressing the pads of her hand to the cold window.

* * *

They set off in her mother's car at noon for the Whitmans' house.

Georgia sat quietly in the passenger seat, head bobbing to "Like a Virgin."

"Do you know what Mamie is going to say?"

"It's Mrs. Whitman," Bettie corrected her. "And no, Georgia. I'm afraid I do not."

223

"Will I see Lawrence?'

"Yes, Miss Mamie said that he will be there."

Georgia had driven to the Whitman house many times in the past—the familiar ride that started in her neighborhood, the urban bonfire of metal and smoke and shattered dreams, to green stretches of countryside. But she'd never remembered the drive taking so long before.

When they eventually arrived, Georgia asked, "Aren't you coming in?"

"No, baby. I'm afraid that this one's all yours."

She smiled as she got out of the car and was about to walk in when she looked as though she'd forgotten something. She leaned into the passenger window.

"Mom, I'm sure Lawrence can drive me home," she said.

"I'll be here," Bettie said firmly. "Don't make me wait too long."

Georgia took the stone stairs that led to the Whitmans' front doors two at a time, her heart full and believing that the mild morning boded well for the day. But her hopes were dashed when she noticed that Mrs. Whitman had not greeted her at the door as she usually did—with a smile warm enough to melt an Antarctica iceberg.

"Won't you come in, Georgia?" Mamie said, looking up toward the stairwell where Lawrence was.

"Thank you, Mrs. Whitman," Georgia said, and began to peel off her navy and polka dot boots.

"You have a guest, son," Mamie called up the stairs.

Lawrence scrambled downstairs and watched as Georgia finished taking off her boots in the entryway. He looked at her as she stood to face him, beaming.

"I'm sorry, but could you put them back on, Georgia? I want us to go outside and talk for a minute," he said as walked to the door and put on his shoes.

Lawrence opened the door for her and together they walked to the tree that had become the emblem of their starkly divergent childhoods. She could see that he had been crying.

"What's this all about?" she asked.

They sat down on the familiar patch of ground in the woody knoll by the old Oak tree and leant their backs against its trunk. Georgia started to cough, so Lawrence removed the coat that he was wearing and draped it over her shoulders like a shawl.

"I'm just a little cold," she said. And he knew—as she spoke the words, a little gruffly—that she didn't mean it as a complaint. It was more of an observation, something to fill in the cavern that they both knew was brimming with sadness. His coat smelled, she noticed, the same as the leather chairs in his father's study that her mother often had to polish with a special oil. She told him this and he threw his head back and laughed, exposing his long neck over his white turtle-neck shirt.

"I...I...enjoyed..." she said, unable to finish her sentence.

"Our night," he said, completing her thought. "Me, too, Georgia. Me, too."

"So, what's wrong then?" she asked.

"My father would like me to...to take a hiatus."

"From what?" she inquired in a small voice.

"From you."

His coat was no longer draped around her shoulders. She was wearing it now. Wearing it and staring at him.

"Is this about Claire?" she asked.

"No," he said, then, "Well, yes. It is. Georgia, you know that she was my girlfriend before we got together."

To the east, a beautiful red cardinal perched on a tree branch. It seemed to turn toward the couple before opening its black rimmed mouth to sing. There was, Lawrence noticed, an implicit urgency to the clear, bell-like call, as if sounding a warning to him.

"Claire may have been your girlfriend," Georgia said. "But I know that you don't love her. I don't know whether it's me you love, but it's certainly not her."

When he didn't reply, she sighed deeply.

"Well, I guess it's OK because your mom and dad have paid for me to attend Hampton University, so I'll be out of your way."

"What will you be studying?"

"Social work," she said wistfully, looking past him at the red cardinal that was still singing its warning to them. Georgia bravely tried to smile at him, but her fortitude gave way like a snapped branch in a storm, and she began to cry.

"Now, now," he said. "Why the tears?"

"Tell me the truth, Lawrence," she said as she moved closer to him. "Why are you acting like this?"

"To be honest, it's my father. I'm doing what my father asks me to do," he said stiffly. "Now that I'm his only son, I need to stay the course. Attend law school and make plans with Claire. Blood is thicker than water, he says, and I need to honor the sacrifices he's made for me."

"But what about me?" she asked. "What about honoring me?"

She smiled her funny crackerjack smile at him, and he felt an uncontainable urge to comfort and protect her. Without thinking, and as if it were the most natural thing in the world, he bent her head back and kissed her fully on the mouth until she sighed.

Finally lifting his mouth from hers, he said, "I have to do what he asks because of…something I need to atone for, something that happened a long time ago."

"What is it?" Georgia asked insistently, remembering the evening they made love and he'd talked in his sleep. "Does this have something to do with Robert?"

He didn't answer, but instead reached out to hold her chin gently in the palm of his hand.

"I love you, and I will always be there for you," he said. "Perhaps I'll come and visit you at college in Virginia."

"Yes, please do," she said, smiling. "Although I know you won't."

"I'll make it there somehow," he said. "But it's getting cold now. It's time to go."

As they walked back to the house together, he stumbled over a piece of rock on the path, and in doing so grabbed her arm in a knee-jerk reaction. They continued walking arm in arm as she began to recite a poem to him that she had recently memorized.

> *"How do I love thee? Let me count the ways.*
> *I love thee to the depth and breadth and height*
> *My soul can reach, when feeling out of sight*
> *For the ends of being and ideal grace.*
> *I love thee to the level of everyday's*
> *Most quiet need, by sun and candlelight,"*

He made them both stop a few yards from the back door of the house.

"Wait…who wrote that?" he asked.

The sound of the little gold beads on the tips of her hair jingled as she turned to look at him, his face proud and strong as a Fulani herdsman bronzed before the fire.

"Oh, just a great female poet you might have heard of," she said. "Her first name is Elizabeth."

* * *

Mamie was feeling good that evening. Her and Theodore's relationship had reverted to solid ground in a way that they had not enjoyed since Robert's passing. They'd begun to rediscover themselves through simple things, like feeding the ducks at Valley Green Park, or more grand occasions, such as going to hear the Philadelphia Orchestra with Riccardo Muti conducting.

And while she didn't show it, she was quietly delighted when she heard that, although her son's little talk with Bettie's daughter had been difficult for him, he had gotten through it and he and Georgia were no longer an item. She was proud of him. She and Theodore had only one remaining son, and damn it, they were going to make something of him. When Shirley phoned, she could practically feel her hot breath through the phone wire as she'd waited to hear the news about when her son would call Claire. She frankly wasn't sure, she told her. He'd been coy about revealing his plans.

"But one thing's certain, Georgia is out of the picture. I'm sure he'll call Claire soon, very soon," she said, reassuringly to Shirley. "I'm certain of it."

PART THREE

30

September 1984

At 10:00 p.m., Mamie was busying herself, washing and drying the dishes from the evening meal and humming to herself. Bettie had always told her to leave whatever dishes she didn't finish in the sink for her to do in the morning, but she wanted to ease her load rather than add to it. Teddy was exhausted from his day in court, so he had gone to bed.

"Come to bed soon, petal," he called as he went up the stairs. He only called her "petal" when he wanted to be endearing, and she relished his newfound adoration.

She finished the dishes and then sat at the kitchen table with a cup of sassafras tea to read the society page of the *Philadelphia Tribune*. She became lost in thought, picturing where Claire and Lawrence's wedding might take place. If she had her druthers, it would be held at their beloved Cape cottage in June. Perhaps in the airy space just behind the veranda of their salt box home, where they'd pitch a bright red canopy where Lawrence and Claire would stand and say their vows. Lost in her thoughts, the knock on the front door didn't register at first.

Then the knocking began again, this time with urgency. No one showed up uninvited at this time of night to their front door, so her initial thought was for their safety. By now, Teddy would be in the deep fog of sleep, and she wondered whether or not to wake him. And then she remembered that Lawrence had borrowed the car. He was planning to move out soon and she'd noticed that he was spending less and less time with them. She threw the door open, thinking that he'd forgotten his keys.

But instead, it was Robert's childhood friend, Lemuel, who was standing with his lean shoulder pressed against the door frame.

"Hi, Mrs. Whitman," he said. "May I come in?"

Mamie hadn't seen Lemuel since Robert's funeral, but it only took one look into Lem's two brown limpid eyes for the memory of her beloved eldest son to come surging back to her.

During Robert's teenage years, Lemuel had been a fixture in the household on Saturday evenings when Lawrence and Robert's friends congregated in the basement pool room for hours, sustained by bowls of buttered popcorn and trash talk. But unlike Robert's other friends— who either biked to the house or had their parents drop them off and pick them up—Lemuel had to take two busses and then a train to the station closest to them.

She stared at Lemuel, lost in her thoughts.

"I'm so sorry to have startled you, Mrs. Whitman," he said politely. "I know it's late, but may I come in? I won't keep you long."

"Oh, I do apologize, Lemuel," she said, distractedly. "Yes, yes… please do come in."

She wondered why he had come. *It must be something serious for him to commute all the way from North Philly at this time of night*, she thought.

Lemuel followed Mamie through the house to the den, where a large white rug took up most of the space in the room. There were two chairs in the corner, one dark ebony and the other a red wicker. He chose to sit in the nearest one, which was the red wicker.

"Please sit down, Mrs. Whitman," he said, but she remained standing.

"Are you OK, Lemuel? I haven't seen you for so long."

She considered going upstairs to fetch Theodore, but the panicked look on Lemuel's face made her think better of it.

"Can you please tell me why you need to see me so urgently?" she asked.

Lemuel crossed his legs and then put his clasped hands on his knee. She watched as he opened his mouth, only to close it again. He breathed long and deeply before finally saying, "Ma'am, I think that you're going to want to sit down before you hear what I need to say to you tonight."

"Why do I need to sit down, Lemuel?" Mamie asked. "What are you going to tell me that's so awful that I need to sit down. What's happened? Is there something wrong? Do I need to go get Judge Whitman?"

He didn't answer, so she sat down in the ebony chair opposite him.

"So how you've been Lemuel?" she asked, changing the subject in order to encourage him to begin talking. "What are you doing with yourself these days?"

His head was slightly bowed, and for a moment she thought he was praying.

"Stayin' out of trouble, I guess," he eventually replied.

"Yes? Well, that's good. Where are you working right now?"

"Working in an automobile body shop in West Philly. My uncle owns it."

He watched as Mamie nodded appreciatively. She knew that there were few Black-owned enterprises in the city, although they were needed badly because most white folks still hired their own kind.

"So, tell me. What's this all about, Lemuel? No foolishness I hope."

"Oh, no, Mrs. Whitman, this ain't no foolishness. Ma'am, I came here to tell you that word on the street…"

He hesitated, and something about the rigid way he held his head made Mamie anxious. She gripped the arms of her chair.

"…is that Lawrence played a role in Robert's accident."

"But that can't be true," Mamie gasped. "What are you talking about, Lemuel?"

The memory of Robert's funeral, coupled with Lemuel's outlandish claim, curdled inside her. She stood up, ram rod straight.

"You get out of here, right now. You hear me?!"

"Please sit back down, Mrs. Whitman!" Lemuel pleaded. "It hurts me as much as it hurts you to tell you the truth, but it must be said… because the truth will come out somehow, someday. It will."

Like a reprimanded child, Mamie turned back around and sat down. Her first thought was of Teddy, whom she knew was snoring away upstairs. He would be blessedly oblivious to any noise downstairs. This was a farce, she decided. A trick. Something Lemuel had concocted to take advantage of the family, maybe with a financial motive in mind.

She surveyed the handsome boy, thin as a reed, who remained motionless in his chair. She reminded herself that this was still the same old Lemuel, her late son's best friend.

"Believe me, Mrs. Whitman," he said, looking anxiously at her. "I don't relish telling you this, but it must be said."

He cleared his throat and then kept his eyes firmly on Mamie.

"I heard it from a mutual friend of Carlton Lavington," he began. "I know you know the Lavington family, and I know they're rich, but Carlton has hung out a lot in the hood and many people think that he's…"

"Bad news," Mamie said, finishing his thought. "And his word is not to be trusted," she continued, beginning to think that this would turn out to be a mere piece of fiction.

"Yes," Lemuel said firmly. "But this mutual friend told me that Robert tripping and falling down the stairs during his jog that night was not entirely an accident. Carlton was there, waiting for Robert on the running track that evening. He was armed with a club or a stick, and when Robert saw him, he tripped and fell down the stairs. Carlton hates gay people and, well, it was Lawrence who tipped him off to where Robert would be that evening."

Mamie, like a confused child trying fit the pieces of a complicated jigsaw puzzle together, stared at Lemuel and then past him, to the framed photograph on the wall of the two brothers astride two ponies that had been taken at Valley Green Park. Lemuel began to speak again, but she interrupted him.

"Lemuel, let me get this straight. What you're telling me is that Robert was gay. You two...you and my Robert..." She started to cry softly.

"Yes, ma'am," Lemuel said. "I'm gay, and so was he. We both loved each other, you know," he said, waiting for her gaze to return to his.

Mamie had always known that she was a strong woman and that she came from robust stock. She knew that only 60 percent of Blacks had survived capture in Africa and the ordeal of the slave ship. "We are the descendants of slave ship survivors," her mother had told her. "Those whose heads bobbed above the water. Champions and survivors despite the odds." It took all of her strength to deal with Lemuel's revelation, which had shocked her to her core. Her first instinct was not to believe him.

"That can't be true," she said. "That's a lie."

She stared at him, grilling him with her eyes.

"I can understand how difficult this must be for you to accept, Mrs. Whitman," he said softly. "But I swear that it's the truth about Robert and me."

He unclasped his hands and gripped each side of the chair.

"Lawrence was jealous of his brother," he continued before she had a chance to respond. "Something happened to tick Lawrence off. It was an argument, a disagreement of some kind, and so Lawrence tipped him off."

"Who?" Mamie said, her voice panic stricken.

"Carlton. He tipped off Carlton as to where Robert would be that evening. The exact jogging path in the park and the precise time, so that Carlton could hunt him down."

"But why?" Mamie asked, throwing up her hands, bewildered. "Why would he do that?"

"I'm not sure exactly, ma'am, but not long before the accident Robert told me that he'd heard you and Judge Whitman arguing one evening and that he'd heard something about Lawrence that was not meant for his ears...."

Mamie motioned with her hand for him to stop and put her hand in front of her face, as though shielding it.

"Don't tell me anymore, Lemuel," she implored.

Ignoring her, Lemuel got up from his chair and walked over to kneel beside her.

"Mrs. Whitman," he said. "Lawrence didn't mean for Robert to be killed. He just wanted Carlton to mess with him. And I don't think that Carlton wanted to kill him either. But when Carlton jumped him, Robert took a step back and fell down the stairs. It was an accident."

As Mamie wept bitterly, Lemuel sat quietly, waiting until her sobbing ceased.

"Ma'am," he said after a while. "I'm sorry if I've upset you, but I wanted to tell you myself just in case anyone else hears it and tries to make something of it to hurt you and your family. I'd hate for that to happen and for you to be unprepared. But if nobody does, I want you to know that I will go to my grave with what I've shared with you. You can trust me on that."

"I know that I can, Lemuel," Mamie said.

There was nothing more to be said, so Lemuel stood up as if to go and—after a few seconds—Mamie rose from her chair and went with him to the front door.

As he walked away into the night, she called out, "Lemuel."

"Yes, ma'am?"

"Do you need a ride home?" she asked, her voice wavering. "Let me drive you home. I don't like the thought of you walking to the bus in the night."

"Thank you, ma'am," Lemuel replied. "I appreciate your kind offer. But I did it dozens of times when Robert and I were young. For some reason, it just seems right for me to do it now."

He smiled at her and continued walking into the black night, the moonlight illuminating his path. Mamie watched until his slight figure disappeared behind the tall, thick hedges at the boundary of their property. She continued looking until she could see him no longer.

Drained and with her head spinning, she closed the door and wondered whether to wake Teddy. But she was too exhausted, so she went to bed, resolving to tell him in the morning. As her head fell on her pillow, a spiritual came to her from her childhood.

It's me, it's me, O Lord,
Standing in the need of prayer.

She repeated the words. She clung to them as if they were her last remaining ticket to sanity. Her grandmother had sung the spiritual to her as a child; in fact, she had rocked her in a wicker basket, in the bottom of which was a tiny triangular shaped cloth of striped blue and gold that was—according to family folklore—the one remaining relic of an ancestor who had survived the slave voyage. The rough scrap of cloth, fragile with age, had been passed down through five generations to her.

She got up from her bed and took the ancient Bible that had been passed down to her out of the bottom drawer of her bureau. She opened it and carefully extracted the rough scrap of cloth from between the folds of the delicate pages. She slept heavily that night, the relic under her pillow.

* * *

The following morning, Theodore woke up late. It was a Saturday, and that was his day to lie in. He had nothing on his schedule apart from a round of golf that afternoon.

Mamie was already up, he noticed. *Probably already cooking breakfast,* he thought as he stretched out and lay in bed for a few more minutes. Eventually, when he could put it off no longer, he got up and showered. Then he put on a pair of beige chinos and a blue Georgetown sweatshirt and went downstairs.

He looked around for Mamie, but she was nowhere to be found.

"Where is she?" he asked to himself as he went into the kitchen, more than a little irritated that he would have to make his own breakfast.

Bettie was sitting calmly at the kitchen table, gently polishing silverware. Without turning her head, she said, "Good morning, Judge Whitman."

"Good morning, Bettie," he replied. "Do you know where Mamie's gone this morning?"

"She got an early start. She said she wanted a little peace and quiet. She told me that she was going over to Thomas Mill Covered Bridge. Said she wanted to look at the leaves on the trees before they turned."

"What? Why on earth should she want to go there at this time of the morning…didn't you think that was strange?" Theodore said, beginning to get concerned. "And how did she get there? Her car is still outside."

"No, Judge, I did not," Bettie said. "And I suppose she must have walked there."

She stood up from the table and walked over to face him. "Is there something wrong?" she added, beginning to feel concerned herself. "Is there something going on I should know about?"

Ignoring her, he rushed out of the kitchen, grabbed his set of keys that were by the front door, and ran to his car. On the five-minute drive to the bridge, Whitman's head swirled with fears, but the minute he saw his wife he breathed a sigh of relief.

She was seated on a stone ledge at the foot of the bridge with her feet dangling over the side. He approached her, and when she did not turn to acknowledge him, he quietly sat next to her. She swung her heavy walking shoes back and forth over the water, like a schoolgirl. Below them was a brook of blue water that meandered over a bed of red and brown river stones.

"What's wrong, my love? Is this about Clarence?"

He asked the question gently as he tenderly rubbed her back. He knew that he need not remind her that this was where she used to meet him from time to time.

"It's all behind us now," he added softly as she turned to look at him. "We've both come a long way since then."

"I'm sorry if I worried you, Teddy," she said, taking his hand in hers. "But it's nothing to do with that."

"Then what is it about, Mamie? What's wrong?"

She hesitated for a moment and then said, "A strange thing happened last night. Robert's friend Lemuel paid us a surprise visit. He had something to say to us both, but you were already in bed and asleep, so it was me who heard him out. I'm sorry if I worried you, but I came here to think about what he told me, and what we should do about it."

"What on earth did he say that got you so concerned, Mamie?"

"Well, almost the first thing he told me was that Robert and he were both gay…that they were lovers. Did you know anything about that?"

"To be honest with you, I did have my suspicions…but in the end, I couldn't bring myself to discuss it with him. I thought about doing so, but I worried about the consequences. It would have probably ended up in an argument and he would have become estranged from us. I thought it better to let sleeping dogs lie. I didn't want him to lose his love for me, nor did I want to lose my love for him."

"I can see that, Theodore, but I wish you'd have shared that with me. I suppose you were worried about the consequences for me, too."

"Yes, my love. I was. But that can't have been the only thing Lemuel told you for you to be so worried. What more did he say?"

Holding both of his hands in hers, she told him about Carlton and the accident and Lawrence's role. Initially, Theodore had difficulty in coming to terms with Lemuel's account.

"Are you sure that that boy was telling the truth?" was his first question.

"Yes, I am," she told him firmly. "At first, I was doubtful...but then I thought, what reason would he have to lie?"

"So, it's a fact. Lawrence set up the situation for it to happen."

"It was an accident, Teddy," she said, dabbing away tears. "It wasn't supposed to happen."

"But Lawrence still kept quiet about it," Teddy said in a low, wintry voice.

"Yes, he did. He shouldn't have done, but I can guess why. He was probably scared out of his wits because of what you would say. What do you think it must have been like for him, living under a roof where he got the scraps and Robert got the sit-down fare? I'm not excusing him. All I'm saying is that he was probably as shocked as anyone else that Robert fell when he saw Carlton. Lawrence must have been terrified to come clean. Terrified of you."

Theodore held his head in his hands. Twice he lifted his head as if to speak, but each time he shook his head and said nothing. Finally, he looked at Mamie and asked, "So what should we do?"

"You need to talk to him, Teddy," she said. "But please remember, what he needs is empathy, not anger or judgment."

31

Lawrence was surprised to get a phone call from his father out of the blue.

"Be ready at 11:00 a.m.," his father said. "I'll come by to pick you up."

"What's this about, Dad?"

"I'll tell you when I see you," he said. "By the way, I hear that you're seeing both Claire and Bettie's daughter."

"I love them, both," Lawrence replied, "but differently. And Bettie's daughter has a name. Her name is Georgia."

"You love a BMW and an Alfa Romeo differently, not women," Theodore replied before hanging up.

* * *

When Theodore arrived, he asked his son to get in the car with him to go for a drive. Puzzled, Lawrence did as he was asked and they drove to an alley in back of the Richard Allen homes, just a short distance from Lemuel's house.

"Get out, and follow me please," Theodore said as he parked the car.

It had begun to rain just as the two walked into the alley, which turned into a dead end.

"I wanted you to see this, son," Theodore said. "When we moved from Tennessee and I was growing up around here, they used to call it Gladiator's Way. This is the place where boys were fashioned into men."

He walked a few yards from where he was standing with Lawrence to a spot near an overflowing dumpster. Then he traced a circle with his shoe where the chipped pavement met the wall.

He pointed to the spot. "This is where I pummeled a boy's face to a pulp. Did it to keep him from murdering me. In those days that was justice. Street justice." He angrily kicked an empty bottle of Jack to the side.

"Still is, Dad."

He walked back to Lawrence and stood directly in front of his son.

"I'm not proud of what I did that day," he said, zeroing in on his son's face. "But I owned up to it, even though it earned me the whupping of my life from my father. But what I did doesn't compare to the role you played in Robert's death. So, why don't you come clean and tell me what happened?"

Lawrence was stunned. It was the last thing he imagined his father would ask. His face turned ashen, and his first thought was to ask how his father had found out. But then, he thought, what good would that do? His father knew, so he'd better try and explain.

"It was an accident, Dad! How was I to know that Robert would fall? He wasn't supposed to die! That was the last thing I wanted to happen."

"But you did call that nasty piece of work, Carlton Lavington, and tell him where Robert would be?"

"Yes, Dad, I did. But it was to scare Robert…maybe beat him up. It wouldn't have been much of a fight. Robert was much stronger than Carlton."

"And that's your excuse, is it? 'I didn't mean it, so I shouldn't be blamed'? I might not mean to knock someone down when I speed through town, but that doesn't mean I'm not to blame!"

Despite Mamie's admonition, Theodore was having difficulty controlling his anger. So, he took a few deep breaths before asking his next question. "Why did you ask Carlton to go to the park and beat up Robert? That's what I can't understand, son."

"But that's just it. I'm not your son!" Lawrence cried, guttural, wrenching sobs escaping from him.

"What?"

"I'm not your son. I know it. Robert told me that he overhead you and Mom having an argument about it years ago."

"And is that why? Why…?"

Feeling cold and numb, Lawrence shook his head silently.

"I'm not a murderer, Dad. I didn't want him dead. But I was angry when he told me. I hated him for having all that I ever wanted in life."

"And what was that?"

"Your love, of course, Dad. I wanted to tell you and Mom and atone for what I'd done, but I was afraid."

"Afraid of what?" Theodore asked.

"Afraid of *you*! I was another man's son, and you punished me for that," Lawrence yelled back at him. "Hard as I tried, I couldn't do any-thing right. All I got from you was anger, so it was no wonder I was terrified of you. And since Robert died, you've tried to fashion me into his image! When in God's name will you stop? When will it ever end?"

He turned his back on his father and began walking away from him.

"It ends now," Theodore said gruffly.

But Lawrence was too far away to hear, so Theodore ran after him. He slowed down when Lawrence turned to face him.

"Stop," Lawrence called out. "Stop right now. Don't come any closer. I'm not going to let you attack me like you did to that boy all those years ago."

He looked around desperately for something to defend himself, but there was nothing in the filthy alley save for crushed cigarette cartons and scattered yellow McDonalds' wrappers. He turned to face his father with his fists at the ready.

"No, Lawrence," an out-of-breath Theodore wheezed. "I didn't bring you here for a fight. I just wanted you to understand where I came from and some of the struggles I've had to go through to get to where I am today. I know that journey has left its mark and it hasn't made me a joy to live with....

"I'm so very sorry for the way I've treated you. What I said back there was, 'It stops right now,' and I mean it. Nothing you or I can do will bring Robert back, and I know that you didn't mean for him to die."

Lawrence was the first to reach out. He hugged his father, who returned his embrace.

"This tragedy, the passing of my brother, this is not yours to own, Dad," he whispered into his father's ear. "It's mine and mine alone to atone for and live with for rest of my life."

"We both own it," Theodore said. "I bear responsibility, too. If I hadn't driven a wedge between you and your brother none of this would have happened."

Theodore released Lawrence from his grip as the heavy rain became torrential.

"I guess," he said repentantly. "It's as Hamlet says, 'Conscience doth make cowards of us all.'

"Let's go son. Let's go home."

32

He wondered whether he was doing the right thing, but at the end of the day Lawrence Whitman was happy that he'd made the decision to attend Georgia's graduation at Hampton University.

Not that he asked for their advice but, predictably enough, his parents insisted that he shouldn't go.

"Stay the course, son," his father had advised one Sunday evening at the Whitman household, minutes after grace was said and forks and knives were deployed for Mamie's roast chicken dinner.

"Stay the course and I promise that your mother and I will throw you a wedding party you won't believe. *Philadelphia Magazine* will be calling to put you and Claire on their society page."

"I don't need that, Pop," he said.

"What don't you need?"

"Validation," he said, biting his lip so as not to add, *like you do.*

* * *

Lawrence made it just in time to find a seat at the commencement ceremony. He was near the aisle, and Georgia waved at him trium-phantly as she passed by to take her seat among all the other excited

245

graduates. As he waved back, he reflected that his father had gotten it all wrong.

She was a maid's daughter, yes. There was a conflict of culture and status. But despite her humble beginnings, the maid's daughter was making something of her life, just like his father had done when he overcame the challenges of his early years. And, of course, her phenomenal ability to charm him with one bashful cast of her brown eyes, remained undiminished by time. She'd long forgiven him for being a no-show all of these years, and that made him want her all the more.

He'd never had the experience of going to a historically Black college. He hadn't given it much thought, not an iota until now, when he took in the cacophony of boisterous, exuberant yells punctuating almost every sentence that the wheelchair bound Valedictorian delivered in his commencement speech. As befits such an occasion, several speeches were made, with some speakers unable to resist the temptation of displaying their knowledge of apposite quotes from the works of Voltaire, Socrates, Cicero, and Seneca. Somehow—to him—his Georgetown degree seemed not to stack up against this phalanx of freshly minted Hampton graduates. For some reason, he felt as though he came up short, and he was left feeling more alone than ever before seated amongst the crowd.

After the ceremony, he followed the crowd outside and caught sight of Bettie. He went to join her and found her overcome with emotion.

"Jimmy would have been so proud of her," she said. "I just wish he could have seen her graduating today."

"What makes you think that he's not looking down on her from heaven right now?" he replied, in an attempt to comfort her and lift her spirits.

It seemed to help, so they made their way through the crowd in search of Georgia. They found her among a group of peers and, as they approached, he felt a tinge of jealously as he saw the laughter and easy rapport she had with her friends. It was almost as though she and her friends, of all sexes, colors, and incomes, had grown up in the same family. Bettie rushed over to join Georgia, and he stood back to allow her to rejoice with her daughter and her friends.

* * *

He caught up with Georgia that evening after Bettie had left to return to Philadelphia. After braving a popular seafood restaurant, exuberant graduates and their families occupying every table, Lawrence paid the bill, and they walked back to her dorm room. He took the tour of the small space, inspecting the various knickknacks of her modest life displayed on the shelves and on top of her desk. They included a white rabbit's foot, several strings of puka shells, a community service award, a small emerald colored bowl that held various hair ornaments, and a picture of Jesus on the wall.

The small, screenless window was open and fresh breezes infused the room. Beethoven's "Moonlight Sonata" could be heard faintly on the cassette player.

"Stepping up in the world, are we?" Lawrence asked, teasingly.

"Culture isn't only for folks like you, you know," she replied.

"And who are folks like me?"

"Rich Black folk," she said, as she grinned triumphantly at him with her crooked smile.

"Touché," he replied, suppressing the urge to kiss her. She had grown only more beautiful with time.

They sat on her bed and quietly talked about her life at Hampton and her dream to become a social worker.

"I want to help the forgotten ones," she said in a plainspoken manner, "those whom society has ignored and left behind."

He nodded in agreement, and he felt her watching him as he glanced at her posters and photographs. He noticed that one painted blue wall was devoted to Ella Fitzgerald and Nina Simone. Then he saw a photograph of Georgia, Bettie, and Jimmy that had been taken

247

when she was a child. At that moment, he thought of the sadness she'd had to endure and realized that he had only added to it.

She touched the top of his hand, which lay on her yellow bedspread, and directed his gaze toward her nightstand.

"Remember that?" she asked.

It was a photograph of her and Lawrence, standing side by side next to the tall spruce tree in his backyard. They were smiling brightly into the camera—he with his shoes on, she with shoes off.

"Momma took the picture. Remember?"

He smiled in acknowledgment and began to survey the room again.

"Any boyfriends?" he asked quietly.

"Of course," she said. "I have trouble keeping count." Then, seeing the alarmed look on his face, she laughed. "No, that's not true. I've been in one 'on again, off again' relationship, but I've mainly focused on my studies. I wanted to make the most of the opportunity of being here."

"And you?" she added, looking at him boldly.

"I'm still with Claire, if that's what you mean," he said. "But, like you, it's very much been an 'on again, off again' relationship, much to my parents' disappointment."

She reached out to hug him, and it was all he could do to stifle his tears as the familiar aroma of her perfume surrounded him. He caressed her and then lay back on the bed, expecting her to join him. But she refused to make love in her dorm room, even though her dorm mate had abandoned her bed for the evening. So, at sunset, they walked to the only place where she could envision a spiritual connection between the act of making love and staying at peace with God.

They left her room and strolled, hand in hand, to the Emancipation Oak that proudly stood on the university campus. As they walked, Georgia explained that the 150-year-old tree was the site of the first official reading in the South of the Emancipation Proclamation issued by President Abraham Lincoln. But what made it special

248

to her, she explained, was that it was the setting where newly freed Blacks took classes, learning to become literate and numerate after being denied that opportunity for so long.

They lay side by side on the blanket that they had brought with them and looked for a while at the hovering moon that peered at them through the branches of the ancient tree. Georgia remained quiet and still as Lawrence undressed her, button by button, clasp by clasp. But when he held her full breasts in his hands, she gave a little gasp. They kissed and then looked deeply into each other's eyes. He cradled her chin and looked down at her, moonlight illuming her long-braided tresses. She smiled shyly back at him.

She was aroused by him in a way he was certain that Claire had never been or ever could be. He reached over and gently caressed her nipples, feeling them grow hard and stiff. She moaned quietly and he looked at her reflectively as she lay nearly naked on the ground, save for her pink lace panties, which she now half-heartedly grasped with one hand at the waistline. Whatever atonement she had had in mind had reached its expiration date with him.

She seemed to know his mind. "I've wanted you for a long time, but I kept myself from thinking it. I knew that I had alienated you from your parents and that is the last thing I wanted."

"And I've always wanted you, too," he whispered, as he undressed himself and unbuckled his jeans.

Not wanting to wait a single moment longer, he moved her tentatively held hands from her panties so that he could remove them. Ultimately, though, it was not the absent panties, but her brown, dewy eyes that invited him in.

Afterward, they lay exhaustedly side by side on the rectangular brown blanket they had brought from her dorm room. They looked up from there, peering into the black night at an assemblage of stars clustered and shimmering in the dark night's sky. A fat tear rambled from the corner of Georgia's eye, found its way down her cheek, and landed finally on her skinny shoulder blade.

"You are beautiful, Georgia," he said, hugging her.

"Am not," she said, releasing herself from his arms.

Her next words dented a near perfect evening.

"You're never going to leave her, are you?" she asked. "Claire, I mean."

"Don't be so doubtful, Georgia."

"I'm not an angry Black woman if that's what you're thinking."

A sad expression clouded Lawrence's face.

"Well, why not? Why shouldn't you be angry?"

He sat up and abruptly began to put on his clothes. He passed her plain white brassier to her and draped her green cardigan over her bare breasts as she reached out to touch the tree.

"Do you ever wonder about what it must have been like for those first slaves when they landed in North America?" she said. "Can you imagine what their first winter must have been like? I mean, white immigrants came here from cold climates, but our folks came from the land of the sun."

Lawrence frowned, shaking his head. "They must have been in a state of shock."

"Still are," she quickly added.

"I guess that's why they became so deeply religious. Solace from suffering," he said. "I used to think that I wanted to be like my father. I wanted to be a big man, to get as far away from the curse of slavery as I could get. But then it was in trying to be like him that I lost my way."

Georgia patted his knee. "It's OK, babe," she whispered softly. "You'll find your salvation. But you need to decide about Claire."

"She's in the rearview mirror," he replied, gently holding her face in his hands. "I'm looking at about all the salvation I can handle right here in you."

33

Lawrence got out his keys and let himself into his nice toasty apartment. But a spate of brisk autumn air quickly trotted after him, like an irate child. He hugged himself as he stepped inside.

"Feels like winter already," he said to her.

"I put on one of your classical favorites," she said softly, pointing to the record player. "'Bach French Suite number one.'"

"Something that befits your cerebral status," she added. "Something classy, like you…like us."

He walked into his kitchen and his eyes were drawn to an ivory-colored card that rested against a glass vase, which was filled with an artfully done arrangement of pinecones and ivy. Next to the card were two tickets to the Academy of Music. Jazz-soul great saxophonist Grover Washington was featured to play that evening.

He picked up the card, which was written in beautiful calligraphy. He immediately recognized the handwriting.

An Ode to Hampton,
(Also, an Ode to You)
My School
My love

Sit by the Sea,
Beneath an old oak tree
Where you transported and conquered me.
We sat and we loved,
My man at the Tree.
I Love You, Georgia

Lawrence lived in a second-floor apartment of a restored Tudor on the Main Line. Although many apartments had attracted him, it was the cozy, curved sitting nook—perfect for long, relaxing reads—and the tall, Victorian-style picture windows that had won him over. He'd quickly signed the rental contract, once his father had kicked in a few grand toward the down payment and the first few months' rent.

He had just got home from the nonprofit in North Philadelphia where he now worked as a pro bono legal advisor for delinquent boys. He could kick himself for agreeing to be "on call" for whenever the organization needed him. As it turned out, the need was great.

"What's this?" he asked.

Claire had joined him for breakfast before he left for work and had planned to luxuriate with an *Inquirer* and a stack of *Essence* magazines. But a white envelope addressed to Lawrence, with a Booker T. Washington stamp on it, had intrigued her. A carton of Minute Maid orange juice, two small white plates with empty egg holders on them had not moved since he'd left. He noticed that a tiny bit of yellow egg yolk had stained the white cashmere sweater she wore over her red shirtdress.

"Did you open my mail?"

He walked over to her where she sat, quietly sipping from a small glass of orange juice. He could see that she'd been crying. She'd already gone through two boxes of Kleenex.

She snatched the card from him and waved it in front of his face.

"An old oak tree?" she exclaimed incredulously. "Really? And 'I Love You, Georgia'?"

He reached out to take the card back from her. Claire couldn't help but ruefully notice the reverence with which he placed it back on the table.

She had graduated from nursing school and was now working in the pediatric wing of the University of Pennsylvania Hospital. Over the last few months Claire had been become fully preoccupied with nesting and one side of his closet had become clogged with her clothes, her shoes, and her purses. And although she had still not been given a key to his apartment, she zipped back and forth from her family's place to his in her little white BMW. She was there often enough that she could smell the scent of her Samsara perfume on his towels and linens. Her one concern was that there was still no proposal and no ring. But otherwise, in her estimation, things were good between them. At least until the card appeared

"I went there to attend her graduation, OK? Is that a crime? And, yes," he said, lamely, "there really is an old tree at Hampton University. It's called the Emancipation Oak. It's where the freedmen and women first learned how to read and write. Look it up, Claire. You spend enough time snooping around me, you could spare some of it toward doing something meaningful."

He glared at her exasperatedly. "You really shouldn't have opened my mail."

"'My man at the tree,' it says! That bitch is still pining for you! Don't you dare deny it."

"And don't you ever use that vile word against Georgia, or anyone else for that matter," he shouted. "You're above calling people names like that. Or at least you should be."

The heated words had been volleyed gently but they still packed a punch. And when Claire gazed into Lawrence's eyes, she knew that she had made a grave mistake.

He placed his head in his hands as though carrying the weight of the world in them.

"Claire, look. I'm sorry this has hurt you. You know how much I care for you. You know this. But for God's sake, show me a little compassion."

She looked back at him, dumbfounded. If she'd had a sliver of grace, she would have deployed it right then. But his words had sapped the energy out of her. All she could say was, "What about us?"

Lawrence didn't answer, so Claire wiped away her tears and began tidying up the kitchen, picking up the plates that had been left on the table since breakfast and filling the sink with warm sudsy water. She suddenly felt a warmth behind her as Lawrence walked up to her and began to massage her shoulders. He kissed her gently on the back of her neck.

"Try not be so defensive," he said sweetly. "Just ditch the jealousy, OK?" Claire sighed as she smelled Lawrence's potent cologne of sandalwood and lime.

She turned to face him, soapsuds covering her red dress and arms, but as she did a glass she was holding fell out of her hands and dashed to the floor, breaking into two perfectly shaped half-moons.

"I'm sorry, Lawrence."

She had meant to tell him that she would try. She may not succeed, but she had determined to finally park her jealousy of Georgia. She picked up the shattered shards of glass, trying desperately to find internal equilibrium in body and spirit. As she searched feverishly for the right words, she dumped the broken glass in the trashcan. Then, Claire finally faced him and spoke.

"Lawrence, it's not just about you and me anymore," she said, trying but failing to calibrate her voice. "Mom and Dad were just talking about this the other night. Judge Whitman is a shadow of his former self. Now that Robert has gone, the only thing that keeps your old man going is his ambition for you. It's high time you stepped up to the plate."

She looked steadily into his cool, serene face as it dissolved into a hot, irritated restiveness.

"I suppose what you mean by that is get a better paying job at some fancy law firm and marry you," he said.

She watched as he slowly backed away from her and walked over to the small oval breakfast table. He picked up the card off the yellow placemat. Then he went to the side of the sink where she had left the opened envelope and reinserted it.

He looked at his Movado watch. His clipped voice told her all that she already knew in her heart.

"Claire, it's time for us to get dressed and ready if we don't want to miss Grover."

* * *

She watched him out of the corner of her eye the entire evening. His face was uncharacteristically grim and wooden, as they sat and listened to Grover Washington, Jr. play in the only life affirming, ebullient way he knew how.

When they got back home, she hugged him and asked him if he wanted her to stay.

"If you want," was his curt reply as he unlocked the door.

His powerfully sad and quiet demeanor was like a requiem. She followed him as he walked into the apartment, and his softly crinkled blue Ralph Lauren shirt tucked into the belted waist of his crisp black slacks made her yearn for him.

"I'm tired," he announced. "I've had a long day and I desperately need to get to bed."

Claire pressed the toe of her shiny black pump on the hardwood floor to release the heel and did the same with the other. She leaned against the white doorframe, careful not to snag her blue chiffon dress, and looked at his sleek Spanish guitar that was propped against the closet door.

"Play for me," she said. "Just one short piece…anything you choose."

"What now?" he asked groggily.

"For me, Lawrence, please."

"No, I don't think so," he said from the bedroom. "Not right now, Claire. I'm exhausted."

She moved toward the light switch on the wall, turning it off, and then entered the bedroom and began to undress.

They lay in bed side by side, but as distant as two strangers. She was left feeling lonelier with him next to her than if she had been lying in her bed alone. Before she closed her eyes, he reached out to her and traced the contours of her face with the tips of his fingers.

"You are beautiful, Claire," he said. "And you give me all that a man's heart and mind could ask for. But sometimes I think that my soul could use more sustenance…more comfort food."

34

September 1985

A ray of molten orange sunlight streamed through Georgia's window, waking her up. She turned to look at the alarm clock on her nightstand that she'd forgotten to set, which informed her that she had overslept. She hoisted herself from bed, tightened the belt of her robe around her and padded over to the window in her slippers, touching it with the tips of her fingers. The pane felt cold to the touch, and she quickly withdrew her hand. Shivering, the fleeting thought came to her that this cold autumn day was only a foretaste of a classic Philadelphia winter to come. She took some solace in the fact that the sparse leaves on the two Sycamore trees on the street had just begun to turn red.

Since her return to Philadelphia after completing her social work degree, Georgia was still trying to make the tiny apartment in the Tioga neighborhood of North Philly feel like home. She'd resisted her mother's call to come live with her. If she had to live cheaply, then she'd at least do it on her own terms. She had purposely decided on the Allegheny apartments in Tioga. The turn-of-the-century gray brick building was showing its age, but never mind. It was affordable and close to Hope Village, a clinic where she had been newly hired as a social worker, counselling an array of down-on-their-luck teenage unwed mothers. She'd gotten the one-bedroom apartment for a song.

"If you don't mind the occasional mouse dropping in for visit, you'll be fine," the realtor told her as she signed the lease.

She went to the kitchenette and made herself a cup of instant coffee and, gripping the mug in her hand, she padded back to the window and looked outside. A thin, smiling wiry boy of about fifteen was whirling around like a top. She smiled as she watched him, but as he continued to spin the smile dropped from her face. *He's high as a kite*, she thought, *drugged out of his mind*. The bulbous sleeves of his mint green shirt fluttered like an open sail in the morning breeze as he spun around, and his black, polyester pants fit him like a tight glove. From where she stood, they looked almost like black leotards. His high, yellow-colored cheekbones revealed a complicated heritage.

There had been drugs at Hampton University, but she'd never touched them, worried that they'd interfere with her studies. The dealers and their customers were discreet, which was certainly not the case in the neighborhood where she now lived. Dealers dotted every street, every corner, every dark alley where they could industriously work the streets. Areas were fought over, and kill or be killed was the way things were in the Hood. The vineyard was plentiful with habits, and they all needed their fixes.

Georgia was mesmerized by the sight of the teen, spinning on the concrete in his high-top sneakers like a figure skater, hands now clasped high above his head. She turned from the window, returned her mug to the kitchenette, and walked back toward her small bedroom. She quickly showered and threw on a decade-old pair of faded denim jeans and the same blouse that Lawrence had dexterously unbuttoned under a full yellow moon, the night they had made love beside the Emancipation Oak.

She looked out of the window again and saw that the boy was still in the same spot as before, but something had changed. His wild spinning had stopped, and she watched as he fell listlessly to the ground. She gasped, wondering whether the boy was alive or dead.

She was about to turn and run downstairs to see if he was OK when her eyes became riveted to the sight below, as every Black man's nightmare came wrenchingly into view. A blue Ford Crown Victoria police car crawled down the street and stopped, lights flashing, a few yards in front of the boy. Two white cops emerged from the car, clad in their thickly padded black uniforms, their guns sinister and glistening from their hips. They sauntered over to the boy, who had suddenly revived himself and was seated placidly on the street—until the minute they touched him. She watched the struggle and saw him thrown against the side of the car, his high cheekbones melded like soft clay on the blue steel. One of the cops punched him savagely as the other held him still. They then handcuffed him and searched him. Digging into his pockets they discovered something in a brown envelope, which earned they boy a few more blows. As they threw him into the car, the last thing she saw was a flash of his billowy, mint green shirt.

Another beautiful day in the neighborhood, Georgia thought, as she began to tidy up the apartment.

* * *

There was a knock on the door just as she was tucking the small bottle of Hennessey under her bed that she'd been nursing the night before. She threw open the door, still racked by the memory of what she just seen.

Bettie's eyes sternly met the downcast ones of her only child.

"What did you do to your hair?" she asked.

"I cut off my braids. I needed a change. That alright with you?" Georgia said curtly.

Bettie brushed past her daughter and into the room. She inhaled and sighed heavily. Her daughter's apartment smelled like boiled carrots.

"Haven't kicked the habit yet, I see," she said, pointing to the ashtray on the coffee table.

"Neither have you," Georgia mumbled.

"What do you mean?"

Georgia's gaze was fixed on Bettie's purse.

"Oh, you mean this?" she asked casually, pointing to her brown Gucci bag.

"Yeah, Mom. I see that you're still relying on Miss Mamie's handouts."

"I don't know what you're talking about," Bettie said exhaustedly as she deposited her purse on the kitchenette counter, along with a small green plant she'd brought as a housewarming gift. She took of her coat and sat stiffly on one of two high stools in front of the counter and crooked her neck toward her daughter.

"It was gifted to me by Mrs. Whitman," she said. "What's wrong with me having a few nice things, even if they are secondhand? And why are you getting on my case when I've just walked in?"

Georgia went to her bedroom to retrieve a red shawl that she layered over her bedspread at night to keep her warm. She threw it over her shoulders and returned to the small living area. She sat next to her mother on the other stool. The air hung down between the two women like heavy drapes.

"What's wrong, baby?" Bettie asked. "You should be happy. You've got your degree. You've got your own place, and you've got a good job, even though it doesn't pay all that much."

"I'm sorry, Mom. Just before you arrived, I was looking out of my window, and I saw a boy outside beaten up and dragged away by the police. He was on drugs. God only knows what they'll do to him once they get to the station."

"It ain't just about dope now, is it?" Bettie said after a pause.

She looked past her daughter toward the small kitchenette. A large cockroach shimmied across the smooth surfaced floor. "Don't think I don't know you've been dipping into the bottle. Or, as brother Scott-Heron says, living in the bottle."

"How'd you know?" Georgia asked, wearily, head bowed low.

"Smelled it on your breath when I came in! How else?" Bettie laughed and gave a shrug.

She took her bifocals out of her purse, put them on, and walked over to where Georgia had stacked dozens of social work books and piles of articles about the struggles of vulnerable people in the cities.

"You've really got some deep-dish anger stewing around in you, don't you?"

"Do I, Mom?" Georgia said as she stood up and walked to the window. "So now I'm an angry Black woman. That it? Is it because I decided to cut off my hair and sport an afro?"

Bettie shook her head.

"No, baby. I like your hair cut," she said. "It suits your small face."

"Got it chopped off by a lady down the corner. I did it to honor Ramona and Birdie."

"Who are they?"

Georgia stared hard at her mother.

"The two sole survivors of MOVE, Mom."

"Well, you're not a Rastafarian like the people who lived in that compound," Bettie said. She looked at Georgia's neatly cropped hair. "And at least you wash your locks."

"Mom, how could you ever say a thing like that? It was a tragedy. Children were burned to death in there. The city was heartless."

Georgia had watched the horror unfold on television four months ago while at college. It involved the Philadelphia cops and the Black liberation group called MOVE. The police had attempted to arrest four of the organization's members at their compound, which was a row house in the middle of a residential neighborhood. A gun battle ensued, and the MOVE members resisted all attempts to extricate them. Finally, at 5:00 p.m. on May 13th, the police dropped two bombs on the compound. "Let the fire burn," the firemen were told.

"How in the world could you forget that our so-called City of Brotherly Love allowed our folks to die in that fire?"

Georgia peered into her mother's crestfallen face.

"Our folks, Mom," she added, her voice dropping a register. "And they weren't just adults," she whispered fervently. "Children, innocent kids, all mercilessly slaughtered. Ten thousand rounds of ammo in ninety minutes. Our great City of Brotherly Love burned the fucking place down with little children inside."

Bettie was about to remind Georgia to watch her language. But instead, she said, "Yes, Georgia. It was shameful…a stain on this city."

She walked over to her daughter and took her hands in hers. They both looked out of the window, where the weather had changed on a dime from bright sunshine to a sudden shower. Rain lightly pattered the window.

"Look at me, Georgia. Look at me now. I want to see your eyes."

Bettie waited until Georgia reluctantly complied.

"You've got it all going on," she said, sweeping her hand toward the stacks of thick books layered neatly on the floor and on the coffee table. "But you just don't see it!"

Georgia angrily shook her head. "But you don't understand," she said. "Things are getting crazier and crazier for people like us, Mom."

"No, *you* don't understand, Georgia," Bettie said firmly. "I may not agree with everything that those MOVE people stood for, but I respect them for their pride in being Black and their wanting to make the world a better place. You need to take a leaf out of their book, girl. Be proud of who you are and be the best social worker that you can be so that you can transform blighted lives for the better. Do it so that those children did not die in vain."

"Yes, Mom," Georgia said, sniffling. She looked at her mother and swallowed hard.

"But this isn't only about MOVE and the boy you saw being arrested this morning, is it?" Bettie said. "You're upset about Lawrence, aren't you?"

"That's over. She's got him, Mom."

"Who, Claire Scott?" Bettie shrugged. "What she got that you don't?"

Georgia looked around the sparsely furnished apartment and then back at her mother. For the first time that morning, they smiled at each other, enjoying the irony of Bettie's words.

"Stand up for yourself, girl. Just like those MOVE folk did on Osage Avenue. You want something? Fight for it."

She turned and hugged her daughter tightly, at first receiving no response but finally Georgia hugged her back, clenching the back of her mother's dress tightly.

"But he's not my man," Georgia said, sobbing.

"Nah, baby," Bettie said softly, remembering Lawrence as a child. Any excuse would do to linger in the kitchen whenever Georgia was around. "He is."

Georgia broke from her mother's embrace and stared at her. Bettie saw the same huge, brown, piercing eyes that she had been greeted by from the miraculous day she was born.

"It's like your father always said when he got home from the mines. He'd be so torn down and tired, yet…" She paused to think. "So entirely giving with his joy. He radiated it. One day I asked him why that was so. 'You got to be gripped by the dark to be embraced by the light,' he said."

Bettie smiled cheerfully at her daughter, who wiped her tears away and smiled back.

"Don't stay gripped by the dark. You go and get him, girl," she said, as the sun swung low into the apartment, illuminating Bettie's broad, intelligent forehead.

Georgia offered her trademark lopsided grin, but that was all that was needed as far as Bettie was concerned. She knew, in that intuitive way that sensitive women have, that nothing more had to be said. Georgia was going to take on the challenge, and Lord knows it was about time.

EPILOGUE

Autumn 1999

It was early September and mild weather for Pennsylvania, so the car windows were left halfway down that Saturday afternoon. A family was on their way to the venue for Pennsylvania's annual Quaker School music recital. A cool whistle of air threaded through the tall, stately trees, their long limbs draped in burnished orange leaves.

Leave it to the rich, she thought, as she gently smoothed the crinkle from her beige silk dress, to host a piano recital competition in a refurbished barn in New Hope.

Her husband began to hum "Thunder Road." She hated "Thunder Road," but she loved him so she tolerated it. Looking over at him as he drove—his eyes focused on the two yellow lines in front of him—she focused on his prematurely gray hair and reached out to caress the side of his head. He turned to look at her briefly and smiled. His kind slate-blue eyes were a constant reassurance to her that she had chosen the right man. She'd met him at the intersection between hope and despair and had not looked back.

The barn was New England–styled—stacked quarried stones on the bottom half, deeply weathered gray wood on top. As they exited their cars, all the parents held the same expression on their expectant faces. *What an adventure. A recital in a barn.* As they streamed toward the barn, their children clutching their music in hot little hands, the heels of the pumps of some of the mothers got wedged in the black soil. The aromas of Chanel and cow manure mingled in the evening air.

At the entrance, Clotilde, like the other child performers, was whisked to the front of the room by the young ushers. They were late but were able to find two white folding chairs at the rear right side of the room, close to the large picture windows that had been flung open for the evening.

As the recital began, each child's name was called out by a young woman wearing a floral wrap-around dress. From where they sat, all that was visible was the rim of a black, gleaming Baby Grand piano. Following each piano piece, subdued coughs could be heard above the applause, the volume of which was in proportion to the quality of the performance.

"That's my daughter," she said to her neighbor, as Clotilde played Claude Debussy's "The Girl with the Flaxen Hair." Her performance began well, but she struggled in the passages with 4ths and 5ths, and when she finished, Claire winced while joining in the polite applause of the other parents. She leaned her head softly on Peter's shoulder, and like the compassionate person he was born to be, he commented positively on their daughter's performance. He turned and sweetly kissed her on the side of her head. "She has an artist's soul," he said.

All they could see of the next child to perform was his outsized curly afro. The boy sat down to play, and when he did, the music that flowed from his fingers was stunning. "Maple Leaf Rag" had never sounded like this before, played with a rigor and vibrancy that belied his age.

The winner of the competition was announced at the end of the recital, after which the performers were released from their front-row seats. They ran fast as bandits to their parents, faces peppered with the feverish glow of achievement. They were then all directed en masse to the front of the barn for the reception, which had been cordoned off for the purpose. They were met by another set of ushers, dressed in white shirts and black slacks or skirts offering them soft drinks and hors d'oeuvres.

She spotted the mother of the winner of the piano competition and drew near to her. She was standing next to Lawrence, chatting gaily. She was struck by how well she looked. Slim, confident, still showcasing the long braids that had been her trademark since childhood.

"Come with me," Claire said to Peter and Clotilde.

They weaved in and out through the clusters of parents and sticky-fingered children, striding past the silk and pea jacket set.

"Hello, Georgia, Lawrence."

The child stood between them, griping a smooth, pewter trophy in his hand.

The two men shook hands as the women gazed contemplatively at each other.

"You look lovely, Georgia," Claire said. "I nearly didn't recognize you."

"Thanks," Georgia replied, looking appreciatively toward Peter. "I see you've bagged your man."

Claire leaned down to eye level with the child. "And you are?"

"Robert Whitman," he said, sidling up to his mother as cautious children do.

"Congratulations, Robert," she said softly. "You played brilliantly. Now, I bet you were named for your uncle!"

"Yes, ma'am!" the boy said, schooled since the age of two to respect his elders.

Claire gently patted the crown of Robert's head, then introduced him to Clotilde. The two children looked shyly at each other as Georgia turned toward Claire. Georgia smiled back at her and was surprised to see tears gathered in the corner of her eyes.

"Happy tears," Claire said, as though reading her mind. "Truce?"

"Truce!" Georgia replied with a smile. "We've both got all we need."

* * *

Amid the soft chatter of adults mixed with the sound of wilting laughter of tired children, the families began to leave the reception, treading on layers of amber colored leaves as they walked in the night air to their cars.

As they left the barn, Georgia felt a crisp autumn breeze sweep across her face. She looked up and smiled at the Little Dipper, which dappled the night sky. She then turned to see the glowing face of her son looking up at her. The evening and the memories of all that had gone before, both the good and the bad, began to intertwine in her deepest most thoughts.

Robert interrupted her thoughts. "Are you happy that I won, Momma?"

"Couldn't be happier, Baby," she replied softly. "But Robert, you must always remember that the world if full of champions"

Georgia held one of his hands as Lawrence held the other, sandwiching their son between them, as though two strong bookends.

"Who was that lady, Mom?" Robert asked, his youthful face serious and concerned.

"Don't worry," Georgia said, smiling warmly. "One day when you're old enough, I'll tell you the whole story."

THE END

ABOUT THE AUTHOR

Julie Sullivan is a clinical assistant professor at Arizona State University where she teaches healthcare ethics. Prior to teaching, she headed an international nonprofit organization that sent thousands of volunteer educators to work on education and health reform throughout Sub-Saharan Africa. Julie has received several awards for her work in Africa, including the World Association of NGO's Education Award for Innovation and Leadership. She is married to a Brit and together they have six children, in both the US and the UK. Julie also authored *Against the Tide*, a nonfiction book that chronicled the life and times of her great-grandfather, a Black steamboat captain who battled prejudice in the Chesapeake Bay region.